Perfect Mother

Perfect Mother

Uduak E. Akpabio

authorHOUSE®

AuthorHouse™ LLC
1663 Liberty Drive
Bloomington, IN 47403
www.authorhouse.com
Phone: 1-800-839-8640

Published by AuthorHouse 09/09/2014
First published 2009 by Athena Press.

ISBN: 978-1-4969-2265-6 (sc)
ISBN: 978-1-4969-2266-3 (e)

To my father,
Dr Edward Udo Akpabio, MB, BS,
Justice of the Peace [JP], Officer of the Order of
the Niger [OON]. December 1, 1926 to September 5, 2009.
You encouraged me to write and never flagged in your belief
that I would one day do so. That I have published this
today is all thanks to you. I wish you had lived to see it.
You were my rock, Daddy, and I miss you more than
I can say. Rest in peace. Your memory will live on.
Uduak.

LIST OF CHARACTERS

ANIEKAN 'ANI' UMOH	businessman
CELIA UMOH	Aniekan's wife
ENO UMOH	their daughter
EKAETTE UMOH	their daughter
ITORO UMOH	their daughter
IDORENYIN UMOH	Aniekan's mother
SANDRA EDO	Celia's friend
GERALD 'GERRY' UMANA	Aniekan's friend
IJEOMA NWANKWO	Aniekan's former secretary
UBONG/UGOCHUKWU	her son
JOHN 'BABA' MADUEKWE	the native doctor
REGINA OLUSOLA	Celia and Sandra's friend
THOMAS OLUSOLA	her husband
ATIM	Celia's maid
FUNKE	Aniekan's secretary
ELIJAH	the Umohs' driver
HARUNA	the Umohs' gateman
IYABO	Sandra's employee
DR IDIONG	paediatrician at the hospital
DR BOLU	Celia's obstetrician
MATRON	matron of the hospital
NURSE	in the obstetric ward
NURSE 1	in the OPD
NURSE 2	in the paediatric ward
NURSE 3	in the general ward

CASHIER	hospital staff
RECEPTIONIST	hospital staff
POLICE CHIEF	the head police officer
POLICEMAN 1	investigating officer
POLICEMAN 2	investigating officer
POLICEMAN 3	at the police station
POLICEMAN 4	at the police station
POLICEMAN 5	at the police station
STORE GIRL	Toyland employee
MAIGUARD	the Olusolas' gateman
MAID	Sandra's maid
SERVANT	the Olusolas' maid

GLOSSARY

Abasi	God
abi	approximately means 'is that so' or 'is that not so'
Annang and *Igbo*	different ethnic groups, with different languages
ashawo	prostitute
babalawo	native doctor
bubu	a long loose garment
chop	food or eat
jo	literally meaning 'please', it can signify anything depending on how it is used, for instance agreement, impatience, disgust, commiseration, even joy
LASTMA	Lagos State Traffic Management Authority
pele	Yoruba word of commiseration, literally means 'sorry'
maiguard	gateman
na wa	expression used when something don't go as expected, roughly means 'imagine that happening' or 'imagine you doing that'
oga	master of the house
over-sabi	thinking oneself too knowledgeable.
oya	expression of impatience to do something or get something done
Oyinbo	Caucasian

sabi	know
sef	self
sharp-sharp	rapidly or immediately
wahalla	trouble or bother

PROLOGUE

There is a function taking place in the open. Canopies are erected in the yard. Well-dressed people are eating, drinking, and talking. Music is from a live band. There is a cameraman recording the event. GERRY goes to the microphone and gestures to the band. The music gradually stops.

GERRY: Ladies and gentlemen. Now that we have all been refreshed, let us get back to the reason why we have gathered here today. Each and every one of us has come here to rejoice with Aniekan and Celia Umoh.

There is applause and cries of 'yes, yes', from the crowd.

GERRY: Yes. This is truly their happy moment. After eight years of marriage they have finally been blessed with a bouncing baby girl.

The crowd applauds again.

GERRY: Yes, God has His own time for answering our prayers. If we are patient, He will surely reward us, as He has rewarded the Umohs. And I'm sure that this baby has opened the way for others to follow!

There are more cheers.

1

GERRY: Now ladies and gentlemen, let us have a
              word from the couple. [*GERRY turns to the
              band.*] Bandmaster, welcome them with a
              rousing rendition of '*aniewo atie nte* Jehovah'.
              Yes. Who can be like Jehovah?

CROWD: No one!

*The band starts playing. People get up and start dancing. A procession
with ANI and CELIA in native attire made with identical materials,
surrounded by dancers, makes its way out. IDORENYIN, ANI'S
mother, is carrying a baby wrapped in a pink baby blanket. She and all
the other women are dancing vigorously. They dance up to the microphone.
She hands the baby over to CELIA. The music crescendos and dies down.
The people clap and cheer, then they sit. ANI takes the microphone.*

ANI: Yes. I have searched and have not seen
              anybody like Jehovah. He has been so good
              to me. My business is prospering. When
              my mother was sick, He was with us. The
              operation was a complete success and she
              is totally recovered. Now, He has blessed
              us with a daughter. He saw my wife safely
              through the pregnancy and the delivery.
              Truly, God is good!

*There is more applause and cries of agreement. He takes the baby from
CELIA and holds her up.*

ANI: I have named her Eno Abasi, for she is truly
              the gift of God.

More claps and cheers. CELIA takes over the microphone.

CELIA: All that my husband has said is true. The
              glory goes first and foremost to God. But

I would also like to use this moment to thank my husband. For eight years we were married with no child. Eight heart-breaking years. We all know what childlessness means to the African woman. And throughout those years, my husband showed me only understanding, love and support. [*She faces ANI.*] So to you, my darling husband, I say a very heartfelt thank you. I love you. [*She kisses him. There are more cheers. She takes the baby.*] And to you, my precious gift from God, I promise to be a perfect mother. [*She starts singing*] I am saying thank you, Jesus...

The band accompanies and crowd sings with her. GERRY takes the microphone as the song dies down.

GERRY: Yes, ladies and gentlemen, we have come to rejoice with Aniekan and Celia Umoh. So let us rejoice! While they dance, we will present to them the gifts and good wishes we have brought for their daughter.

The band starts up again, playing 'Magnify the Lord with Me'. CELIA and ANIEKAN start dancing. IDORENYIN takes the baby. People gather, showering the UMOHS with money. Others present gifts. Some crowd around IDORENYIN admiring the baby. The cameraman moves around covering the scene.

Fade.

Scene I

Nine years later. The UMOHS' house. It is morning. ENO, nine, and EKAETTE, seven, are putting on their school uniforms. ITORO, five, is wearing ordinary clothes. ATIM is helping EKAETTE put on her uniform. ENO sits on the bed and reaches for a pair of socks.

EKAETTE: Those are my socks, Eno!

ENO: No, they're not. Your socks can't fit me.

EKAETTE: [*reaching over to grab them*] Yes they are! Mummy said I could have them!

ENO: [*keeping them out of her reach*] She can't give them to you. They are mine!

A short tussle ensues. ATIM tries to separate them.

ATIM: Stop. Stop. Stop it now!

EKAETTE: No! [*CELIA enters.*]

ITORO: Mummy, Ekaette and Eno fighting over socks! [*The two girls separate.*]

ENO: Mummy, Ekaette wants to take my socks!

EKAETTE: You said I could have them, Mummy!

CELIA:	Let me see the socks. [*Eno gives them to her.*]
CELIA:	Yes. I did say Ekaette can have these socks. They are a little small for you, Eno. I bought you some new pairs.
EKAETTE:	See? I told you!
CELIA:	Don't gloat, Ekaette. It's not nice. Let me go get the new ones for you, Eno.
ITORO:	I want new socks, too.
CELIA:	But yours are almost new, Itoro. [*She affectionately pats the child's head.*]
ITORO:	Eno getting a new one!
CELIA:	All right. I'll get you a new pair next week.
EKAETTE:	You always give Itoro what she wants.
CELIA:	She's just a baby.
ITORO:	I'm not a baby!
CELIA:	[*chuckling*] All right, pumpkin. [*IDORENYIN enters.*]
IDORENYIN:	Isn't anybody ready for breakfast yet?
EKAETTE:	Good morning, Grandma.
ATIM:	Good morning, Mama.
ENO:	Good morning, Grandma.

ITORO: Good morning, Grandma. I'm going to get
                new socks.

IDORENYIN: Good morning, everybody. Why aren't you
                in your uniform, Itoro?

CELIA: She has no school this week. Her classroom
                is being used for some external exams. [*She
                exits.*]

ENO: The whole nursery school block is being
                used.

IDORENYIN: Well, come down to breakfast, you two. Or
                you will be late.

*EKAETTE, who has just finished putting on her shoes, jumps up. She
picks up her school bag. She and ITORO exit the room.*

ENO: I have to wait for Mummy to bring my socks.

*CELIA returns. IDORENYIN and ATIM leave. CELIA helps ENO
put on her socks. They soon finish and leave together, CELIA carrying
ENO'S school bag. They go downstairs to the dining room. ANIEKAN,
IDORENYIN, ITORO and EKAETTE are seated at the table.
ANIEKAN has already started his breakfast. IDORENYIN is dishing
for the children. ATIM is bringing plates in from the kitchen.*

ENO: Good morning, Daddy.

ANI: Good morning, Eno.

ENO sits at the table. CELIA serves her, then herself. She too, sits.

ITORO: Daddy, I want to come and drop Eno and
                Ekaette in school.

7

ENO: You can't come. Daddy goes straight to work from school.

EKAETTE: Yes. How will you get back home?

CELIA: Atim, bring Mama the plantain dish I prepared specially for her.

IDORENYIN: I didn't know you made something special for me. I have already started on this.

CELIA: You mentioned yesterday that you hadn't had plantain pottage in a long while, so I had Atim buy some plantain yesterday evening.

ANI: [*glancing at his watch*] Hurry up, girls. Time is going.

He pushes away his empty plate. ATIM comes in with a covered dish which she places in front of IDORENYIN. IDORENYIN helps herself to the plantain.

EKAETTE: I want some plantain pottage.

ANI: You can't have it now. There's no time.

IDORENYIN: I will keep some for you for when you come back from school.

ANI leaves the table followed by EKAETTE, CELIA, ENO and ITORO. EKAETTE and ENO gather their schoolbags together.

ENO *and* EKAETTE: Goodbye, Grandma.

IDORENYIN: Goodbye. Have a good day at school.

ITORO gets to the door first.

ENO: You can't come with us, Itoro.

ITORO: [*pouting and tapping ANI to gain his attention*]
                    But I want to come. Daddy, I want to come.

ANI: How will you come back home? You know
                    I'm going to go to work.

ITORO looks like she is going to cry.

CELIA: [*who has come to the door to see them off*] Let her
                    come with you. I'll come over to the office
                    and pick her up on my way to the market.

ANI: All right.

ITORO: Yippee!

*ITORO races outside. ATIM gives ENO and EKAETTE their
lunchboxes. ANI kisses CELIA.*

ANI: Goodbye, darling.

ITORO, ENO *and* EKAETTE: Goodbye, Mummy!

*They leave. CELIA closes the door and returns to the table. She resumes
her meal.*

IDORENYIN: Ani's office is quite a bit out of your way to
                    the market.

CELIA: I know. I just didn't want Itoro to feel left
                    behind.

9

IDORENYIN: A driver would be useful here. He could bring her back from the office, saving you the extra journey. In fact, the driver could be the one taking them to school. Even though both of you drive, I think you could still find a driver useful.

CELIA: You have a point, Mama. [*There is a pause as CELIA considers.*] I'll talk to Ani about it.

There is a short silence.

IDORENYIN: My daughter, there is something I want to discuss with you. Itoro is five years old now. It's time for you to try for another child. Remember, you are yet to produce a son, and a woman does not remain fertile for ever. And when you consider the eight years you waited before you had Eno Abasi, you will see with me that you don't have much time left.

CELIA: Mama, it is God who gives children and God's time is the best. He decided when I should conceive, just as He has decided the sex of my children.

IDORENYIN: Don't get me wrong, Celia. I'm not blaming you. I am only pointing out the obvious. [*She holds up her hand formed into a fist with one finger pointing up.*] One, you are not getting younger. [*She raises another finger.*] Two, you have to give my son a son. I love my granddaughters, but my son needs a son to carry on his name.

CELIA: Mama, Ani has so many uncles and cousins. There is no danger of the family name dying out.

IDORENYIN: [*looking shocked*] What are you saying? Ani's cousin's children are not his children!

CELIA: I know, Mama, but...

IDORENYIN: Do you want him to be the laughing stock of the whole village?

CELIA: Of course not. But why should people laugh at him? Times have changed, Mama. People don't place emphasis on that any more.

IDORENYIN: Is that what you think? Because you are living here in Lagos? Let me tell you, nothing has changed in the village. If you were living there you would understand what I'm telling you. In fact, this conversation would be unnecessary. By now you should have already given birth to your fourth child.

CELIA is silent, then she releases a long sigh.

IDORENYIN: I'm saying all this for your own good, Celia. My son must have a son. It is to your own advantage to be the one who gives it to him.

CELIA: [*looking at her sharply*] What are you suggesting, Mama?

IDORENYIN: I'm suggesting that you give Ani a son.

CELIA:	Or else what? You will find another woman to give him one?
IDORENYIN:	You know our culture allows a man more than one wife. But you also know it is not compulsory he marry more than one. In this case, the decision is in your hands. Entirely in your hands. A word is enough for the wise. [*She gets up from the table.*] Thank you for the plantain, my dear. It was lovely. That's one of the things I like about you. You are thoroughly versed in kitchen matters.
CELIA:	Those eight years before I had Eno, you did everything you could to make Ani accept the village girl you had chosen to be his wife.
IDORENYIN:	Don't exaggerate Celia. I merely suggested the idea to him. He was against it, and I accepted his decision.
CELIA:	And now you are bringing it up again.
IDORENYIN:	My daughter, as I said before, I'm telling you this for your own good. I have nothing against you. You have been an excellent daughter-in- law. I just want you to round it off perfectly by having a son.
CELIA:	Or else everything that I suffered for? [*She indicates the house.*] None of this would have been possible if I hadn't stood by Ani when times were really rough. But is it all to go to another woman because I don't have a son?

IDORENYIN: There is nothing stopping you from having
               a son, is there?

CELIA: I'm not God, Mama. There is no guarantee
               that the next pregnancy will yield a boy.

IDORENYIN: Then you keep on trying. That's why it is
               important not to leave all these long gaps
               between pregnancies. I have said my piece,
               Celia. I am going to my room now. Think
               over what I have said. Remember, I am not
               saying it to humiliate you. Rather, I want to
               save you from humiliation.

*IDORENYIN leaves. CELIA rests her elbows on the table, her chin in
her hand. She starts remembering.*

*Flashback. The kitchen of the house. ATIM and CELIA are preparing
food. ATIM is chopping up leaves on a cutting board. CELIA is breaking
a seasoning cube into a pot. She stirs. Touches the spoon to her palm and
tastes it. Adds a little more salt and stirs again. She pauses abruptly in the
middle of the action, her face twisting in pain. She gives an audible gasp.
Bends over clutching her stomach and cries out. ATIM leaves what she
was doing and rushes over to her.*

ATIM: Ma! Ma! What's wrong?

CELIA: [*bending almost double*] Oh, God. God, please,
               please. [*She clutches ATIM'S hand.*] Help me
               to the bathroom, Atim. [*ATIM holds her and
               they make slow progress to the bathroom, CELIA
               groaning and crying out intermittently.*]

ATIM: Sorry, Ma… sorry… sorry. Na your belle?

CELIA: Yes. My... belly... Oh! [*They enter the bathroom.*] Thanks.

ATIM goes out. She stays by the door. Shortly CELIA emerges. She is still in pain. She eases herself gently onto the sofa.

CELIA: Get me my phone.

ATIM leaves and returns shortly with the phone. CELIA makes a call.

CELIA: Go and check the pot on the cooker. You can cook edikang ikong, can't you?

ATIM: Yes, Ma.

CELIA: Finish it up. I'm going to the hospital.

ATIM: Yes, Ma.

ATIM leaves. CELIA starts talking on the phone.

CELIA: Sandra... It's me... I'm in trouble, Sandra. I'm in pains and I'm bleeding. Can you come and drive me to the hospital?... No, Ani won't be able to get here quickly enough. He's not in the office. He's gone on inspection of some properties... Yes. I'm pregnant, but I think I'm losing it. Oh, Sandra, hurry...

CELIA ends the call and drops the phone on the carpet. Then gingerly stretches herself out on the sofa.

Fade, with her still groaning.

Refocus. CELIA is lying on a hospital bed in a private room. She is on a blood infusion. Wires connect her to a monitoring device that beeps intermittently. NURSE is in the room with her.

NURSE: That should ease the pain, Mrs Umoh.

CELIA: Thank you.

NURSE packs her syringes and other equipment and leaves. SANDRA enters. She sits on a chair beside the bed.

SANDRA: How are you feeling now?

CELIA: A bit woozy. The nurse just gave me something for the pain.

SANDRA: What did the doctor say?

CELIA: He agrees that I am miscarrying, but he's waiting for the results of some tests before taking further action.

SANDRA: Are you still bleeding?

CELIA: Yes.

SANDRA: Didn't they give your something for it?

CELIA: They did, but it hasn't stopped. Did you get through to Ani?

SANDRA: No, but I left a message with his secretary, she is trying to get him.

DR BOLU enters.

SANDRA: Good afternoon, Doctor.

DR BOLU: Good afternoon. Please let me have a word
               with her.

SANDRA: Certainly. [*She stands up, ready to leave the
               room.*]

CELIA: Don't go, Sandra. Doctor, you can say
               anything in front of her.

DR BOLU: All right. [*He takes another chair.*]

CELIA: Is there any hope that my baby will be OK?

DR BOLU: I'm afraid not. The baby cannot survive.
               The ultrasound also revealed something
               else. The fibroids have returned, and they
               are growing rapidly under the effect of the
               pregnancy hormones. Just two weeks ago,
               you attended antenatal clinic, and they were
               not detectable then.

CELIA: So what do we do now?

DR BOLU: Nothing we have given you has controlled
               the bleeding. The only option we have left
               is surgery, and we need to do it immediately.
               You have already lost a lot of blood.

CELIA: Well, I guess that settles it. I hope this won't
               happen again during my next pregnancy.

DR BOLU: You don't quite understand. The operation
               I want to perform is hysterectomy. I want to
               remove the uterus.

SANDRA: Hey! The uterus!

CELIA: Why? Why not just remove the fibroids like you did last time?

DR BOLU: Because we cannot control the bleeding. I have to take into account your past history. When you delivered your last child, we had problems controlling the bleeding then, too. Your uterus did not contract on time. Now, it is not responding to the medications we have tried. In addition, your blood results show that your platelets are low. Those are the cells responsible for blood clotting. If we attempt another myomectomy now, there is a very great possibility of you bleeding to death. I warned you after your last delivery that it was inadvisable for you to have any more children, Celia. [*CELIA starts crying.*]

CELIA: That means I can never have a male child.

SANDRA: Is there absolutely no other solution, Doctor?

DR BOLU: Not if we want to keep her alive. [*Gently, to CELIA.*] I know this is coming as a shock to you but there is no way I can break it to you gradually. We're pressed for time. We need you to sign the consent forms so we can get started. The less blood you lose the better. Is your husband going to be here soon?

CELIA: I'm not sure. He's on field inspection today.

DR BOLU: We need him to sign the forms, too, if possible.

SANDRA: The operation can't be done if he doesn't sign?

DR BOLU: It can be done. Once Celia signs, we can go ahead. The ideal though would be for him to sign as well. I'll get the nurse to bring you the consent forms.

DR BOLU stands. CELIA grabs his hand and pulls him back.

CELIA: For my husband to sign, the operation has to be explained to him, doesn't it?

DR BOLU: Yes. It will still be explained to him when he gets here.

SANDRA: What is it, Celia? You don't want him to know, do you?

CELIA: No. I don't.

DR BOLU: How will you hide it from him? He will know you underwent surgery.

CELIA: But he doesn't have to know what for. You can tell him I simply miscarried and you had to do a... a...

DR BOLU: An evacuation of the uterus?

CELIA: Yes. Doctor, please.

DR BOLU:	An evacuation doesn't need abdominal surgery. He's going to know you had abdominal surgery.
SANDRA:	Well then... you can say you did the myomectomy again to remove the fibroids can't you?
DR BOLU:	Myomectomy during pregnancy is usually avoided. [*He turns back to CELIA.*] Celia, is this what you what you want? To lie to your husband?
CELIA:	[*grabbing DR BOLU'S hand again with both of hers*] I'm asking you to save my marriage. And my dignity.
DR BOLU:	But from what I've seen of your husband, he strikes me as a very reasonable fellow. He hasn't abandoned you all these years, why would he do so now?
SANDRA:	Ha! Doctor, in marriage it is better to be safe than sorry. She's right. There is no need for him to know.
CELIA:	You don't know my in-laws. In particular, my mother-in-law. She will grab this as an excuse to force another wife on Ani.
DR BOLU:	You and your husband can decide not to tell her. Not to tell anyone.
CELIA:	But every time Ani looks at me, it will be there at the back of his mind. He will be

thinking, This woman can't give me a son. This woman can't give me a son.

DR BOLU: [*sighing*] You are overwrought. Your husband has a moral and legal right to know.

SANDRA: You are her doctor. Your first duty is to her. To her total wellbeing, physical and emotional. I think the Hippocratic Oath that says something to that effect, doesn't it?

DR BOLU is silent.

SANDRA: Plus, she has the right to confidentiality.

DR BOLU: The laws of confidentiality do not exclude the husband in cases like this.

CELIA: Unless you promise me that you won't tell him, I will refuse to sign the consent form.

DR BOLU: Celia! Pull yourself together. You can't use your life as a bargaining chip.

CELIA: [*sobbing*] What life? I'd rather die than have Ani turn me out of the house and marry another woman.

DR BOLU: Then you must hold your life very cheap. And what about your three lovely daughters?

SANDRA: Doctor, please. Please. She will never have peace of mind otherwise.

CELIA: Promise me, Doctor, promise me. Promise me.

DR BOLU: OK. All right, all right. I promise. Stop
                    crying. You need to conserve your energy.

*CELIA'S sobs subside into hiccups. DR BOLU reaches for a hanky from
the drawer near the bed and gives it to her. She wipes her face.*

DR BOLU: I'll tell him you had an ectopic pregnancy
                    and we had to operate immediately.

CELIA: Thank you, Doctor.

DR BOLU: I hope I don't regret this.

Fade.

Refocus. CELIA is still sitting at the table, her chin in her hand.

IDORENYIN'S VOICE: There's nothing stopping you from
                    having a son is there?

CELIA removes her hand from her chin.

CELIA: Atim. Atim!

ATIM'S VOICE: Yes, Ma!

CELIA: Come and clear these plates from the table.

CELIA exits.

Fade.

Scene II

ANI'S office. It has two doors, one leading to the reception where his secretary stays and the other leading to a corridor. He enters via the corridor door carrying ITORO. She is singing.

ITORO: Baa, baa, black sheep,
                    Have you any wool?
                    Yes sir, yes sir,
                    Three bags full.

ANI sets her down. ITORO runs over to the table and kneels on a chair in front of it. ANI keeps his briefcase on the desk and pulls out his in-tray.

ITORO: Daddy, can I play piano on your computer?

ANI: [*settling into his chair*] Not now, honey. I have work to do.

ANI switches on his computer. Picks some papers from the in-tray and glances through them.

ITORO: [*pouting*] You never let me play on your computer.

ANI: You have a lot of computer games at home. It's the same thing.

ITORO: No. It not the same thing. [*She picks up a ceramic dog from the table.*]

ANI: It is not the same thing. Don't forget the 'is'.

ANI activates the speaker on the telecom and dials his secretary. He waves
a hand at ITORO.

ANI: Be careful how you handle that, honey. It
                        can break.

FUNKE: [*over the speaker*] Good morning, sir.

ITORO carelessly drops the ceramic dog on the table and quickly leans
over the phone. ANI grabs it just in time to prevent it falling to the floor.

ITORO: Funke! Funke!

FUNKE: Ekaette?

ITORO: No. It me, Itoro.

ANI: It is me.

ITORO: It is me.

FUNKE: Good morning, Itoro. How are you?

ITORO: Fine.

ANI: Good morning, Funke. Bring me my coffee
                        and the printout on the beach property
                        estimates.

ITORO: [*who has been trying to interrupt*] Me, too. Me,
                        too. I want coffee, too.

ANI: Let Funke bring the things I want first, then
                        she can make you a cup of cocoa.

ANI switches the phone off.

ITORO: [*pouting again*] No! I want coffee!

ANI: You know you're not supposed to drink coffee.

ITORO: But you drink it.

ANI: But you see, I am big.

ITORO stops leaning on the table and kneels straight. She raises her arms in muscle man style, fists clenched.

ITORO: I am big, too!

ANI: [*laughing*] Oh, Itoro.

ANI turns his attention back to the computer. ITORO starts singing and picks up the ceramic dog again.

ITORO: How much is that doggie in the window?
                    The one with the waggly tail.
                    How much is that doggie in the window?
                    I do hope that dog is for sale.

                    [*She shakes the dog.*] Wag, wag. Wag your tail.

FUNKE enters with a cup of coffee and some papers. She sets them down in front of ANI.

ITORO: You didn't bring my coffee!

ANI: Look, honey, why don't we strike a deal?

ITORO: What that?

ANI: Is, honey, is.

ITORO: What is that?

ANI: A deal is a kind of agreement between us.
                [*He points to himself.*] I will agree to let you
                have coffee, if [*he points to her*] you will agree
                to stay in Funke's office and sing and play
                and whatever, until Mummy comes.

ITORO: Why can't I stay here?

ANI: Because you are disturbing me. I have to
                work. Funke's office is very nice. Lots of
                chairs to climb on, plants to inspect and a
                nice big window to admire the city from.

FUNKE: [*smiling*] And I make very good coffee.

ITORO: Ooh, yes!

*ITORO scrambles off the chair, again carelessly dropping the dog.
FUNKE catches it this time.*

ITORO: I'll wait for you there!

FUNKE: OK. I will be out soon.

*FUNKE opens the door for ITORO; ITORO exits and FUNKE closes
it behind her.*

ANI: [*heaving a sigh*] It's a good thing I don't have
                to bring her to the office every day.

FUNKE: I thought today was a school day.

ANI: Not for her. They are holding some exams
                in her classroom.

FUNKE: Should I really make coffee for her?

ANI: Yes. But make it very weak and put in lots of
                milk. [*He sips his coffee.*] Now, what are my
                engagements for today like?

FUNKE points some papers out for him.

FUNKE: These are your engagements. As usual, I've
                put the most pressing ones at the top. These
                are the beach estimates. [*ANI looks through
                them.*] There is a lady waiting to see you.
                She has been here thirty minutes already. I
                think we can squeeze her in before your first
                engagement.

ANI: What does she want?

FUNKE: [*lifting her shoulders*] She said it is something
                personal and refused to expatiate.

ANI: What is her name?

FUNKE: Ijeoma Nwankwo.

ANI: Ah. Ijeoma. She was the first secretary I had
                when I started out on my own. Please send
                her in.

FUNKE: Yes, sir.

*FUNKE exits. Shortly, IJEOMA enters. She closes the door and smiles
at ANI.*

IJEOMA:	Good morning, Ani.
ANI:	Good morning, Ijeoma. [*They shake hands. ANI surveys her.*] It's good to see you again. You look wonderful.
IJEOMA:	[*sitting down*] So do you. [*She glances around.*] You have moved. This is nice. Much better suited to your image than the old place.
ANI:	Thank you.
IJEOMA:	I met your daughter in the reception. Very sharp girl.
ANI:	Oh, yes. She is, she is.
IJEOMA:	And how are your wife and… Eno Abasi?
ANI:	They are fine. I have three daughters. You just saw Itoro, the last one. The middle girl is called Ekaette.
IJEOMA:	Congratulations.
ANI:	Thank you. How about you? You have married?
IJEOMA:	No. I am still single.
ANI:	[*raising his eyebrows*] Don't tell me it is for want of offers. You have just decided to push us men aside, eh?
IJEOMA:	Well, I wanted to concentrate on my career first. When I left I went back to school, you know.

ANI:	No, I didn't know. You just lost touch completely. Not even an email to let me know how you were doing.
IJEOMA:	I'm sorry. I thought it would be better if I just cut off completely.
ANI:	Would you like a cup of something? Coffee? Tea? Something cold?
IJEOMA:	No thanks.
ANI:	You sure?
IJEOMA:	Yes. I'm OK. Thank you. Ani, I came to see you because I have something very serious to discuss with you.
ANI:	[*looking attentive*] Mmhm, go ahead.
IJEOMA:	You see I… when I left… I mean these last few years… oh, I don't know how to go about this.
ANI:	Why not take it from the beginning? [*He gives a small smile.*] That's always a good place to start.
IJEOMA:	OK. [*She takes a deep breath.*] All right.

IJEOMA leans towards him, placing both arms on the desk, an earnest look on her face.

Fade.

SCENE III

CELIA drives into the parking lot of SANDRA'S boutique. She alights and enters the boutique. SANDRA'S employee greets her.

IYABO: Good Morning, Ma.

CELIA: Good morning, Iyabo. Is your madam busy with a customer?

IYABO: No, Ma. She is in her office. Let me tell her that you are around.

CELIA: Don't worry. I'll just go in at once.

CELIA goes to the rear of the boutique and enters the small office there. SANDRA is seated at her desk going through some papers. She looks up and smiles.

CELIA: Yoo hoo. Are you very busy?

SANDRA: [*taking her reading glasses off*] You could say that. But I can never be too busy to spare a moment for you.

CELIA sits in the chair opposite her. She indicates the papers.

CELIA: Are you ordering new supplies?

SANDRA: Actually no. I was going through the buying receipts of those dresses I got from France almost five months ago. Can you imagine this Celia, I've only sold two. Two! In spite of giving them prominence on the mannequins in the window. I was just going over again how much I spent on those clothes. On the whole Paris trip, in fact. If I had spent that money going to Italy or Dubai to buy my normal stuff, I would have long since recovered my money.

CELIA: [*shaking her head in commiseration*] I told you I didn't like those dresses. They might be OK for France; Lord knows anything passes for fashion over there. But I can't imagine [*She holds up a hand with fingers splayed.*] five Nigerian women who would spend their money on those… [*She pauses searching for the right word.*] those creations. Where would they wear them to?

SANDRA: It's a pity you weren't with me in Paris. You might have saved me from buying them.

CELIA: Why *did* you buy them? They are so way out of your usual styles.

SANDRA: That's just it. I thought I needed to diversify a little. Expand my European line. And frankly I thought our women would fall for them. Something different. What a lapse in judgement that was. [*She flicks a finger through the papers.*] What a costly lapse in judgement.

CELIA:	Cheer up. You still have a lot of good business decisions to your credit. Like those South African designs? They did very well.
SANDRA:	But what am I supposed to do with these?
CELIA:	I don't suppose you can return them?
SANDRA:	After five months? And I bought them outright.
CELIA:	I guess you'll just have to write off that money. But keep trying to sell them. Hopefully before a year runs out you will recover your money.
SANDRA:	Hopefully. Well you win some, you lose some. So what's up with you? Want some coffee?
CELIA:	No. Nothing. I'm on my way to the market, but I'll go to Ani's office first to pick Itoro up. Her class is not holding this week because of some external exams. Sandra, I need to talk to you. I'm heading for problems with my mother-in- law.
SANDRA:	What kind of problems?
CELIA:	She's on my back again to have another child. A boy child.
SANDRA:	What's her business? Is she your husband? I blame you, Celia. You are too soft. Send her back to the village!

CELIA: You know how she is, Sandra. She will just
                keep on harping on this issue. She will make
                me the talk of the whole village.

SANDRA: So? Let them stay there in the village and
                talk. After all, they have nothing better to
                do. How will it affect you here in Lagos?
                I don't understand how you can let your
                mother-in-law come and live with you in
                the first place. She's a married woman, is
                she not? You are in your husband's house.
                Tell her to go back to hers.

CELIA: She's not living with us. You know she only
                came for a visit.

SANDRA: For how long? It's getting to a month
                now, isn't it? That's how it starts, Celia.
                Be careful. Next thing you know, you'll be
                stuck with her. Tell her to go.

CELIA: The thing is, since Ani's father died, she's
                taken to paying long visits to her children.
                She says it's too lonely in the house.

SANDRA: Lonely *ko*. She's not behaving like a lonely
                woman. Lonely women don't go about
                making trouble for their daughters-in-law.
                How can she expect you to sympathise with
                her when she doesn't sympathise with you?

CELIA: I just don't want *wahalla*. God knows I went
                through enough during those years when I
                couldn't conceive and Ani was struggling to
                get the business started. All I want now is
                peace and happiness. I think I deserve it.

SANDRA:	If peace and happiness don't come to you of their own accord, make them. You're a fighter, Celia. You've always fought for what you want. Fight for this, too. Start by booting anyone who makes you miserable out of your home. Hah! Me? I don't put up with any nonsense in my house.
CELIA:	You are right. I won't kick her out though. I'll do it in a much nicer way.
SANDRA:	[*smiling*] Of course. I trust you. Cee, baby. [*They laugh.*]
CELIA:	You know how it is, Sandra. Where possible, try to stay in the good books. Tell me; in this day and age is the sex of one's child of such overwhelming importance anymore? I mean, this is the new millennium.
SANDRA:	No it's not. Women are achieving such a lot these days. It's not like before when girls were not even sent to school. There is nothing a man can do in today's Nigeria that a woman can't.
CELIA:	My sentiments exactly. And girls are the ones much more likely to look after you in your old age.
SANDRA:	[*nodding*] Definitely. Does Ani still think you are trying for another child?
CELIA:	He hasn't said so outright. After Itoro, he actually said we should not try again. But I

33

think deep inside he hopes we are. I know he would love to have a son.

SANDRA: Well, he can't. You can't have any more children. He just has to be satisfied with his daughters.

CELIA: But now this morning my mother-in-law more or less warned me that if I don't give Ani a son, she will get him another woman to give him one.

SANDRA: These old women. I don't know why they can't understand that grown men can take charge of their own lives.

CELIA: Well, she has a surprise coming. After all I went through. I know how hard I worked to keep myself and Ani when he was just starting out. Ani had nothing, nothing whatsoever when we got married. For the first five years, it was my salary as a bank clerk that we lived on. Ani went through a lot of frustrations trying to start this company. His own family was reluctant to help him finance it. It was through me that he eventually got the capital.

SANDRA: Yes, I know. You went to a money lender behind Ani's back.

CELIA: I had to do something when my bank denied his loan application. Ani did not approve of money lenders, but I didn't see that we had any choice.

SANDRA:	You know you took a very big risk. Money lenders are dangerous. And their interest rates are killing. If you had failed in your repayments, your very life could have been in danger.
CELIA:	Ani believed in the business, and I believed in Ani. I knew he had what it takes to make it. He just needed one chance. I was right. He is the most successful person in his entire family. But you are right on one point. Any business takes time to get off the ground. We did have problems meeting up with the repayments. Ani believed that if I begged my uncle, he would bear with us for a while. I couldn't tell him the real situation. I went to the Alhaji and pleaded for more time. I told him everything about the business. I went down on my knees. I wept and begged.
SANDRA:	[*shaking her head in amazement*] And he agreed? He actually agreed?
CELIA:	Yes. He agreed. But he hiked up the interest rate astronomically. I had no choice but to accept his terms. So even after paying off the original debt, it took us a while to pay off the interest. And at that point I had to tell Ani. Still, we eventually paid it all off and now Ani is doing so well, the sky is the limit.
SANDRA:	So what are you going to do about your mother-in-law?
CELIA:	What you suggested. Send her back to the village. Taking everything into account, I

can never allow another woman reap the fruits of my labours. These village girls she wants him to marry, where were they when Ani had just two pairs of trousers and we could barely scrape together bus fare for him to meet with possible backers? No. No other woman. And for that matter, no other woman's child either. My children and my children only are going to inherit their father's wealth.

SANDRA: What will you do if some *ashawo* girl outside gets pregnant for him?

CELIA: She better not try it. In fact, Ani better not try it. Because it is over my dead body that any woman's child will come into that house. [*There is determination in every line of her face.*] Hear me, Sandra? Over my dead body.

Fade.

Scene IV

The UMOHS' house. ANI and CELIA'S bedroom. She and ANI are in the room. She is putting away clothes into the drawers and closet. ANI is lying on the bed with his back up against the head board.

CELIA: [*inspecting a dress on a hanger*] The drycleaners really did a good job on this dress. [She turns the dress around.] It's perfect. I didn't think they would succeed in removing so extensive a stain. Hmm. Good.

CELIA hangs it up, closes the door and opens the next door. She starts putting away ANI'S suits.

CELIA: I went to see Sandra today. She's organising a beach barbeque this weekend. We should do something like that sometime. Make it a really classy affair. Invite your clients. Maybe this Christmas. What do you think?

ANI: [*resting his head on his arms, staring into space*] Mmm?

CELIA: Uh-oh. I forgot to send this to the drycleaners, too. [*She frowns.*] But you haven't worn it in ages. [*She brings out the suit on a hanger and twirls it around, looking at it critically.*] Maybe you shouldn't even wear it any more. I don't really like the cut of the jacket. Maybe you should give it out. Ani?

There's no answer. CELIA looks at him.

CELIA: Ani!

ANI starts, as though bringing himself back mentally.

ANI: Eh? Eh? What? What did you say, darling?

CELIA: Just where are you, dear? You've been lost in thought ever since you came back from work this evening. Even when we were eating you were only physically present at the table. Your mind was aeons away. You hardly said a word to me. I bet you did not even notice what you ate.

ANI: Oh, yes I did.

CELIA: Really? If I ask you now, can you tell me what we had for dinner?

ANI: Ah… ah, *afang* and pounded yam.

CELIA: That was yesterday. Today we had *atama*.

ANI: [*laughing ruefully*] Ah well.

CELIA goes over to the bed and sits beside him.

CELIA: Something is bothering you.

ANI opens his mouth as though to speak and she quickly raises her hand.

CELIA: No. Don't deny it. I know you too well. Are you having problems with your contractors?

ANI: No. It's not something to do with work.

CELIA: Then what is it? [*There is a small silence.*] Come on, tell me. We've always shared our problems.

ANI: I intend to tell you. I've only been wondering how best to do it. Celia, you know I love you very much. I would never deliberately do any- thing to hurt you. You know that, don't you?

CELIA: Yes, I know. What is this about?

ANI: I just want you to bear that in mind because what I want to tell you will be a shock. Sometime ago...

ANI stops as the door is flung open. ENO and ITORO rush into the room.

ENO: Daddy, Itoro is telling lies.

ITORO: I'm not. I'm not.

ENO: You are! You know we are not allowed to drink coffee.

ANI: Hey, hey, hey. What is this all about?

ENO: Itoro says she drank coffee today in your office.

ANI:	That's true.
ITORO:	You see? You said I was lying!
ANI:	All right. Now she knows you are not lying. Run along and play now. Mummy and I have something important to discuss.
ENO:	I want coffee, too.
ANI:	You can have coffee, too.

ENO and ITORO exit, running.

CELIA:	Put less than half a teaspoon, OK?
ENO'S VOICE:	Yes, Mummy!

CELIA goes and closes the door and returns to the bed.

CELIA:	You were saying?

The door opens again, and again ITORO and ENO burst into the room.

ITORO:	Daddy! Daddy! That woman in your office said I'm a smart girl, didn't she?
CELIA:	We all know you are a very smart girl and this is not the first time Funke is saying so. Now girls, please. Daddy and I need to talk.
ENO:	Itoro is always boasting about things that didn't happen.
ITORO:	It happened! It wasn't Funke. It was that other woman in Funke's office.

ANI: Er, yes. I think she said something like that.

ITORO: She asked a lot of questions about Mummy and Eno and everybody. I answered all of them! And she said I'm smart. [*She turns to ENO.*] See?

ENO: [*sticking out her tongue at ITORO*] So? I'm going for my coffee.

CELIA: [*to ANI*] Who was this woman?

ITORO: I want another coffee, Daddy!

ANI: [*exasperatedly*] No. You've already had. Girls, please! Do you think you can allow Mummy and me a minute?

ITORO: [*pouting*] I want another coffee!

CELIA: Maybe you can have one another time, OK?

ITORO: [*exaggerating her pout while thinking*] Promise?

CELIA: Promise.

ITORO: OK.

CELIA: Eno, remember to tell Atim to make the coffee for you, and to put less than half a teaspoon in it.

ITORO and ENO exit. CELIA locks the door this time.

CELIA: So, who was the woman?

ANI: Ijeoma Nwankwo.

CELIA: [*frowning*] Ijeoma? What did she want?

ANI: She came to say hello.

CELIA: Hello. Hmm. As long as it stops there. I never liked her. She was always making eyes at you. Let's forget about her. We were discussing something far more important.

ANI: Actually, this has to do with her. Celia, Ijeoma and I, well, we had an affair some time ago. [*He quickly raises his hand as CELIA opens her mouth.*] It was just, ah, I don't know, a mad fling. She was working for me and… I guess proximity had a lot to do with it.

When he stops speaking CELIA is silent. Then she turns her back to him.

CELIA: Hm. Now I know why I didn't like her. Intuition.

ANI: It's over. It has been over ever since she left. And it is not starting up again. It is you I love, Celia.

CELIA goes to a window and stands there backing the room and him.

CELIA: You love me.

ANI goes over to her. He stands behind her and caresses her shoulders.

ANI: Yes, I love you. Only you. I made a mistake. I'm sorry, sweetheart. Please forgive me.

CELIA shrugs his hands off and walks away from him.

CELIA: It's over?

ANI: Definitely.

CELIA: Then why are you telling me about it? Why
               did she come to see you today?

ANI: Because she has a child.

CELIA turns slowly and faces him.

ANI: She says it's mine.

CELIA: You've had a child all this while and never
               told me?

ANI: I didn't know until today.

CELIA: How old is the child?

ANI: Eight years.

CELIA: Eight!

ANI: It happened a long time ago.

CELIA: Why is she only telling you about it now,
               after all this time?

ANI: She didn't want to bring disharmony into
               our home. But she realises she is being
               unfair to him. He needs his father.

CELIA: A boy. It's a boy.

ANI:	Yes.
CELIA:	She's lying. She just wants to push someone else's spawn on you.
ANI:	I don't think so. He looks like me.
CELIA:	She brought him to the office?
ANI:	No. She brought his pictures.

ANI brings some photographs from his briefcase and hands them to her. CELIA takes them slowly, and equally slowly looks at them. She shakes her head.

CELIA:	This can't be happening to me.
ANI:	Darling, I'm sorry. But I didn't exactly plan this.

CELIA flings the pictures at him.

CELIA:	[*shouting*] What do you mean by you didn't exactly plan this? So you don't know that when you have sex with a woman this can be the result? Eh? I don't blame you. Because it took me eight years to conceive. You forgot that sex brings babies? [*She starts crying.*] Oh, God, what have I done to deserve this?
ANI:	Darling, I know how you feel, but…
CELIA:	Rubbish! You have no idea how I feel! Maybe if I suddenly presented you with an outside bastard you would have some idea!

ANI tries to take her in his arms. CELIA pushes him away.

ANI:	I'm really sorry, Celia. But now that I know about him, we need to discuss this.
CELIA:	Discuss what? I have nothing to discuss.
ANI:	Not discussing it won't make it go away. He's my son, Celia.
CELIA:	Congratulations!
ANI:	I wish there was some way I could make it easier for you.

CELIA heads for the door to leave the room. ANI stops her.

CELIA:	What is it? Leave me! I want to go and see to my children!
ANI:	I want to bring him here next week.
CELIA:	Bring him where?
ANI:	[*firmly*] Here. To live with us and his sisters.
CELIA:	And what's wrong with where he is now?
ANI:	Darling, he's my son. For eight years of his life he didn't know me. He is not to blame for any of this. I want to give him the life he deserves.
CELIA:	No!
ANI:	Celia, listen…

CELIA:	This is my home, too! I don't want him here!
ANI:	I'm handling this the wrong way. Darling…
CELIA:	Don't call me darling. It sounds too hypocritical.
ANI:	Celia, why don't you think things over? This is a big shock to you. We'll discuss it again later. [*He picks up his car keys.*]. I'm going to see Gerry. I'll be back before nine. [*At the door he pauses.*] Just remember that I love you. You are the only woman I have ever or will ever love.

ANI exits. CELIA wipes her eyes and is still standing in the centre of the room when the door bursts open and EKAETTE, ENO and ITORO rush in.

EKAETTE:	Mummy, Eno and Itoro had coffee! What about me?

CELIA doesn't answer. She is staring into space. EKAETTE shakes her.

EKAETTE:	Mummy! Mummy!
CELIA:	[*exasperated*] Yes? What is it?
ENO:	She wants coffee.
CELIA:	[*distracted*] Do whatever you want.

ENO and EKAETTE race off.

CELIA:	[*to herself*] Disaster. This is disaster. I can't believe this is happening. The very thing I was discussing with Sandra just this morning. Men and their libidos. They can never control themselves. Sleeping with your own employee. Well, I'm not going to take this lying down. If Ani thinks he's going to bring his bastard into this house, he better think again. I meant every word I said to Sandra this morning.
ITORO:	[*sitting on the carpet looking at the pictures*] Mummy, who this?
CELIA:	Nobody important. You wanted coffee, didn't you?
ITORO:	[*eagerly*] Yes!
CELIA:	Go and have it.
ITORO:	Yippee!

ITORO races off, banging the door behind her. CELIA picks the photographs off the carpet and looks at them again. Then she tears them up and tosses them into the wastebasket.

Fade.

Scene V

Downstairs in the parlour. IDORENYIN is sitting watching TV. ANI comes down.

ANI: I'm going out briefly, Mama.

IDORENYIN: Ah, my son, you have only just come back from work. Why don't you rest a little?

ANI: I've rested, Mama. Besides I'm not going to the office. I'm going to see Gerry. [*IDORENYIN follows him outside.*]

IDORENYIN: If you can spare some time, there's something I want to discuss with you. [*They stop at the car. ANI leans on it.*]

ANI: What?

IDORENYIN: I tried to discuss it with Celia this morning, but she was not receptive. No doubt she thinks it's none of my business.

ANI: What is it?

IDORENYIN: I think you need to try for another child. God willing, it will be a boy this time. [*ANI doesn't answer.*] Aniekan, don't make the mistake of thinking that the sex of the child is not important. It is for us black Africans. Nigerians in particular. Back in the village we are all still waiting to carry your son. [*ANI unlocks the car door.*]

ANI: Thanks for your concern Mama. But this is really an issue between Celia and me.

IDORENYIN: I know. I just want to make sure you don't lose track of reality. I want to hold my grandson in my arms before I die, Ani.

IDORENYIN leans on the window looking at him.

ANI: You will.

IDORENYIN: Good. I know that no one can predict the sex of a child at conception, but I have this feeling that God will be merciful. The next child will be male.

ANI: [*slowly*] Y-e-s. Don't worry, Mama. [*He starts the car.*] I guarantee you a grandson. I should be back before nine. Bye.

IDORENYIN: Bye.

IDORENYIN watches him drive away.

Fade.

Scene VI

The parlour of GERRY'S house. GERRY and ANI are drinking. The TV is on.

ANI: So, Gerry, that's the situation. You know I don't as a rule discuss my personal problems, but I feel I need advice on this one. Impartial advice. Celia is taking this hard.

GERRY: Well, that's to be expected. Give her time. She'll get around to accepting it.

ANI: How much time? That's the question. The sooner he starts living with me, the better, all round.

GERRY: Why is Ijeoma only just telling you about him now?

ANI: She says she didn't want to disorganise my family.

GERRY: [*sceptically*] Really?

ANI: [*shrugging*] So she says. What do you think?

GERRY: The Ijeoma I remember always struck me as something of an opportunist. She was perfectly willing to keep your own child from you when things were OK with her. I think maybe she has fallen on hard times. But hey, I may be wrong. Maybe what she says is true. But it must have been rough for the child. Eight years old and never met his father.

ANI: That's why I want him living with me by next week. I've lost eight years of his life already.

GERRY: [*nodding*] Yes. Your children have to live with you. So now you have a son.

ANI: Yes. Though I must say, this isn't the way I anticipated I'd have one.

GERRY: A son is a son. It doesn't matter how he came about. Have you told your mother yet?

ANI: No. I want to settle with Celia first. But she will be overjoyed. Just this evening she was telling me to try for a son.

GERRY: Well, congrats, man. And don't worry too much about Celia. She'll come round. She's a smart woman. [*He raises his glass.*] Here's to your son. Can't wait to meet him.

ANI: I can't wait myself. Ijeoma only brought photographs. But she will bring him to meet me tomorrow.

GERRY: At the office or the house?

ANI: Neither. I wanted somewhere neutral. As
                        unintimidating as possible. We'll go to one
                        of those food joints children love.

GERRY: Good luck on your first meeting. Eight years
                        is pretty old to be meeting your old man for
                        the first time.

ANI: That's true. But I just have this feeling that
                        we will hit it off from the word go. [*There is
                        a short pause.*] Yes, I can't wait to meet him.

Fade.

Scene VII

The UMOHS' house. It is night. ANI drives in. HARUNA opens the gates for him. ANI parks and alights from the car. IDORENYIN opens the front door for him.

IDORENYIN:	My son, welcome. You are later than you said.
ANI:	Yes. I lost track of time. [*ANI enters the house.*]
IDORENYIN:	I kept a snack warm for you.
ANI:	Thanks, but I'm not hungry. I'll just go straight to bed. Celia has turned in for the night?
IDORENYIN:	I guess so. Actually she didn't come down at all this evening. I went up to see if she was all right. She said she was.
ANI:	Mmhmm. The girls are in bed?
IDORENYIN:	Yes.
ANI:	I'll turn in, too.
IDORENYIN:	All right. I want to finish this movie.
ANI:	OK. Goodnight. See you in the morning.

IDORENYIN: Goodnight, my son.

ANI climbs upstairs and looks in on the children's rooms. They are asleep. ATIM shares ITORO'S room. He moves on to his bedroom. CELIA is in bed. The lights are dim. He changes into his nightclothes and gets in beside her. For a while there is silence. CELIA lies on her side backing him.

ANI: Celia. [*There is no answer.*] Celia. I know you are not sleeping.

It is true. CELIA'S eyes are open. She says nothing. ANI sighs.

ANI: Darling, I know you are upset. That's understandable, but please try to remember that I love you. Only you. I'm sorry about Ijeoma. She was just a fling. Nothing more. I have never loved any other woman the way I love you.

CELIA doesn't answer. The silence stretches. ANI puts a hand on her. She shrugs it off. He puts it back. She leaves it there.

ANI: I would never deliberately hurt you. You know that.

CELIA: So sleeping with Ijeoma wasn't deliberate? What was it? An accident? You accidentally had sex with her? Or did she rape you? For… how long did you say it went on?

ANI: I said I'm sorry, Celia. I made a mistake and I regret it.

CELIA: And that makes it all right. You're sorry, so everything is OK.

ANI: Celia, what do you want me to do?

CELIA: What I would have liked you to do is keep your trousers zipped. But it's too late for that now. All those hours you worked late, coming back to tell me how tired you were and I felt so sorry for you, my poor overworked husband. What an idiot I was.

ANI: I did work very hard, Celia. I still do. You know that.

CELIA: Still you found time to...

ANI: I said I'm sorry. I'll say it any number of times you want. I would undo the past if I could, but I can't.

CELIA: Where were you tonight?

ANI: I told you I was going to Gerry's.

CELIA: Did you tell him?

ANI: Yes.

CELIA: What did he do? Congratulate you?

ANI: What does it matter what Gerry did? This is between you and me.

CELIA: I'm going to be the laughing stock of the whole city.

She starts crying. ANI embraces her and strokes her gently.

ANI:	Nobody is going to laugh at you. This is Nigeria. Polygamous children are common. Please don't cry, darling. I can't bear it when you cry.

CELIA stops crying immediately.

CELIA:	Polygamous? What do you mean by polygamous? Are you planning to marry her?
ANI:	Of course not. I'm just telling you why nobody will laugh.
CELIA:	[*sniffing*] Ha! What do you know? They will laugh. At social functions, women's meetings, even in church. Everyone will be staring at me and snickering behind their hands.
ANI:	No they won't. None of them can swear that they can never end up in the same position.
CELIA:	Was she the only one?
ANI:	Er… what do you mean?
CELIA:	You know what I mean, Ani. Was Ijeoma the only one?
ANI:	Er… yes.
CELIA:	Are you sure? I don't want to be confronted with another bastard five years from now.
ANI:	You won't be. I don't like that word bastard. It implies that he doesn't have a father.

CELIA: Well, he didn't until now, did he?

ANI: You can take out all your anger and hurt on me, but please don't call an innocent child names.

CELIA: You said you wouldn't deliberately hurt me.

ANI: You know I wouldn't.

CELIA: Well then, don't bring him here. Don't push him into my face.

Ani doesn't answer.

CELIA: [*turning towards him*] Ani?

ANI: I can't do that, Celia. He is my son. That is tantamount to punishing him for the sins of his parents. *CELIA backs him again.*]

CELIA: I see. What was the point in saying you were sorry? You are not prepared to make amends.

ANI: I'll do anything else you want me to. [*He pulls her close again.*] But I can't do that. [*She lies rigid in his arms.*] He's my son. His place is here with me and his sisters.

Fade.

Scene VIII

SANDRA'S boutique. SANDRA is at her desk looking over catalogues. CELIA knocks perfunctorily and enters. She is wearing sunshades.

SANDRA: Ah. Just the person I wanted to see. Look through these catalogues. I'm trying to decide my next stock. Your contribution will be much appreciated. [*Sandra smiles.*]

CELIA takes off the sunshades. Her eyes are red and swollen.

SANDRA: [*aghast*] Cee, what's wrong?

CELIA: Sandra. Oh, Sandra.

CELIA bursts into tears. Sandra rushes over to her alarmed.

SANDRA: What is the matter? Cee, talk to me. What is it?

CELIA: [*talking between sobs*] Remember what we talked about just yesterday? About another woman having a child for Ani?

SANDRA: Yes?

CELIA: Well, he comes home last night and tells me his secretary has an eight-year-old son for him!

SANDRA: What! I don't believe this!

CELIA: I didn't at first either. I kept telling myself
            this can't be true, but it is.

SANDRA: Which secretary?

CELIA: Ijeoma Nwankwo. Remember her?

SANDRA: [*frowning*] Ijeoma Nwankwo. Oh, yes.
            The tall slim one who was always wearing
            miniskirts and tight shirts, isn't it?

CELIA: Yes! That's the one. *Ashawo* girl.

SANDRA: Hah! Celia, I remember telling you to get rid
            of her once. Those miniskirts gave a whole
            new meaning to the word mini!

CELIA: My sister! I tried *o*! I told Ani to change her
            but he just spouted jargon about what a fine
            secretary she was!

SANDRA: Not surprising! Seeing as she was practicing
            her secretarial skills on him rather than the
            paperwork! Men! They are so weak! A
            woman only has to flash her body and they
            become senseless! [*CELIA'S sobs subside.*]
            And she had to have a boy! Is Ani 100% sure
            the child is his?

CELIA: He says he looks like him, and I have to
            admit he does.

SANDRA: You've seen him?

CELIA:	His photographs.
SANDRA:	Oh, he brought you pictures of him. Hmm. *Na wa*. Still that doesn't prove anything. People have been known to resemble people they have no connection to at all.
CELIA:	Unfortunately, the connection here is all too obvious. Worse still, Ani insists on him living with us. I tried to stop it but he is adamant. What am I going to do, Sandra? I can't tolerate the idea of that boy under my roof!
SANDRA:	Do you want to move out with your girls?
CELIA:	Move out *ke*! And leave the house for another woman to move in? After all my suffering? Not likely! In any case, Ani would never let me take the girls. I am not going to leave Ani up for grabs. No way. He is mine. I will not simply hand him over to someone else.
SANDRA:	All right. So what are your plans?
CELIA:	I don't know. My mind is blank, Sandra. I just don't know.
SANDRA:	Well, I have a suggestion. There is a *babalawo* near Ijebu, who I've been told is very good. We can get him to make a charm that will stop Ani from bringing him to the house.
CELIA:	[*shaking her head*] No, Sandra. Not that again. I saw enough *babalawos* during my eight years of childlessness. They couldn't do anything for me. God finally gave me

children in His own time. I'm not going through that *babalawo* rigmarole again.

SANDRA: I think this one is different, Cee. The person who told me about him praised him so highly. And this is just a charm to lock a boy out of your house. Shouldn't be hard to do.

CELIA: [*still looking sceptical*] Hmm. Another *babalawo*.

SANDRA: What do you have to lose? You don't have any other ideas at the moment.

CELIA: What do I have to do?

SANDRA: Get something of the boy's. You said Ani brought back some photographs. One of them should do.

CELIA: I tore them all up.

SANDRA: We should be able to tape them back together.

CELIA: Do you know how to get there?

SANDRA: I should be able to find the place. I was given very detailed directions. But you have to make some arrangements for your daughters. It will take us about three hours to get there and back. What will you do about picking your girls from school?

CELIA: I'll just tell Ani to do it. He's not in a position to refuse me anything now. If he really can't

61

	make it, he can send his secretary in a taxi to get them.
SANDRA:	Another secretary. What's this one's name?
CELIA:	Funke. She seems OK. I used to like her.
SANDRA:	Used to?
CELIA:	Right now I am not sure I will ever really like any secretary again.
SANDRA:	I don't blame you *jo*. We have to use your car. Mine's kaput.
CELIA:	What happened?
SANDRA:	I wanted to tell you. A prophet in my driver's church saw a vision. He told my driver he doesn't have to look after the car any more. That angels are doing it for him in the night. The stupid boy stopped checking the car. The oil got too low and this morning the engine knocked. Peter sacked him on the spot.
CELIA:	Are people really that stupid?
SANDRA:	Apparently they are. I blame myself. He has been acting funny for some time now, no doubt seeing visions everywhere he turned. I didn't take any notice of it.
CELIA:	But there are warning signs when the oil levels are low.

SANDRA: He just ignored them. After all, prophet had spoken. I'm just happy nothing happened to my children in that car.

CELIA: And we are about to get a driver. It's things like this that made me refuse to have one for so long.

SANDRA: Why are you getting one now then?

CELIA: To take the girls to and from school. He can also ferry Mama around as well.

SANDRA: I thought you were going to send Mama back to the village?

CELIA: All in good time. We can go with my car. But what are you going to do about your car?

SANDRA: I'm going to use this as an excuse to get a new car out of Peter. I've been hinting at it for a while now.

CELIA: [*smiling*] Every disappointment is a blessing.

SANDRA: Yes *o*. Let's see if we can turn yours into a blessing.

CELIA brings out her make up case and looks at herself in the mirror.

CELIA: This is terrible. That's it. No more crying for me.

CELIA powders her face and they leave the room together.

Fade.

Scene IX

Inside a fast food joint. ANI sits facing the doorway. Drinks and food are on the table in front of him. IJEOMA and the boy walk in. ANI waves to them. They make their way to his table. The boy is wearing his school uniform. ANI stands to greet them.

IJEOMA:	[*smiling*] Hello, Ani.
ANI:	[*staring at the boy*] Hello, Ijeoma. Hello, Ugo.
UGO:	[*shyly*] Hello.
IJEOMA:	What did I tell you, Ugo?
UGO:	Sorry. Good afternoon, sir.
ANI:	No need to be sorry, Ugo. Have a seat. [*He holds out a seat for UGO.*]
UGO:	[*sitting down*] Thank you, sir.
ANI:	[*to IJEOMA*] He is so well mannered.
IJEOMA:	He was living with my sister. She's a no-nonsense type.
ANI:	So how are you, Ugo?

UGO: [*looking down at the table and speaking very softly*] Fine thank you, sir.

IJEOMA: Ugo, speak up! And look at the person you are talking to.

UGO: [*looking up at Ani briefly*] Fine thank you, sir.

ANI: I expect you are hungry. I've ordered almost everything they have. Didn't order ice cream though. [*He chuckles.*] It would have melted. But I can get it now that you're here. And anything else you want as well.

UGO: [*still sitting with his hands in his laps*] Thank you, sir.

UGO makes no move towards the food.

ANI: Well, go ahead. Take whatever you want.

UGO looks questioningly at his mother who nods consent.

IJEOMA: Yes, go ahead, Ugo. [*She opens the dishes.*] Ah there's barbeque chicken here. [*To Ani.*] He loves that.

IJEOMA dishes it out for him along with rice and salad.

ANI: What drink do you want?

UGO: Ribena.

ANI gives it to him. There is silence while they dish the food and start eating. ANI keeps staring at UGO. UGO mostly looks down at his plate, but now and then he looks up at ANI.

ANI: So how was school today?

UGO: [*softly*] Fine, sir.

IJEOMA: Speak up, Ugo.

ANI: It's OK. I can hear him. What class are
                   you in?

UGO: Primary 3.

ANI: Do you like school?

UGO: Yes, sir.

IJEOMA: [*proudly*] He was first in his class last term.

ANI: [*pleased*] Wow! That's wonderful!

*UGO looks at ANI again. ANI is smiling widely. UGO tentatively
returns the smile.*

ANI: That's an achievement that cannot go
                   unrewarded. I have to get you a present.

UGO: [*smiling a little wider*] Mummy gave me a new
                   shirt.

ANI: That's good. But that was from Mummy.
                   Now I want to give you something, too.

UGO stops eating and gazes at ANI.

UGO: Mummy says… [*UGO stops and looks down
                   again.*]

ANI: Go on. Don't be shy. What does Mummy say?

UGO: She says you are my father. [*UGO pauses then looks up again.*] Are you?

ANI takes one of UGO'S hands.

ANI: Yes, Ugo. I am. And it is a very great honour to have you for a son.

UGO regards him sombrely for a while. Then he smiles.

UGO: I like you.

ANI: I'm glad.

Fade.

Scene X

The UMOHS' house. CELIA drives in. She and SANDRA get out of the car and go inside. ATIM opens the door for them.

ATIM: Welcome, Ma. Good afternoon, Aunty.

SANDRA: Hello, Atim. How are you?

ATIM: Fine, Aunty.

CELIA: Where is Itoro?

ATIM: In her room. She dey sleep.

CELIA: What about Mama?

ATIM: She just go up to her room. She say she want to rest.

CELIA: OK. Their father will be picking Eno and Ekaette from school today, in case Mama asks. Is their food ready?

ATIM: Yes, Ma.

SANDRA: When will Itoro's school reopen?

CELIA: Monday. She wanted to follow me to your
                place, but I wasn't in the mood to take her.
                Let me check on her.

CELIA looks in on ITORO. She is asleep on the bed hugging her Barbie doll. CELIA sighs.

CELIA: Poor girl. All alone with no one to play with.
                I really should have taken her with me. I'll
                get something for her on our way back.

SANDRA: I forgot to tell you, you better carry some
                money with you for the *babalawo*.

SANDRA and CELIA move on into CELIA and ANI'S bedroom. The room is neat and the bed made.

CELIA: Oh! Atim has done the room already!

SANDRA: What's wrong with that? I wish my maid was
                this hardworking. I have to remind her to do
                everything.

CELIA: No. What I mean is that if Atim has done the
                room, then she has emptied the wastebasket.

SANDRA: Oh! I see. You threw the pictures in it.

CELIA checks the wastebasket.

CELIA: I thought as much. Empty. [*More to herself.*]
                What do I do now? I can't send Atim to go
                looking for it in the big bin outside. She'll
                wonder what I want it for. I'll have to do it
                myself.

SANDRA: I can distract Atim.

CELIA: OK.

*SANDRA and CELIA go downstairs. SANDRA settles in the parlour.
CELIA goes to the kitchen.*

SANDRA: Atim!

ATIM'S VOICE: Yes, Aunty.

ATIM enters the parlour.

SANDRA: Bring me a soft drink.

ATIM: Yes, Aunty.

*ATIM returns to the kitchen. CELIA is by the open freezer taking some
things out.*

CELIA: Atim, where is the goat meat I bought on
                   Thursday? [*She holds up a package.*] Is this it?

ATIM: Yes, Ma.

CELIA: I told you not to put it in this type of bag.
                   That this is only for ground foods.

ATIM: Sorry, Ma. The other plastic done finish.

CELIA: And you didn't tell me. What did Sandra
                   want?

ATIM: Soft drink, Ma.

CELIA: Go and serve her.

CELIA continues looking through the freezer. ATIM brings a soft drink from the fridge and sets it on a tray with a glass.

CELIA: I'm leaving this goat meat out to thaw. I want to make some pepper soup with it this evening.

ATIM: Yes, Ma.

ATIM leaves with the tray. In the parlour she sets it on a side table beside SANDRA. SANDRA has turned on the TV and is watching it. ATIM pours the drink into the glass.

ATIM: Here is your drink, Aunty.

SANDRA: Thank you, Atim.

SANDRA reaches for the remote control beside the tray and in the process knocks over the glass, spilling the drink.

SANDRA: Oh, dear! Quick. Bring a cloth.

ATIM rushes to the kitchen. CELIA has just closed the freezer.

CELIA: What's wrong?

ATIM: The soft drink pour, Ma. I wan clean it.

ATIM takes a cloth from the rack and leaves. CELIA immediately goes to the back porch of the kitchen. A large covered, black refuse bin stands just slightly away from the wall. CELIA quickly rummages through it.

CELIA: Aha.

CELIA pulls out pieces of torn photographs from a black plastic bag, then stuffs it and the other black bags back into the bin and closes it. She turns to re-enter the house and finds IDORENYIN standing in the doorway watching her. CELIA gives a start.

CELIA: Mama! You startled me.

IDORENYIN: Did I? Sorry o.

CELIA: [laughing nervously] I guess I just didn't expect to see you there. [She gives another nervous giggle.] Atim told me you were upstairs resting.

CELIA enters the kitchen, IDORENYIN standing aside for her. IDORENYIN closes the screen door.

IDORENYIN: Yes, I was. But I heard voices downstairs and came to see who it was.

CELIA: Sandra came back with me.

IDORENYIN: Oh. OK. What were you looking for in the bin?

CELIA: My earring. I just discovered one of my earrings is missing. And it is one of those I like very much. I've looked all over for it, so I thought I'd check the bin, too, to be thorough.

IDORENYIN: Did you find it?

CELIA: No. I'll check again upstairs.

CELIA and IDORENYIN enter the parlour. ATIM is still wiping the carpet. SANDRA looks up.

SANDRA: Good afternoon, Mama.

IDORENYIN: Good afternoon, Sandra. How are you?

SANDRA: Very well thank you. But I seem to be rather
                   clumsy today. I spilt my drink – twice.

IDORENYIN: Accidents happen.

CELIA: Don't worry about it. The carpet's stain
                   resistant. It has to be, with three boisterous
                   kids. Atim, get the Febreeze and spray on it.

ATIM: Yes, Ma. [ATIM exits. IDORENYIN sits
                   down.]

IDORENYIN: How is your boutique doing?

SANDRA: Very well, thank you.

IDORENYIN: You don't cater to people my age. I would
                   have visited.

SANDRA: You can come! I just got a shipment of some
                   lovely brocades and laces. Come over and
                   take a look.

CELIA: The lace we gave you last Christmas, Mama,
                   was from her boutique.

IDORENYIN: Really? I really like it. I must come and have
                   a look soon.

CELIA: Let me know whenever you want to go and
                   I'll take you.

IDORENYIN: OK, my dear.

CELIA: Now I have to take Sandra back to the boutique.

IDORENYIN: So soon?

SANDRA: I have appointments with some suppliers so I have to go. I didn't drive. My car's not good.

IDORENYIN: Ah. Car *wahalla*. All right. See you soon.

CELIA: Ani will be picking the girls back from school today.

IDORENYIN: Eeh? I hope nothing's wrong?

CELIA: No. No. I just have some errands to run.

IDORENYIN: OK, my daughter.

SANDRA: [*standing up*] Goodbye, Mama.

IDORENYIN: Goodbye. See you later, Celia.

SANDRA and CELIA leave and ATIM closes the door behind them. She goes to the spot on the carpet and starts spraying the Febreeze.

IDORENYIN: Atim, did your madam tell you what she was looking for in the outside refuse bin?

ATIM: [*looking puzzled*] Refuse bin? No, Mama.

IDORENYIN: Did she tell you about any earring she has lost?

ATIM: [*still looking puzzled*] No, Mama. I don't
                   know that she lost any earring.

IDORENYIN: All right, Atim. Forget about it.

IDORENYIN sits there quietly, looking thoughtful.

Fade.

Scene XI

Inside a toy store ANI, IJEOMA and UGO are browsing the merchandise. ANI picks out a toy car.

ANI: Do you like this? [*UGO nods.*] OK. We'll take it.

UGO: [*wide eyed*] For me?

ANI: Yes, for you. [*He smiles.*] I'm a little too old for it.

ANI gives it to STORE GIRL who takes it to the counter and returns.

ANI: Point at anything you like, Ugo, OK?

UGO nods again. They move down the aisle. UGO doesn't point anything out.

ANI: What's the matter? Don't you like anything else?

IJEOMA: He's shy. Just pick out what you want for him yourself for now.

ANI: All right.

ANI looks around and picks out a computer game set.

| ANI: | We'll take this too. And this. [*He adds a set of toy soldiers.*] Every boy should have his soldiers. |

ANI smiles at UGO, who smiles shyly back. His phone rings as he hands his selections to STORE GIRL.

| ANI: | Please tally that and let me have the bill. |

| STORE GIRL: | Yes, sir. |

ANI turns away and answers the call.

| ANI: | Hello, darling. |

| CELIA: | Ani, you'll have to pick the girls from school today. I have some errands to run with Sandra. Her car is not good. |

| ANI: | [*frowning*] I'm busy right now. I can't go to pick them up. Take a break from the errands, take them home, then continue. |

| CELIA: | That won't be possible, Ani. I won't be anywhere near the school by 2.30. |

| ANI: | What kind of errand is this? |

| CELIA: | I can't tell you about it now. We'll talk when I get back. |

| ANI: | Hold on. Hold on! What kind of arrangement is this? Did this errand suddenly come up? Why didn't you tell me about it since? |

| CELIA: | It was rather sudden. |

ANI: I'm occupied with a very important
                        engagement right now. I can't go for the
                        girls.

CELIA: Well then, send your secretary. You always
                        have such loyal, hardworking, trustworthy
                        secretaries. Send her to go pick up your
                        daughters.

ANI: [*warningly*] Celia…

CELIA: Goodbye, Ani. I will talk to you later.

CELIA ends the call.

ANI: [*shouting*] Celia! Celia!

*ANI looks at the phone with disbelief, then angrily returns it to his pocket.
He turns back to IJEOMA and UGO and forces a smile.*

ANI: It's at times like this I realise I need a driver.

IJEOMA: What happened?

ANI: It seems I have to pick my daughters from
                        school. [*He stoops to UGO'S level.*] I know I
                        said I'd spend the afternoon with you, but
                        something has come up. I'm really sorry
                        about this, but there will be other times, I
                        promise.

UGO nods. IJEOMA prods him.

UGO: Yes, sir.

ANI: We'll work on this 'sir' business next time.

ANI stands up. REGINA in the shop sees him and smiles.

REGINA: Aniekan!

ANI: Regina. How are you? I thought I heard
                you'd travelled to the US.

REGINA: It was a short trip. I returned day before
                yesterday.

ANI: How was the trip?

REGINA: Oh, fine, fine.

REGINA stares inquisitively at IJEOMA and UGO.

UGO: [*softly*] Good afternoon, ma'am.

REGINA: Good afternoon.

STORE GIRL: Here's your bill, sir.

She gives ANI the paper.

ANI: Where do I pay?

STORE GIRL: Over there, sir.

She points to a desk with another girl behind it.

ANI: OK. [*To Regina*] I'll be seeing you around.

REGINA: Certainly. You'll be at Sandra's beach
                barbeque, won't you?

ANI: Er… yes.

REGINA: Then we'll meet there. My regards to Celia.

ANI: Yes. Yes. And tell Thomas I said hello, too.

REGINA: Sure. Goodbye.

REGINA leaves, with a last lingering look at IJEOMA and UGO. ANI goes to the counter to pay.

Fade.

Scene XII

CELIA'S car. She is driving.

SANDRA: I thought you'd already concluded arrangements with Ani to pick the girls.

CELIA: [*shrugging*] If he likes, let him not arrange to have them picked up. He can't complain about anything I do right now.

SANDRA: [*smiling wryly*] And you intend to rub his face in it?

CELIA: But of course! Maybe this will teach him to keep his trousers on in future.

SANDRA: You know, Cee, I'm not sure what I'd do if Peter just upped and presented me with an outside child one day. It doesn't bear thinking about.

CELIA: [*sombrely*] It hurts Sandra. I may look like I'm holding up but I'm dying inside.

SANDRA reaches over and pats her hand.

SANDRA: Don't worry. Every problem has a solution. We're almost there. Slow down [*She peers through the windshield.*] Yes here. Here's the

dirt road between two palm trees and the
blue sign board just as she described it.

*The car turns down the narrow dirt track and stop in a small clearing.
At one corner is a hut. Trees line the edge of the clearing. CELIA cuts the
car engine.*

CELIA: Is this it?

SANDRA: Yes.

CELIA: Just this?

SANDRA: [*gathering her handbag*] What do you mean?

CELIA: I mean… [*She indicates the view.*] just look,
                Sandra. This is where a powerful *babalawo*
                lives? Here? If he is so powerful, why can't
                he improve himself?

SANDRA: Oh, Celia. You and your *Oyinbo* way of
                thinking. What do you want him to have?
                Cars? A big house? I'm sure he has all those
                in the city. But this is where he works.
                Maybe that's why his charms work so well.
                He's totally in touch with the spirits or
                whatever.

CELIA: [*still looking sceptical*] Hmm.

SANDRA: Don't tell me you're changing your mind.

CELIA: After coming all this way? Not a chance.

SANDRA: Good. Let's go.

SANDRA and CELIA alight and go to the door of the hut. As SANDRA raises her hand to knock a voice booms out.

BABA'S VOICE: Don't touch that door!

SANDRA quickly withdraws her hand. Both women step back from the doorway and look around.

BABA'S VOICE: What do you want?

SANDRA looks at CELIA, but CELIA stays silent. SANDRA nudges her, but CELIA just shakes her head.

SANDRA: Baba, I have brought my friend. She needs your help.

There is silence. They face the door waiting for it to open.

BABA: [*voice no longer booming*] What do you need my help with?

Both women turn around to find the babalawo *standing behind them. He is naked except for a loin cloth tied low on his hips. There are red and white markings on his face, arms, chest and abdomen. His feet are bare and painted white. Anklets made with open-ended wooden beads decorate his feet, bracelets of the same material, his wrists. A long necklace of the same wooden beads, crowned with a large wooden pendant shaped like a half-moon, hangs from his neck. High up on his arms are tight red armbands.*

SANDRA: Ah, Baba, good afternoon.

CELIA: Good afternoon, Baba.

BABA: Good afternoon. What brings you here?

SANDRA: My friend here needs a special charm.

BABA: [*nodding*] Let's go inside. [*He opens the door and they enter.*] Take off your shoes.

SANDRA and CELIA comply and walk in barefoot. Inside, the room is dim despite the two open windows. It is devoid of chairs, there is only a stool in one corner. The main focus of the room is a white cloth-covered shrine at one end. Various jars, bottles and receptacles cover the only other piece of furniture in the place, a long low table adjacent to the shrine. Native artefacts and artwork adorn the wooden walls. There is a large mat on the floor in front of the shrine. Baba sits yoga-style on this mat, and indicates that they should do the same. They sit.

BABA: Now, tell me all about it.

CELIA: Baba, I have been married for seventeen years. I have three daughters. I struggled alongside my husband to get to where we are in life now. Now, when I should be enjoying the fruits of my labour, he tells me he has a son with a former secretary of his and he wants to bring this boy into our marital home. Baba, I don't want this. I want to stop it at all costs.

BABA nods thoughtfully.

BABA: How old is the child?

CELIA: Eight years. [*BABA nods again.*]

BABA: Now you have to be more specific. What is it exactly that you want me to do? Kill the boy?

SANDRA: [*looking startled*] Kill *ke*! Nooo, Baba! Nothing like that!

84

BABA: [*to SANDRA*] Is this boy a problem for you as well?

SANDRA: [*looking puzzled*] Problem for me?

BABA: Yes. Is he causing any problems in your marital life?

SANDRA: No. Of course not. He's a problem for my friend.

BABA: Then I suggest you let your friend do the talking. [*BABA pauses, staring at SANDRA. SANDRA nods embarrassed. BABA turns back to CELIA.*] I repeat, what do you want to do, kill him?

CELIA is silent as she considers the question. SANDRA looks on in horror. CELIA remains silent.

SANDRA: Cee? You can't be seriously thinking of killing him?

CELIA: It would be a final solution to the problem.

SANDRA: [*gaping at her*] Celia Umoh! Tell me you're joking!

CELIA bursts out laughing.

CELIA: Of course I'm joking! Oh, Sandra, you're so gullible!

BABA: [*looking impatient*] Let's cut out these jokes and get down to business. My time is precious!

CELIA: Sorry, Baba. What I want is a charm that will keep him out of my house permanently. I don't want to live with him. I don't want my daughters to grow up with him. He can just go back to wherever he came from.

BABA: [*looks thoughtful again then nods*] A lock-out charm. Easy. Have you brought anything that belongs to the boy?

CELIA: Yes. Some pictures, but they are torn. [*She takes out the pieces and arranges them on the mat. They form two whole pictures.*] Will this do?

BABA: [*nodding*] His face is intact in both. That's good. What is his name?

CELIA looks at SANDRA.

CELIA: Oh, my goodness! I don't know his name. I never asked. I just didn't want to hear about him, so the less Ani said the better. Damn!

SANDRA: Can't you call Ani and find out?

CELIA: After just ordering him to pick up the girls? Besides what reason can I give for wanting to know right this minute?

SANDRA: Aaah, this boy is expected to live with you. Pretend you're coming round and just want to know more so you can make him feel really at home.

CELIA is already shaking her head.

CELIA: That won't work. Ani knows I'm still upset.

BABA: All right! All right! Forget it. I can find out
                his name.

CELIA: How? [*BABA just looks at her. CELIA raises
                her palms in surrender.*] Sorry.

*BABA closes his eyes. He rocks back and forth and murmurs
incomprehensible things to himself. Then he opens his eyes.*

BABA: It is easy. It is a charm that needs the tail
                feather of a jungle fowl.

CELIA: Where would I get that? I have never even
                seen a jungle fowl in my life.

BABA: [*waving her into silence*] Not a problem. I can
                get it. [*He meditates some more.*] 100,000 naira.

CELIA: For a feather!

BABA: For the entire charm.

CELIA: That's an expensive charm! Couldn't you...
                ah... bring the price down a bit?

BABA: Madam, I'm sure you passed many markets
                on your way here. If you want to haggle, go
                there. This place is not a market.

SANDRA: [*looking exasperated*] Celia...

CELIA: [*quickly*] OK all right. 100,000. [*There is
                silence, as BABA stares at them.*] Well?

87

SANDRA: I think you have to give him the money
                     first, Cee.

CELIA: Oh.

*CELIA brings a single bundle of 1,000 naira notes still wrapped in the
bank's label, out of her bag, and sets it on the mat. BABA doesn't count
the money; he just tosses it into a corner of the room. He reaches behind
him for an instrument that resembles a wooden rattle. Closes his eyes and
tilts his head upwards. He starts shouting.*

BABA: Spirits of the great forest! I come to you
                     for your help! [*He shakes the rattle with each
                     statement. He rants unintelligibly.*] Tell me the
                     name! Tell me the name of the boy in this
                     picture! [*He touches the rattle to the picture.*]
                     O great forest spirit, your humble servant
                     beseeches you! [*He rants unintelligibly again.*]
                     Thank you, great spirit. You never fail me.
                     [*He is silent for a long while, then he opens his
                     eyes.*] His name is Ugochukwu Umoh.

CELIA: [*looking properly impressed*] Wow.

SANDRA: [*looking smug*] I told you he is good.

BABA: [*to CELIA*] It seems you are not convinced
                     of my powers.

CELIA: Sorry, Baba. I am rapidly becoming
                     convinced.

BABA: Good.

*BABA lays the rattle down and picks up a small bowl with some white
powder in it. He starts chanting and sprinkling powder on the pictures.*

88

Putting the bowl away, he carefully picks up the pieces of one of the photographs and carries it to the shrine. He lays it in a special receptacle, chanting all the while, then sprinkles some dried leaves from different containers in it. He takes a feather from a tall jar and adds it. Finally he takes one of the lit candles, drips wax into the bowl. He uses the candle to light up the contents of the bowl. He uses a stick to turn it to make sure everything is burned. He then brings down a bottle with some clear liquid in it. He opens the bottle and puts a small funnel in the mouth. He carefully pours the ashes into the bottle, corks it and shakes it vigorously. He stops chanting, faces the shrine and raises the bottle.

BABA: Great forest spirit. Thank you for this charm. [*BABA holds the bottle out to CELIA.*] Take this. [*CELIA takes it.*] When you get home, sprinkle it around your home and say what you wish to happen to him, should he enter that house. This charm can make him sick, unconscious or mad. Take your pick.

SANDRA: But it will not kill him.

BABA: She did not ask for a death charm.

CELIA: Thank you, Baba.

BABA: That is OK. You can go now.

CELIA points to the second picture still on the mat with white powder on it.

CELIA: What about that?

BABA: I will keep it.

CELIA: All right. Thank you again, Baba.

SANDRA: Thank you, Baba.

CELIA and SANDRA both leave closing the door behind them. BABA is still seated yoga-style on the mat. There is the sound of car doors closing, then the engine starting, and finally driving off. BABA dusts the powder off the pieces of the picture. Then he turns the pieces face down. Written in one corner of the picture in light pencil is 'Ugochukwu Umoh on his eighth birthday'. BABA rocks back and forth gently, an enigmatic smile on his face.

Fade.

Scene XIII

The UMOHS' house. CELIA drives in, parks and alights. The front door opens and the girls rush out.

ITORO: Mummy! Mummy!

ENO: Welcome, Mummy.

EKAETTE: Where did you go, Mummy?

ITORO, ENO and EKAETTE surround her at the car.

CELIA: I went somewhere with Aunty Sandra.

CELIA takes some plastic bags out of the car.

EKAETTE: Where?

ENO: What is that?

ITORO: Yippee! You brought something for us! [*The girls grab at the bags.*]

CELIA: Easy. Don't fight over it. Each of you can carry a bag.

They each take a bag. CELIA locks the car. The girls peer into the bags.

EKAETTE: Meat pies! Doughnuts! Yeah!

ENO: Mine has chicken. What's in your bag, Itoro?
                    [ENO and ITORO peer into the bag.] Sausage
                    rolls. [ITORO screws up her face.]

ITORO: I don't want sausage rolls. I want meat pie
                    and chicken. Mummy, I want chicken!

CELIA: Everything will be divided among you. Eno,
                    here. [She gives ENO another bag.] Go inside.

ATIM has come out to meet her. She takes CELIA'S handbag.

ATIM: Welcome, Ma.

CELIA: Thank you. [The girls are now inside; CELIA
                    and ATIM head for the house.] Did they finish
                    their food?

ATIM: Eno and Ekaette finish their food. Itoro no
                    finish her own.

CELIA: [frowning] Her appetite has been going down
                    recently. I hope nothing is wrong with her.
                    Maybe I'd better take her to the doctor just
                    to be sure.

ATIM: [shrugging] If na chocolate and cake, Ma, she
                    no get problem. She can finish a whole box.
                    [They enter the house.]

CELIA: Where's Mama?

ATIM: She go out. She say she want visit her friend
                    in Yaba.

CELIA: How did she go?

ATIM: Haruna call taxi for her.

CELIA: [*settling in the settee*] When did she leave?

ATIM: Almost one hour ago.

CELIA: Hmm. Share the snacks I brought among
                   the girls and yourself. Let everyone have a
                   piece of everything. Don't take my handbag
                   upstairs. Give it to me.

ATIM: Yes, Ma. Thank you, Ma.

*ATIM exits. CELIA waits a while then takes the bottle out of the bag.
She goes outside and standing on the front steps shakes the bottle vigorously.
Then she starts sprinkling it around the house.*

CELIA: [*under her breath*] Make him mad. Make
                   him mad.

*She repeats this as she goes around the entire house ending up back on the
steps. She looks around. HARUNA is in the maiguard post watching
her. She heads back inside. A car drives up to the gate and horns. CELIA
stops. HARUNA opens the gates. ANI drives in. The girls come rushing
out. They are still eating their snacks. They rush to ANI as he alights.*

EKAETTE, ENO *and* ITORO: [*together*] Welcome, Daddy!
                   Welcome! [*ANI hugs them.*]

ANI: Thank you. And how are my lovely ladies?

EKAETTE, ENO *and* ITORO: Fine, Daddy.

ITORO: Mummy bought snacks for us.

ITORO shows him the doughnut she's eating. EKAETTE and ENO bring out his briefcase and newspapers from the back. ATIM comes out of the house.

ITORO: Do you want some, Daddy?

ANI: Thank you but no. Right now I want real food.

ITORO: [*pouting*] Just a little.

ANI: OK. [*He dutifully takes a small bite of the proffered doughnut.*] Mmhmm. Lovely.

ATIM: Welcome, sir.

ANI: Yes, Atim. How are you?

ATIM: Fine, sir.

EKAETTE: Atim, take.

EKAETTE gives ATIM ANI'S jacket and the newspapers. ITORO goes over to ENO.

ITORO: I want to carry Daddy's briefcase.

ENO: You can't.

ITORO: [*whining*] Why not?

ENO: [*looking annoyed*] Because you can't.

ITORO: [*plucking at ANI who is walking towards the house*] Daddy, I want to carry your briefcase.

ENO: It's too heavy for her, Daddy.

ANI: Let Eno carry it today. You can carry it
                  tomorrow, OK?

Itoro considers this. ANI has reached where CELIA is standing.

CELIA: Hello darling. How was your day?

*ANI ignores her and enters the house. ATIM and the girls follow. CELIA
watches them, then slowly walks in. She follows them to her and ANI'S
bedroom. ANI is sitting on the bed loosening his tie. His daughters are all
talking at once, vying for his attention.*

CELIA: Girls! Girls! [*EKAETTE, ENO and ITORO
                  keep quiet and look at her.*] Have you finished
                  your snacks?

EKAETTE: I haven't eaten my chicken yet!

ENO: Me, too.

CELIA: Why don't you all go downstairs and finish
                  up so Atim can clear the kitchen?

ENO: OK, Mummy.

EKAETTE, ENO and ITORO exit. CELIA closes the door.

CELIA: Ani, what is it?

ANI: It seems, Celia, that you are beginning to
                  forget who the man in this house is.

CELIA: Ah, Ani…

ANI: [*sharply*] Wait! I have not finished. Let this be
                the last time you hang up the phone on me
                ever again. Do you hear me? Never again,
                Celia. Ever since this situation with Ijeoma
                and the boy came up you seem to take it
                as a licence to behave anyway you like. I
                have tried to give you some leeway because
                I understand that it is difficult for you, but
                you are abusing it. So we are going to have
                some new rules around here. From now on,
                you will go nowhere without my express
                permission beforehand.

CELIA: [*looking shocked*] Ani.

ANI: Nowhere, Celia! You have no job to go
                to all day, but a simple thing like picking
                your own daughters from school becomes
                an issue. You forced me to leave a very
                important meeting because you could not
                make better arrangements. So I will be
                making all the arrangements from now on.
                And that means that you do not step out of
                this house without my permission. Do you
                understand, Celia?

CELIA: I don't believe you are talking like this, Ani!

ANI: [*almost shouting*] Do you understand, Celia!

CELIA: No! I won't become a prisoner in the house!

ANI: You will go out when I deem it necessary for
                you to do so. No more unnecessary errands!

CELIA: I haven't even told you what I went to do
                this afternoon!

ANI: And I don't want you to! I don't want to
                know! All I'm saying is that from now
                on you go nowhere without my consent
                beforehand. Is that clear!

*There is silence as they regard each other. Then CELIA covers her face with
her hands and slowly sits on the bed. She starts sobbing.*

CELIA: This is how it starts. Yes, this is how it
                starts. You want to throw me out and marry
                someone else. That is why you are treating
                me like this. Oh, God, after all these years!

ANI: Shut up! [*CELIA looks up startled. The sobs
                abruptly cease and her mouth hangs open.*] You
                brought this on yourself!

CELIA: It is Ijeoma. You are still having an affair
                with her.

ANI: [*tight-lipped*] For the last time, no. I am not
                having any affair. Now listen. I am taking
                my son to the court tomorrow to change
                his name officially from Ugochukwu to
                Ubong Umoh. On Saturday, I will bring
                him here. Arrange his room in advance. I
                want everything to be ready and I want him
                to receive a warm welcome when he comes.
                Is that clear, Celia?

CELIA: [*sobbing again*] And if I refuse?

ANI: I will pack you back to your parents. You will
                 stay with them until you remember that a
                 wife is supposed to obey her husband.

CELIA: [*throwing up her hands and shouting*] Heeey!
                 You want to pack me back to my parents in
                 disgrace!

*CELIA sobs noisily. ANI has finished changing his clothes. He doesn't
answer her. He leaves the room closing the door behind him. As soon as
the door closes CELIA stops crying.*

CELIA: [*to herself*] Good heavens, this is serious. I've
                 never seen Ani like this before. He is willing
                 to throw me out because of Ijeoma and her
                 bastard. Imagine! No way. Over my dead
                 body. I will not step out of this house for
                 any woman. Hmm. I'm going about this
                 the wrong way. Bullying and crying will not
                 work. OK, I'll change tactics. I'll be as sweet
                 as sugar. Yes, that's it. And I'll have a good
                 room prepared for that bastard. I'll see to
                 it myself. It will be nicely done. That will
                 please Ani. Only I know that he will not stay
                 there for long. Thank you, Baba. I can't wait
                 to see Ani's face when his precious son goes
                 stark raving mad. [*She gives a small smile.*] But
                 now I have to mend some bridges. Let me go
                 down and prepare the goat pepper soup the
                 way Ani likes it. I'll use it as a peace offering.
                 I'll appear to accept his ultimatums. Men.
                 They all need to feel like they are the lords
                 of the manor. No problem. I'm a woman.
                 There are ways around that. [*She gets up and
                 wipes her eyes. Her phone rings. She checks it and
                 answers.*] Hello, Sandra.

SANDRA:	How is it going?
CELIA:	Rough. Ani is angry. But I know how to handle it.
SANDRA:	What's he angry about?
CELIA:	He had to leave an important meeting to pick the girls up. I have to seriously start looking for a driver. I need one by Saturday.
SANDRA:	I'll help you ask around. Cee, Regina just called me. She ran into Ani at Toyland children's store at around 2 p.m. He was with a woman and a boy. She says he was buying toys obviously for the boy. She was fishing to find out what's going on.
CELIA:	It's happening already. Sandra, my disgrace is already being made public. Anyway, I'll bear it. It's for a short time.
SANDRA:	Yes. Take heart. Baba won't fail. Oh, I have to go, Cee. Peter is waiting for me. We are going to look at some cars.
CELIA:	He's buying you the new car?
SANDRA:	Yes!
CELIA:	Good for you! Go on then. I'll call you back later. [*She ends the call.*] So, he took his bastard shopping. Wait a minute. Regina saw them in the shop at around two. Eeeeh! So that is the meeting that was so important that he is quarrelling with me. His son is

now more important than his daughters. We shall see.

CELIA goes downstairs. ANI and the girls are in the parlour.

CELIA:	[*sharply*] All of you girls out of here. Out now!
ENO:	Why, Mummy?
CELIA:	Don't ask me questions. Just do as I say!
EKAETTE:	Where should we go, Mummy?
CELIA:	Anywhere except the parlour.
ANI:	What is the problem? [*CELIA ignores him.*]
ITORO:	I want to stay with Daddy.
CELIA:	I said out! Now! [*The girls exit.*]
ANI:	What is the meaning of all this?
CELIA:	Why should they hang around you? Your son is more important than they. This very important meeting of yours was to buy toys for your son. Go and buy more things for your son. Go and buy the whole shop for him! Leave my daughters for me!
ANI:	Celia, be very careful…
CELIA:	[*shouting*] What for! You betray me, lie to me, dismiss your daughters as of no consequence…

ANI: That's not true! I did not dismiss them!
[*CELIA continues talking over him.*]

CELIA: And you have the guts to tell me you are laying down rules. I should go nowhere without your permission! Oya now. Try and stop me!

CELIA turns to storm out. EKAETTE, ENO and ITORO are standing in the doorway.

ENO: Mummy, why are you shouting at Daddy?

EKAETTE: You told us never to shout at people!

CELIA: Didn't I tell you to go elsewhere?

ITORO: I don't want you to shout at Daddy!

CELIA: Oya, go outside and play. All of you.

CELIA bundles them out of the room and leaves with them. IDORENYIN comes in.

IDORENYIN: My son, what is happening?

ANI: Nothing, Mama. Don't worry about it.

IDORENYIN: Why don't you tell me? I might be able to help.

ANI: Thank you, but I can handle it.

IDORENYIN: OK, Ani. Just remember I'm here for you.

ANI just nods.

Fade.

Scene XIV

It is night. The girls are in the upstairs parlour watching cartoons on the TV. Three mugs are on a tray in varying stages of emptiness. Each mug has the name of one of the girls on it. IDORENYIN and CELIA are also in the parlour. ITORO is sitting on the sofa beside CELIA, dozing intermittently. IDORENYIN too, is nodding off. CELIA glances up at the clock.

CELIA: It's almost bedtime. Finish your hot chocolates. The girls each grab their cup and start drinking again.

EKAETTE: Aww, Mummy, just this once. Please let's stay up.

ITORO: [*yawning*] Please, Mummy.

CELIA: You were practically asleep, Itoro.

ITORO: No. I'm watching TV.

ENO: I'm almost ten. I should be allowed to stay up.

CELIA: Fine. You'll be allowed to stay up later when you are ten. But right now, you're still nine years old.

EKAETTE: I'll be eight next month. Don't I get to stay up, too?

CELIA: What you'll get is lots of presents.

ITORO is dozing off again. CELIA takes the mug out of her hands to prevent the chocolate spilling.

CELIA: [*softly*] Itoro is sleeping. Let me take her to bed. [*IDORENYIN snores gently.*]

ENO: Grandma is sleeping, but you are not sending her to bed.

CELIA: She's an adult. [*ANI enters the parlour. ITORO wakes up.*]

ITORO: No, no. I'm not sleeping.

ANI: [*sitting on the sofa beside ITORO*] Mama, Mama. [*IDORENYIN wakes up.*]

IDORENYIN: Eh? Eh? I dozed off. Well I think I'll go to bed then.

ANI: Before you go, Mama, I have something I'd like to tell you. To tell everyone. Girls, listen. [*ANI waits until they are all looking at him.*] You have a brother. [*They all look puzzled.*]

ENO: How did we get a brother?

EKAETTE: A brother, Daddy? [*IDORENYIN and ITORO are silent.*]

ANI: [*smiling at ITORO*] Don't you have something to say, too, honey? I've never known you to keep quiet about anything. [*ITORO yawns. ANI smiles ruefully.*] Well, I guess that explains it.

ITORO: [*sleepily*] Can I play with him?

ANI: [*tenderly*] Of course, sweetheart.

ENO: Daddy! Daddy! How did we get a brother?

EKAETTE: And where is he?

ENO: Is he a baby?

EKAETTE: A baby! Mummy, did you have a baby without telling us?

CELIA: No.

ANI: He is not a baby. He is eight years old.

EKAETTE: Older than me!

ENO: How can he be our brother if Mummy didn't have him?

ANI: He is your brother because he is my son.

ENO: Daddy, but Mummy didn't have him!

ANI: That's true, Eno. He has a different mother, but I am still his father.

ENO: [*frowning*] How is that?

ANI: It just is, Eno. He is my son. Therefore, he is your brother.

EKAETTE: I have a brother. Older than me. Wow!

ENO: How come we don't know him?

ANI: He has been with his mother all this while, but now he is going to come and live with us and we are going to get to know him very well.

ENO: What's his name?

ANI: Ubong.

EKAETTE: Can he fight?

ANI: Fight! You want to fight him?

EKAETTE: No, Daddy. But I can tell all those bullies at school they better watch out or my brother will beat them all up. Oh, this is good!

ANI: [*looking bemused*] Well, well. I don't know how well he can fight, Ekaette, but I don't want him fighting. There are other ways to deal with bullies. And you never told us you were being bullied at school.

ENO: That's because she isn't. She does the bullying, Daddy.

EKAETTE: No, I don't!

ENO: Yes, you do! I've seen you!

EKAETTE: You are the bully!

ENO: I'm not!

EKAETTE: You are!

ANI: All right, all right, all right! [*ENO and
                EKAETTE stick their tongues out at each other.*]
                Bullying is a serious issue and if any of you
                is ever bullied, I want you to tell me or your
                mother the very day it happens. OK?

ENO *and* EKAETTE: OK.

ANI: Now about Ubong.

EKAETTE: Yes. When do we see him?

ANI: On Saturday.

ENO: Why can't we see him tomorrow?

ANI: He has to go to school then get ready to
                come and live with us.

EKAETTE: I want to see him tomorrow!

ANI: Be patient, sweetheart. Saturday's just the
                day after tomorrow.

ENO: He's coming here to live with us?

ANI: Yes.

EKAETTE: A brother. Imagine that.

ANI: You haven't said anything, Mama.

IDORENYIN: My son, you have taken me by complete
                    surprise. But I, too, am eager to meet
                    Ubong.

ANI: All right. Saturday then. OK, girls. Bedtime.

*Reluctantly EKAETTE and ENO leave. CELIA carries the sleeping
ITORO out of the parlour.*

IDORENYIN: To say you took me by surprise is even an
                    understatement. Why have you not told me
                    about him before now?

ANI: I didn't know about him, Mama. His mother
                    only told me of his existence three days ago.

IDORENYIN: Are you sure he's yours?

ANI: Yes. When you see him, you will understand.

IDORENYIN: He resembles you?

ANI: A lot.

IDORENYIN: That's good. Who is his mother?

ANI: A former secretary of mine. Ijeoma
                    Nwankwo.

IDORENYIN: Why didn't she tell you before?

ANI: She hasn't given me a satisfactory answer to
                    that. She says she intended to tell me when
                    she realised she was pregnant, but Eno had

just been born and she felt it would create big problems in my marriage.

IDORENYIN: [*somewhat sceptically*] That's very considerate of her. Why is she telling you now?

ANI: Because she realises it's not fair to either Ubong or me.

IDORENYIN: Or maybe she's tired of people mocking her or calling the boy fatherless.

ANI: I'm sure that played a major part, too.

IDORENYIN: Did she name him Ubong?

ANI: She named him Ugochukwu. That approximately means 'the glory of God' in Igbo.

IDORENYIN: I see. You simply changed it to Annang.

ANI: Yes. Ubong Abasi. 'The glory of God.' It's a good name. I'll be taking him to the court tomorrow to make it official.

IDORENYIN: So tell me, what is my grandson like?

ANI: Ah Mama, he's a wonderful boy. You will see for yourself.

IDORENYIN: Ani, this is wonderful news. I'm very happy about it. But I must ask, how is your wife taking it?

ANI: She's getting used to it. It was a surprise to her, too.

IDORENYIN: This is a matter that needs delicate handling o! You have to be gentle with her, but at the same time firm.

ANI: Yes, Mama. Don't worry. I'm handling it.

IDORENYIN: Ubong Abasi. Thank you, God, for this gift. My ceaseless prayers to you have been answered. Thank you, God. Thank you, Jesus. My son's name will live on.

She continues smiling.

Fade.

Scene XV

ANI'S office. He is there working. Intercom buzzes.

FUNKE: Sir, Mr Umana is here.

ANI: Let him come in. [*GERRY enters.*]

GERRY: I brought a driver for you.

ANI: That's fast. I mentioned it to you just last night.

GERRY: It's pure luck actually. He was driving the Jensens and you know they are leaving.

ANI: Yes. Returning to the US. Have they gone already?

GERRY: No. They leave later today. I brought him for you to check out. If you like him he can start with you tomorrow.

ANI: How was he with the Jensens?

GERRY: Mark says he was reliable.

ANI: Reliable. That's a word one doesn't usually associate with drivers. That's high recommendation. Where is he?

GERRY: Downstairs in the lobby.

ANI: I'll talk to him on my way out then.

GERRY: What time are you due at the courthouse
                with your son?

ANI: 1.30. But I have to leave now. I want to take
                him and his mum to lunch first. What are
                your plans for lunch?

GERRY: The cafeteria at the office.

ANI: Why don't you join us? I'd love you to meet
                Ubong.

GERRY: Sure. I'm looking forward to meeting
                him, too.

ANI: Great. [*He arranges his desk.*] He's so shy,
                almost to the point of being repressed. He
                was living with Ijeoma's sister and I think
                she was a bit harsh with him.

GERRY: Why couldn't he live with Ijeoma?

ANI: She was hopping around. She didn't have a
                steady place to keep him.

GERRY: How's Celia taking it?

ANI: As well as can be expected, I guess. There
                were some fireworks yesterday, but things
                have calmed down now.

GERRY: If you ever need somewhere to keep him for
                a while, my place is open to you.

ANI: Thanks, but I want him with me. I'm going
                to work on his shyness. I want to draw
                him out.

GERRY: OK. [ANI dials the intercom.]

FUNKE: Yes, sir?

ANI: I'm going out. I should be back around
                three.

FUNKE: Yes, sir.

ANI and GERRY leave through the corridor door.

Fade.

Scene XVI

The UMOHS' house. Everyone is in the downstairs parlour. The girls are neatly dressed. There is an air of expectancy.

ITORO: Mummy. When is he coming now? [*CELIA just shrugs. ITORO goes and shakes her.*] When, Mummy?

CELIA: I don't know, dear. Soon, I expect.

ENO: Daddy said he'll bring him here by one. Now it's almost two. [*CELIA shrugs again.*]

CELIA: Maybe he got caught in traffic.

IDORENYIN: Hasn't he called you?

CELIA: No.

IDORENYIN: Why don't you call him?

CELIA: If anything was wrong, he would call. I'm sure he'll be here soon. Ekaette, stop playing with the remote control. Decide on one channel and leave it there.

EKAETTE: OK. Cartoon Network.

ENO: No. I want to watch something on Disney Channel.

EKAETTE: I want to watch Cartoon Network. Mummy said *I* should decide.

ENO: That's not fair! You didn't even want to watch Cartoon Network before!

EKAETTE: I do now!

ENO: Mummy, tell her to put it on Disney Channel!

CELIA: You know what? Ekaette put it on CNN.

ENO: [*wailing*] Mummy!

CELIA: What is it you want to watch on Disney Channel?

ENO: *The Suite Life on Deck.*

EKAETTE: They don't show that at this time! Mummy, they don't show that at this time!

ENO: Yes, they do!

CELIA: Go to my room and use the decoder there.

ENO: Thank you, Mummy. [*ENO exits.*]

ITORO: I want to play outside, Mummy.

EKAETTE: Yes. Let's ride our bicycles, Itoro.

IDORENYIN: Don't you think everyone should wait here until Ani and Ubong arrive?

CELIA: What difference does it make? When they arrive, everyone will go to greet them.

IDORENYIN: But I thought Ani said…

CELIA: Mama, they're tired of sitting around. Let them do what they want.

A car horn sounds outside. Both girls jump up.

EKAETTE *and* ITORO: They're here! [*ENO rushes into the room.*]

ENO: They're here!

They all rush outside. CELIA and IDORENYIN follow. The driver parks the car. ANI and UBONG are sitting in the back. The girls rush to open the door chorusing welcomes. ANI helps UBONG out of the car and takes his hand. They face the assembled girls, CELIA, and IDORENYIN.

ANI: Everyone, meet Ubong. Ubong, these are your grandmother, your stepmother and your sisters [*He points as he names them.*] Eno, Ekaette, and Itoro.

UBONG: Good afternoon. [*IDORENYIN embraces him.*]

IDORENYIN: Welcome. Welcome, my child.

CELIA hugs him perfunctorily and quickly releases him. She forces a smile.

CELIA:	Welcome.
UBONG:	Thank you, ma'am.

One by one the girls also hug him and welcome him.

ANI:	This is Elijah, our new driver. I picked him up before going for Ubong. That's why I took so long.
ELIJAH:	Good afternoon, Ma. Good afternoon, Ma. Good afternoon.
CELIA:	You are welcome, Elijah.
ELIJAH:	Thank you, Ma.
ANI:	Haruna. [*HARUNA comes over.*] You and Elijah can take the cases upstairs. Atim will show you where to keep them.
HARUNA:	Yes, oga.

ELIJAH and HARUNA start unloading the car. Everybody else goes towards the house. The girls start chattering again.

EKAETTE:	You're not taller than me now. Daddy said you're eight, but you're not taller than me!
ANI:	You're tall for your age, Ekaette. You know that.

They enter the house, CELIA bringing up the rear. Inside the parlour she watches UBONG closely. HARUNA and ELIJAH come in with the cases. ATIM leads them upstairs.

ANI: Well, Ubong, this is home. This is where
                       you're going to live from now on.

UBONG: Yes, sir… er, Daddy. [*EKAETTE laughs.*]

EKAETTE: You called Daddy sir!

IDORENYIN: [*sternly*] That's nothing to laugh about,
                       Ekaette. He's not used to saying Daddy
                       like you.

ENO: [*to ANI*] Isn't he happy to be here?

ANI: Why don't you ask him? He's right in front
                       of you.

ENO: [*to UBONG*] Are you happy to be here?

UBONG: [*in a soft voice*] I'm very happy to be here
                       thank you.

*UBONG looks down at his hands during his reply. ANI and
IDORENYIN exchange glances.*

IDORENYIN: Why don't we let him go up to his room and
                       relax? It will take him a while to get used to
                       all this.

CELIA: I'll go and see about the food. Eno, Ekaette,
                       follow me. Come and make yourselves
                       useful.

*CELIA, EKAETTE and ENO head to the kitchen. IDORENYIN
and UBONG go upstairs with ITORO and ANI following them. They
show UBONG his room. It is neatly done up and nicely decorated.*

ANI: This is your room, Ubong.

UBONG: Yes, sir.

ANI: Sir?

UBONG: Sorry. Yes, Daddy.

IDORENYIN: Do you like it?

UBONG: Yes, ma'am.

IDORENYIN: Call me Grandma, dear. Ma'am is so formal.
                [*She smiles.*]

UBONG: Yes, Ma... Grandma. [*He smiles back
                tentatively.*]

IDORENYIN: Your suitcases are already here. After lunch
                I will help you unpack.

UBONG: Yes, M... Grandma. [*ITORO rushes in.*]

ITORO: Ubong. Ubong. Here. I made this for you.

*ITORO hands UBONG a large paper. On it is a crude drawing of a
boy and a girl smiling and holding hands with a large yellow sun above
their heads. Under the girl carefully printed in childish writing is the word
'Itoro'. Under the boy 'Ubong' and in brackets 'my brother'.*

ITORO: I drew it for you. See? [*She points.*] This me
                and this you! My brother! Do you like it?
                [*UBONG smiles widely at ITORO.*]

UBONG: Yes, I like it very much. Thank you. [*ANI
                pats ITORO affectionately.*]

ANI: That's a wonderful gift, honey. I like it, too.
                        [*IDORENYIN hugs ITORO.*]

IDORENYIN: Well done, my child.

ITORO beams. UBONG puts the drawing on the dresser top.

ITORO: Do you want to play outside, Ubong?

ANI: After lunch, dear. Right now we have to go
                        and eat. But I'm sure he'll be willing to play
                        with you afterwards.

*They all go back downstairs. Lunch is on the table and ATIM is bringing
out a last dish. CELIA is just coming out of the kitchen.*

CELIA: Lunch is ready. Itoro, call your sisters. They
                        went back to the parlour. [*ITORO leaves the
                        room.*]

ITORO'S VOICE: Eno, Ekaette, come and eat.

*The others arrange themselves around the table. IDORENYIN pulls
out the chair next to her for UBONG. The girls enter and everyone gets
seated. ANI says the grace. EKAETTE and ENO peep at UBONG
during the prayer.*

ANI: Heavenly Father, we thank you for this
                        beautiful day and for the nourishing food
                        you have provided for us. Most of all,
                        Father, we thank you for Ubong. Thank
                        you for bringing him to us. We pray that
                        you continue to guide and protect us, and
                        to bless us in Jesus' name. Amen.

EVERYONE: Amen. [*CELIA gets up to dish out the food.*]

ITORO: Eno and Ekaette did not close their eyes.

ENO: And how did you see us? Can you see with
                your eyes closed?

ITORO: [*in a singsong voice, with one finger on one eye*] I
                closed this eye, then this one…

IDORENYIN: [*sharply*] Praying is not a game, girls. It
                is respectful to close your eyes in God's
                presence.

CELIA: They are children, Mama. And they
                normally close their eyes. They were not
                being intentionally disrespectful.

ANI: That is true. Nevertheless, close your eyes
                next time. OK, girls?

ENO *and* EKAETTE: Yes, Daddy.

*CELIA finishes dishing for the three girls. When she reaches for
UBONG'S plate, IDORENYIN takes it.*

IDORENYIN: I'll dish his since he's right next to me.
                [*CELIA frowns.*]

ANI: Mama, let her dish it. She's dishing for all
                the children.

IDORENYIN: But…

ANI: Mama.

IDORENYIN: [*forcing a smile*] Of course.

IDORENYIN gives the plate to CELIA. CELIA dishes food on it and gives it to UBONG.

UBONG: Thank you, ma'am.

CELIA: You're welcome.

CELIA serves ANI and herself. IDORENYIN dishes her own food. Everyone starts eating. UBONG uses his knife and fork and displays perfect table manners. ITORO pushes her vegetables aside.

CELIA: Eat your vegetables, Itoro.

ITORO: [*pouting*] I don't like them.

CELIA: If you want to grow big like Eno and Ekaette you have to eat them.

EKAETTE: Maybe Ubong should get more vegetables.

ENO: Why?

EKAETTE: [*giggling*] So it will help him grow big. He's smaller than me!

ENO: [*giggling, too*] He can have some of mine!

IDORENYIN: One thing he has is better manners than you two. You know you should not talk with food in your mouths.

CELIA: Mama, one small lapse doesn't mean that they have no manners.

ANI: Ubong doesn't need your vegetables, Eno. He is OK as he is. He will grow bigger as he gets older. [*UBONG finishes his food.*]

IDORENYIN: Have some more, Ubong.

UBONG: No thank you, ma'am. I am full.

ITORO: Can we go outside and play now, Ubong?

CELIA: You haven't finished your food, Itoro. [*ITORO screws up her face.*]

ITORO: [*whining*] I don't want it.

ANI: All right. You can go.

ITORO: Yippee! [*She jumps off her chair.*] Come on, Ubong!

UBONG: May I be excused?

IDORENYIN: Of course. Such beautiful manners! But why don't you go upstairs and change into something more comfortable first? In fact, let me come with you. I can help you unpack at the same time.

IDORENYIN, UBONG and ITORO leave. EKAETTE and ENO soon excuse themselves and leave, too. ATIM comes and starts collecting the plates.

ANI: Thank you, darling. That was delicious.

CELIA: Ani, I don't like what is happening.

ANI: [*guardedly*] What's that?

CELIA: The way Mama is behaving. It's as if she's
                        trying to push me aside and position herself
                        as Ubong's surrogate mother. I am your
                        wife. That is my role. You better talk to her.
                        Let us avoid problems.

ANI: She's only trying to help out. I know she can
                        get overzealous at times, but why don't you
                        just let her be. She will soon return to the
                        village anyway.

*CELIA purses her lips, gets up and leaves the room. ANI puts his head
in his hands and sighs.*

Fade.

Scene XVII

It is night time. The children are all in pyjamas in the upstairs parlour watching TV. IDORENYIN, ANI and CELIA are there, too. ATIM comes in bearing a tray with four cups. Three of the cups are the same cups that bear the girls' names. The fourth cup is different and has no name printed on it. ATIM puts the tray on a table and leaves.

CELIA: Come and get your night hot chocolate. [*The girls each take a cup.*] Ubong, that one is yours. [*UBONG takes the cup with no name.*]

UBONG: Thank you.

CELIA: You're welcome.

The cartoon they were watching ends. ENO brings out another DVD from the cupboard.

ENO: Let's watch this one now.

EKAETTE: No, I don't like that one.

ENO: Well, I like it.

EKAETTE: Why do we always have to watch what you want?

IDORENYIN: Ubong what do you want to watch?

ITORO:	I want to play with Ubong's soldiers.
IDORENYIN:	Not now, Itoro. Ubong is watching TV.
ANI:	I'm sure he won't mind Itoro playing with them.
IDORENYIN:	Of course not. But I was just saying he probably prefers joining in what the others are doing.
ENO:	[*holding up the DVD she had chosen*] Do you want to watch this one, Ubong? It's very interesting.
EKAETTE:	[*loudly*] Not to me!
IDORENYIN:	There's no need to shout, Ekaette.
ANI:	Why don't you look through the DVDs and decide the one you want, Ubong?
UBONG:	Thank you, sir, but…
EKAETTE:	[*laughing loudly*] You're still calling Daddy sir!
IDORENYIN:	That's enough, Ekaette! He hasn't been fortunate to grow up with his father like you. That's nothing to laugh about!

EKAETTE stops laughing and looks uncertainly from her father to her mother.

IDORENYIN:	[*orders*] Apologise to him!

ANI: That is not necessary, Mama. She didn't
                        mean any harm. Just don't laugh at him
                        again, dear, OK?

EKAETTE: Yes, Daddy.

CELIA is frowning, her lips tightly pressed together.

ANI: So, Ubong, which one do you want?

UBONG: Any one is OK… Daddy.

ITORO: [*sulkily*] I want to play with the soldiers.

CELIA: [*sharply*] Play with your dolls, Itoro. You
                        have enough of those.

ITORO: [*screwing up her face to cry*] I want…

CELIA: [*looking sternly at her*] If you cry, you are going
                        straight to bed.

*Everyone is silent. ITORO, looking apprehensively at CELIA, sidles over
to ANI and crawls into his lap. CELIA stands up abruptly.*

CELIA: I'm going to bed. Good night, Mama. Good
                        night, children. Good night, Ani.

Even as they chorus their replies she's already gone.

ANI: Eno, put on the DVD you wanted. Let's all
                        watch that now. Next time, someone else
                        gets to choose.

ENO: OK, Daddy. [*She puts on the DVD.*]

126

ANI: [*to ITORO*] You can play with the soldiers tomorrow honey, OK? [*ITORO nods. The movie starts.*]

IDORENYIN: Celia's not taking this very well.

ANI: She just needs time to adjust to it.

IDORENYIN: Hmmm.

ITORO: Daddy.

ANI: Yes, Itoro?

ITORO: Why Mummy mad at me?

ANI: Remember the 'is', honey. 'Why is Mummy mad?' She's not mad at you. She's just a little upset. That's all.

ITORO: With me?

ANI: No, no. Not at all with you. [*ITORO looks up at him.*]

ITORO: With you?

ANI: [*smiling ruefully down at her*] Well, maybe a little with me.

ITORO: Will she tell you to go to bed, too?

ANI: [*putting on an expression of mock horror*] I hope not! [*ITORO giggles.*] I want to watch this DVD!

ITORO: [*still giggling*] Me, too! Me, too!

ANI: Then let's watch it with the others. [*ANI
                resettles ITORO on his lap and kisses her head.
                He looks over and sees UBONG watching him.
                He smiles at him.*] Next time, you choose,
                Ubong.

UBONG smiles back, then turns to face the TV.

Fade.

Scene XVIII

ANI and CELIA'S bedroom. CELIA is sitting at her dressing table. Her face is in her hands. When she takes her hands away her face is wet with tears. She stares at herself in the mirror for a long time, then gets up and goes into the bathroom. She emerges dressed in her night clothes. She dims the light and gets into bed. Shortly ANI comes into the room. He joins her in bed.

CELIA: When is Mama returning to the village?

ANI: Maybe in a couple of weeks.

CELIA: A couple of weeks. She has been here a month already.

ANI: You know there is nothing to rush back to the village for.

CELIA: Even so, it might be better if she returned now. This situation is not easy and she is not helping matters. She can always visit again some other time.

ANI: What has she done that's upset you so much?

CELIA: What has she done? I told you this afternoon. Ever since Ubong came she's tried to push me aside. To take over my role. And as for the girls, look at what happened this

129

evening. There was no need for her to attack Ekaette like that. She didn't mean any harm. She was just playing with him. Are the girls now going to have to watch everything they do and say around her? Their own grandmother?

ANI: Ubong is sensitive about not having had a father till now.

CELIA: I want her to go until we have adjusted to this situation as a family first. [*ANI makes no reply. CELIA turns to look at him.*] Is that too much to ask?

ANI: [*sighing*] I'll talk to her in the morning. [*CELIA gets out of bed.*] Where are you going?

CELIA: I want to see Itoro.

ANI: She's asleep. They all are.

CELIA leaves and goes into ENO and EKAETTE'S room. Both girls are asleep. She kisses them both, then goes into ITORO'S room. ATIM and ITORO are asleep. She kisses ITORO.

CELIA: [*softly*] I'm sorry for snapping at you, sweetheart.

ITORO doesn't stir. CELIA leaves and goes to the third room. She opens the door and slowly goes in. She stands by the bed and watches UBONG sleep. She looks around the room, in particular at the soldiers arranged on the shelf, then at ITORO'S drawing, which is pasted prominently on the wall. She goes over and stares intently at it. Then again at the sleeping boy. Finally she turns to leave and sees IDORENYIN standing in the doorway. CELIA leaves the room, brushing past IDORENYIN.

IDORENYIN: I hope there is no problem?

CELIA: Are you expecting any?

IDORENYIN: Ah no. I thought you were asleep, that's all.

CELIA: I'm going to sleep now.

IDORENYIN: I wanted to check on him. You know, first night in a new home. Just wanted to make sure he's all right.

CELIA: He is. But [*she waves at the room*] feel free to check. Good night.

IDORENYIN: Celia, my daughter, I know this cannot be easy for you, but...

CELIA: Everything's fine, Mama. Good night. [*CELIA exits.*]

Fade on IDORENYIN watching her go.

131

Scene XIX

SANDRA'S beach barbeque. People are milling around, while children in swimwear run around. There is music. CELIA pulls SANDRA off to one side.

CELIA: I need to talk to you.

SANDRA: I've been wanting to ask you; how did things go yesterday?

CELIA: That *babalawo* of yours is rubbish.

SANDRA: Nothing happened?

CELIA: Nothing happened!

SANDRA: What did you wish for?

CELIA: To make him mad. But look at him.

SANDRA and CELIA turn to look at a group of children, UBONG among them.

CELIA: Does he look mad to you?

SANDRA: Maybe it takes time for it to take effect.

CELIA: I didn't hear him say anything of the sort. The whole point of the charm was that

	that boy should not be able to step into my house. I never really believed in this anyway. I want to go and get my money back.
SANDRA:	I don't know what to say. Sorry. He came highly recommended. When do you want to go?
CELIA:	Tomorrow! As soon as the children and Ani leave I'm going to head straight there. I want to be back as early as possible.
SANDRA:	I can't make it that early.
CELIA:	That's OK. I can find my way there.
SANDRA:	You want to go alone?
CELIA:	What's he going to do to me? His charms have no effect on an eight-year-old. Is it me they will now affect? Forget it, Sandra, he's fake.
SANDRA:	Well, if you're sure…
CELIA:	I am. And believe me, he will give me my money or else. [*REGINA comes up to them.*]
REGINA:	Celia, congrats on your stepson! I guessed from the moment I saw him in that shop. He's Ani's spitting image! [*CELIA just smiles and nods. REGINA smiles pointedly at her.*] Well, now there is someone to inherit Ani's wealth!

SANDRA: What are you saying, Regina! That his daughters can't inherit? Didn't you inherit when your father died?

REGINA: What did I inherit? Anything worth having went to my brothers. That is the lot of we women. We can only enjoy through our husbands or our sons.

CELIA: [*turning away abruptly*] Excuse me. [*She walks away.*]

REGINA: Is everything all right with her?

SANDRA: [*sarcastically*] Of course, Regina. What could possibly be wrong? It's time for me to do some more mingling with my guests. Peter's business partner's wife is all by herself over there. I'll see you later, Regina.

SANDRA moves off. The children are still playing. UBONG who is watching them is dragged into a game by ITORO.

Fade on them playing.

Scene XX

The babalawo's *place. CELIA gets out of her car and marches to the door of the hut. She flings it open unceremoniously.*

CELIA: Baba! [*CELIA walks in with her shoes on.*]
                Baba! [*She looks around, then she hears his voice
                behind her.*]

BABA: Who dares to desecrate the place of the
                spirits by wearing shoes! [*CELIA whirls
                around.*]

CELIA: What spirits? Take! [*She throws the empty bottle
                at his feet.*] So much for your charms!

BABA: [*ignoring the bottle*] Before I discuss anything
                with you, you will go outside and come in
                again without your shoes! Do not bring the
                wrath of the spirits down on your head,
                foolish woman! [*CELIA stands mutinously as
                though she won't do it. BABA points to the door.*]
                Out! [*She reluctantly goes out then comes in again
                without her shoes.*] Sit down! [*She sits. BABA
                picks up the bottle and also sits down.*] What is
                your grievance?

CELIA: Shouldn't you already know that? You
                tell me!

BABA:	[*looking sternly at her*] Don't play with me, woman!
CELIA:	Hmmm! I want my money back. The 100,000 I paid you on Thursday, I want it back!
BABA:	I repeat, what is the problem?
CELIA:	Isn't it obvious? The charm did not work! [*BABA studies the bottle.*]
BABA:	What did you wish for?
CELIA:	I wished for him to become stark raving mad! I wanted him to bark like a dog the minute he stepped into my house! But what happened? Nothing! He has been in that house three days now and nothing is wrong with him. I want my money back. I'll go and handle this my own way.

BABA places the bottle on the mat then with his hands hovering over it, starts muttering. The muttering starts low at first then rises. Soon he is shouting.

BABA:	Reveal all to me, o great spirits of the forest! Reveal all to your humble servant! [*BABA mutters some more. Then finally he looks up at CELIA.*] This boy has protection. Powerful protection. That is why the charm did not work.
CELIA:	[*sarcastically*] Oh, really? I wonder why it is you did not realise this before.

BABA:	It has been very subtly done. It was impossible to realise it before. Only now that the charm hasn't worked was I able to dig deep past the wall of secrecy surrounding it to reveal it.
CELIA:	So what happens now?
BABA:	That depends on you. Not this charm or any other charm is going to work on him. You cannot touch him.
CELIA:	So that is all you have to tell me? That I cannot touch him!
BABA:	Not with charms.
CELIA:	Then what can I do?
BABA:	That brings us back to what I said. That it depends on you. [*He fixes CELIA with his gaze, then speaks slowly, enunciating every syllable.*] How far are you willing to go?

There is silence as the import of his words sinks in.

CELIA:	Killing him. Is that the only option?
BABA:	As you said yourself, it's a very final solution.
CELIA:	But what about this powerful protection of his?
BABA:	It cannot stop death by physical means. Supernatural means, yes. But not physical means.

CELIA: Explain physical means.

BABA: There are many ways for a person to die.
                        The simplest in this case would have been
                        for me to put a death curse on him. He
                        would just die for no apparent reason. But
                        that won't work. But if he was to, say fall
                        from the third floor of a building, or get hit
                        by a car… [BABA spreads his hands.] There
                        is nothing supernatural about that.

CELIA: Ah, no! How would I arrange that? I can't
                        afford to be near him when he falls from
                        a building. And I can't hit him with a car
                        myself, so I'd have to hire someone. That's
                        risky. The fewer people involved the better.

BABA: My thoughts exactly. So you use poison.

CELIA: [thoughtfully] Poison.

BABA: I have just the right one for you to use. It is
                        almost tasteless. But even better, it cannot
                        be detected with medical tests. Well what do
                        you say?

CELIA: Killing him is a big step.

BABA: Go home and think it over. When you
                        decide you're ready to do it, come back.

BABA gets up. CELIA sits there thoughtfully for a while then her
expression hardens. She calls BABA back.

CELIA: Baba. Baba. I have made up my mind. I am
                        ready. [BABA returns. He stares at her.]

BABA:	Are you sure?
CELIA:	Yes, Baba.
BABA:	Very sure?
CELIA:	Yes, Baba.
BABA:	Once you start this, there's no going back.
CELIA:	I'm sure.
BABA:	All right. First of all, it's going to cost you 500,000 naira.
CELIA:	500,000 naira!
BABA:	Yes. 500,000 naira.
CELIA:	But you're not the one doing the killing. I am!
BABA:	With the undetectable poison I'm going to give you. If I'm involved at all in any killing, that is my standard price.
CELIA:	Ah, ah, I don't have half a million naira.
BABA:	Go source for it. I will take half now and half after successful completion.
CELIA:	What about the 100,000 I paid you for the charm that did not work?
BABA:	I've told you why that did not work. Still, I'll be generous. Subtract that from the

half million. So give me 200,000 now and 200,000 after. [*CELIA sighs and brings out a cheque book from her handbag.*] No, no, no. No cheques. Come back when you have the cash.

CELIA: All right. I'll see what I can do today and try to bring the first instalment tomorrow.

BABA: No problem. [*CELIA holds out her hand but BABA shakes his head.*] You don't get it until you pay the first amount.

CELIA: Don't you trust me?

BABA: It's not a matter of trust. After all, you will still be owing me the remaining half. I know you won't be foolish enough to try to cheat a *babalawo* of my stature out of his money. There's nowhere on this earth you could run to where I would not still reach you. No, trust is not the issue. It's commitment. A lot of people get cold feet when it comes to the actual act of killing. However once you can bring the money it means you are serious. I don't like wasting my resources.

CELIA: I see. OK then. I'll be seeing you tomorrow.

BABA: [*nodding sagely*] Tomorrow then.

CELIA leaves.

Fade.

Scene XXI

ANI'S office. FUNKE opens the door and IDORENYIN walks in. ANI gets up and shows her to a seat then resumes his position.

ANI: What will you take, Mama? Something hot or cold?

IDORENYIN: You know we had breakfast not long ago. I'm fine for now. I feel we need to talk, my son, just you and me. That is not possible when you are at home which is why I chose to come here.

ANI: [*sitting back in his chair*] What's on your mind?

IDORENYIN: Celia is not handling this well at all.

ANI: It's a difficult situation for any woman to handle. She just needs time to adjust. I wanted to talk to you, too, Mama. I think what is needed now is for Celia and Ubong to get used to each other. It would be best if you leave and come back later when everyone is more settled.

IDORENYIN: You want me to go?

ANI: For now, Mama. You can come back in a month or two.

IDORENYIN:	[*shaking her head*] Celia wants me to leave.
ANI:	I am the one asking you. Give us a chance as a family to adjust to this new addition.
IDORENYIN:	I know it is Celia's wish for me to go. But I don't want you to do things blindly. Think about this. Really think about it. Right now your overriding concern should be Ubong. Celia and the girls have been with each other all their lives. Ubong is the new fish entering their settled pond. As difficult as things may be for anyone else, it doesn't compare to how very hard it is for him. I think he's doing a remarkable job coping. And the girls, Itoro in particular, are helping a lot. Still, he needs all the support he can get. You are at work all day. You come home late in the evening. You only know what goes on during the day if someone tells you. Ubong is very shy. He will not run to you to complain about anything he feels uncomfortable about. You know that. You need someone in that house whose overriding concern is Ubong. Someone like me. Especially now, in these early days.
ANI:	Mama, nothing's going to happen to him. Yes, I know he's shy, but that's all the more reason for him to quickly get used to the situation he now finds himself in. What I don't want is for him to run to you about things creating a division in the household.
IDORENYIN:	The last thing I want is to create a division in your household. I'm not intending to

do that. But telling someone who is as shy as Ubong that he just has to cope with the situation anyhow he can is not fair to him, Ani. Let me keep an eye on him at least this first week. I tell you I have no intention of causing disharmony in your home.

ANI: Well…

IDORENYIN: What is Celia afraid of anyway?

ANI: Why should she be afraid?

IDORENYIN: Exactly. Just one week. Then I'll leave.

ANI: That's just it, Mama. I know you don't do it intentionally, but Celia is feeling sidelined. You are jumping in to do things for Ubong that by rights Celia should be doing. Criticising the girls…

IDORENYIN: I don't criticise the girls. I just said they are helping Ubong settle in.

ANI: Last night with Ekaette, for example…

IDORENYIN: Ah, all I said was she should not laugh at him. Think how it must have made him feel.

ANI: Everybody's sensitive at the moment. That's what I'm trying to tell you. If you want to stay on, you need to be really careful what you say, even how you say it. And give Celia space to be with Ubong. She's his stepmother. She wants to start fulfilling her role.

IDORENYIN: All right, my son. Like I said, the last thing I
                  want to do is bring discord into your home.
                  I promise you I will be very careful. I just
                  want to make things easier for everyone.

ANI: I know you are only trying to help. But I
                  still think it might be better if you gave Celia
                  time to cope in her own way.

IDORENYIN: One week. That's all I ask. Then if she still
                  feels the same, I'll go. [*ANI contemplates this.*]

ANI: All right, Mama. All right. Now what is it
                  you wished to discuss?

IDORENYIN: [*spreading her hands*] This. We've discussed it.
                  I wanted to make some suggestions to help
                  Celia cope, but I think it might be better to
                  leave her to do things her way. Well, let me
                  start heading back. Hope you'll finish early
                  today?

ANI: I'll try to get home as early as I can, but that
                  depends on the outcome of the meeting I
                  have with my contractors.

IDORENYIN: OK. I'll see you when you get home then.

ANI: All right, Mama. Goodbye.

IDORENYIN: Goodbye.

IDORENYIN leaves.

Fade.

Scene XXII

CELIA drives into SANDRA'S boutique. She alights and walks in.

IYABO: Welcome, Ma. Madam is expecting you.

CELIA: Thank you.

CELIA walks through to SANDRA'S office flops down into a chair and removes her sunglasses.

SANDRA: *Pele o.* How did it go? Did you get your money back? [*CELIA nods.*]

CELIA: Trust me now. I got my money back complete. He didn't want to give me at first, but he changed his tune when I told him I'd be back with mobile police. That I would rather give that money to the police than to him.

SANDRA: *Na wa o.* Sorry, sha. Like I told you, he was highly recommended, I didn't know it would turn out like this. Although with the benefit of hindsight, I guess I should have realised.

CELIA: Why? What do you mean?

SANDRA: It was Regina who recommended him *o*!

CELIA:	[*looking surprised*] Regina!
SANDRA:	Yes *o*! Remember a while back she and Thomas had problems with the US authorities?
CELIA:	I heard something like that. Something about their visas being revoked or something like that. I never knew the details. When I saw that she had travelled again, I concluded that it had all just been baseless rumours.
SANDRA:	I never knew the details either until she told me. Apparently Thomas got into some trouble in the US and it affected them both.
CELIA:	What kind of trouble?
SANDRA:	She didn't say. But I have my suspicions. [*CELIA raises her eyebrows. SANDRA nods knowingly.*] Yes *o*! Remember also they had money problems before that. Thomas even asked Peter to stand guarantee for him in the bank so he could get a loan. Peter couldn't because he had so many mortgages going, he couldn't afford to take that risk. So I think Thomas did something to get the money that landed him in trouble with the US immigration. Whatever, Regina said she was at her wits end when someone told her about this *babalawo*. She didn't believe it would help, but she decided to give it a try. One visit and he gave her a charm to take with her to the embassy. It worked like a dream. She said the embassy officials were even falling over themselves to help

her. She was so impressed. And their visas were renewed sharp-sharp. She gave me his address and everything. So I told you about him but I should have remembered Regina's tendency to exaggerate. Now I wonder what part, if any, of what she told me is true.

CELIA: Some of it must have been true. Why would she come and tell you a pack of total fabrications?

SANDRA: Principally because she likes the sound of her own voice.

CELIA: Still, her problem was solved somehow.

SANDRA: Let's leave Regina *jo*. So what are you going to do now?

CELIA: Nothing. I'm just going to lie low and see how things turn out.

SANDRA: You won't try a different *babalawo*?

CELIA: No. This one says the reason the charm didn't work is because the boy has such powerful protection that no charm would work anyway.

SANDRA: Who would have put such protection on him and why?

CELIA: His mother probably, since she was planning to hand him over to his father.

SANDRA: True. True. Well, Cee, I think what you have decided is probably best. As time goes on you can figure out what to do. And think of what people would have said had he indeed gone mad. The finger of suspicion would have pointed straight at you.

CELIA: [*nodding*] Yes. Maybe it's all for the best. [*She checks her watch.*] I have to leave now. I want to stop at Toyland before I go home.

SANDRA: OK. Talk to you later.

CELIA nods and leaves. She drives to an ATM, puts in two cards and withdraws 200,000 naira. She goes back to the car and drives off.

Fade.

Scene XXIII

The UMOHS' house. CELIA drives in. ATIM comes to greet her.

CELIA: Where are the children?

ATIM: Driver done go pick them from school. [*CELIA looks at her watch and frowns.*]

CELIA: At this time? He should have gone long since. They should be back by now.

ATIM: Mama been go out. He bring her back before he go to the school.

As CELIA heads towards the house, the driver and children return. CELIA stops and waits for them. They run and greet her. UBONG is last. He greets her, too.

UBONG: Good afternoon, ma'am.

CELIA: Good afternoon, Ubong. All right all of you. You are late back. You must be starving. Go and get your food.

IDORENYIN has come out while she was speaking. The children greet her, too.

IDORENYIN: [*following CELIA inside*] I had some errands to run this morning. [*CELIA just nods.*

	IDORENYIN continues following her.] My daughter, we need to talk.
CELIA:	Later please, Mama. [*IDORENYIN falls back and lets her go. CELIA goes into the girls' room. They are changing out of their uniforms.*] How was school today?
EKAETTE:	Fine, Mummy. The only thing we talked about is tomorrow's trip to Abuja.
ENO:	Here is the schedule they printed.
CELIA:	[*taking over from ATIM who had been helping Itoro change*] I'll change Itoro. Go and put out their food. [*To ENO.*] Where is the schedule? [*ENO brings it out and shows to her.*] You are to go to school as normal in your uniforms. Your flight is at twelve noon. We are to pick you up as normal from the school on Friday.
EKAETTE:	We are going to Aso Rock and we are going to meet the First Lady!
CELIA:	It's very good of the First Lady to take time out to see you.
ENO:	It's not just our school. Three other schools are going, too.
ITORO:	Mummy, I want to go to Abuja!
EKAETTE:	We've already been to Abuja, Itoro. We stayed at the Abuja Hilton and you liked swimming in the pool all the time!

ENO: They had that big duck in the pool, remember?

ITORO: [*smiling*] Yes! Yes! Mummy, I want to go to Abuja again!

CELIA: [*smiling, too*] We'll go again sometime soon.

ITORO: I want to go with Eno and Ekaette.

CELIA: I'm sure it will soon be the turn of your class to go. Now go down for your lunch. [*She pauses, as the girls start to leave the room.*] Itoro wait. [*The other girls leave her and ITORO in the room.*] I got something for you. [*CELIA hands a Toyland bag to ITORO. ITORO opens it and brings out a box containing the same type of toy soldiers UBONG has.*] Now you have your own soldiers to play with.

ITORO: I have my own soldiers, Mummy! [*ITORO goes to a toy chest and brings out a little plastic tray containing roughly half the soldiers.*] See? This mine.

CELIA: Where did you get them?

ITORO: Ubong gave me. He took some and gave me some. When we play, we use all of them.

CELIA: When did he give them to you? Saturday night you were asking him to let you play with them.

ITORO: We played with them yesterday and he gave them to me after. [*She puts a hand on the new box.*] Eno and Ekaette can have this one.

ITORO scampers off leaving CELIA alone in the room. CELIA picks up the box she bought and holds it while she contemplates. Then she walks over to the toy chest and drops it on top. She goes downstairs. The children are all seated at the table eating. IDORENYIN is dishing for ITORO.

CELIA: I have some more errands to run. All of you, when you finish eating I want you to rest an hour then do your homework. I will inspect it when I return.

UBONG: I don't have any homework.

IDORENYIN: How come?

UBONG: In my school we only get homework on Tuesdays, Wednesdays and Fridays today is Monday.

EKAETTE: Oh, I like your school. Our school gives us homework every day! I wish I could come to your school.

UBONG: It's not as good as your school.

ENO: How do you know?

UBONG: Because Daddy says when this school year is over I will move over to your school.

IDORENYIN: That doesn't make your school bad. Moving you could be just for convenience. It's always better to have all the children in a family attend one school. I'm sure your school is very good, Ubong.

CELIA: I'll see you all later. Goodbye, Mama.

IDORENYIN: Are you going with the driver?

CELIA: No. I'll drive myself.

IDORENYIN: OK. Drive safely, my daughter.

CELIA: Thanks, Mama.

CELIA exits.

Fade on IDORENYIN watching her go.

Scene XXIV

The babalawo's place. CELIA drives up and parks. She goes in after removing her shoes. Another car slowly turns the corner into the edge of the clearing. The window winds down and IDORENYIN leans out and stares at CELIA'S car and the surroundings.

IDORENYIN: Elijah, what kind of place is this?

ELIJAH: I don't know, Ma, but it seems like a... a...
                [*He lapses into silence.*]

IDORENYIN: A what?

ELIJAH: [*reluctantly*] I don't know, Ma. It resembles a
                native doctor's place.

IDORENYIN: [*nodding*] That's what I thought. Let's go.

IDORENYIN winds up and they drive off. CELIA is in the hut with BABA. He is seated on his mat mixing some concoctions.

CELIA: Baba, I'm back.

BABA waves her into silence. He continues concentrating on his concoction. CELIA, after a moment's uncertainty, sits on the mat and waits. BABA finally looks up. He stretches his hand out to her. CELIA silently brings 200,000 naira out of her bag and gives it to him. Again he doesn't count it, just tosses it into a corner.

BABA:	Wait here. [*He goes inside the other room and comes out shortly holding a small plastic container. On it the words 'Best Girl Hair Gel' can be read. He resumes his seat and opens the container. Inside is some fine whitish powder. He shows it to her, then covers it again and hands the container to her.*] It will dissolve in any liquid. It is better to give it to him as a drink rather than sprinkling on food. It is almost tasteless and a drink like Coke, Fanta, juice, Milo, whatever, will completely mask what little taste it has. Put one teaspoon in a glass for him to drink. Do this on three separate occasions. The effect is gradual and cumulative. He will start feeling ill after the first dose. To show your concern, take him to the hospital. While he is on admission, continue to give him the remaining doses. After the third dose, there is nothing anyone can do for him. He will become unconscious and die. Make sure you dispose of any remaining powder afterwards.
CELIA:	It cannot be detected by medical tests, right?
BABA:	That is what I said.
CELIA:	Thank you, Baba.
BABA:	Make sure you wash your hands each time you handle the powder. You have to be careful to make sure no one else accidentally comes in contact with it.
CELIA:	Yes, Baba.

155

BABA: And once the boy is dead, I expect you to
                 bring the rest of my money.

CELIA: I will definitely bring it, Baba.

BABA: OK. Go.

CELIA: One more thing, Baba. What is the poison
                 called?

BABA: It is my secret concoction. I will not tell you
                 what it is. Go.

CELIA: Goodbye, Baba.

She leaves, gets into her car and drives off.

Fade.

Scene XXV

The UMOHS' house. CELIA drives in. The driver has already parked the other car. ATIM comes to greet her.

CELIA: Is oga back?

ATIM: No, Ma.

CELIA: What are the children doing?

ATIM: Them dey upstairs. [*She and CELIA walk into the house.*]

CELIA: Did they have their afternoon rest?

ATIM: Only Itoro sleep. Ekaette and Eno no sleep.

CELIA: What about Ubong?

ATIM: I don't know, Ma. He dey his room. I don't know if he sleep or not.

IDORENYIN comes into the parlour.

IDORENYIN: I thought I heard you drive in. Welcome. I trust your errands were successful.

CELIA: Thank you, Mama. They were. Atim, start the yam. Oga will be back any time from now.

ATIM: Yes, Ma. [*ATIM exits.*]

CELIA: Let me go see and what the children are up to.

IDORENYIN: Celia, my daughter, just hold on a moment. You and I need to talk. [*CELIA resignedly indicates some chairs and they sit down.*] I saw Ani in his office today. He suggested that I go back to the village. I know I have been here for a long time now, and I want to thank you for your hospitality. However, I feel that now would not be a good time for me to leave here. I know this is a stressful time, and I feel I can be useful to you. If it seems to you that I have overstepped my boundaries since Ubong arrived, I apologise. All I desire is to make things easier for you.

CELIA: Like I've told you before, I am fine. I have no problem, with you or anyone else. You are free to stay on if you wish.

IDORENYIN: Thank you, my daughter. Anything you want me to do, just let me know. I am more than willing.

CELIA: Thank you, but like I said, everything is fine. Please excuse me. I need to see to Eno and Ekaette's packing for tomorrow.

IDORENYIN: Yes, they're going on the school trip to
                 Abuja. Since Atim is busy in the kitchen, let
                 me come and help you.

CELIA: I've already done most of it. I just want to
                 put some finishing touches.

*CELIA gets up. IDORENYIN gets up, too, and follows her. Together
they go up to the girls' room. There are two small suitcases open on the bed.*

CELIA: I hope you have not messed up those
                 suitcases.

ENO *and* EKAETTE: No, Mummy!

ENO: I was just looking through to make sure I
                 have everything.

IDORENYIN: [*smiling*] Hmmm, so do you?

ENO: [*grinning*] Yes!

EKAETTE: Mummy, can I take my phone?

CELIA: No.

*CELIA is looking through the suitcases and adding things here and there.
IDORENYIN sits on the bed beside the cases and hands her a few items.*

EKAETTE: Mummy, whyyyyy! Eno is taking her own!

CELIA: And she is under strict instructions to share
                 it with you. But listen both of you. That
                 phone is for you, either of you, to call home
                 if you need anything and for us to get to
                 you directly. Not for you to finish the credit

	phoning your friends up and down like you normally do. Got that?
ENO:	Yes, Mummy.
CELIA:	Ekaette?
EKAETTE:	[*pouting*] Yes. But why can't I take my own, too?
CELIA:	Because one phone is enough for both of you. And if you carry one phone less, you have one phone less to lose.
EKAETTE:	[*whining*] I won't lose it, Mummy. Promise!
IDORENYIN:	It's OK, Ekaette. Maybe next time you'll get to take yours.
ENO:	Mummy, thank you for the soldiers, Itoro says they're ours.
CELIA:	Yes, they are.
IDORENYIN:	What soldiers? [*ENO shows them to her.*] Aren't these Ubong's soldiers?
ENO:	It's for me and Ekaette. Mummy, Ekaette hasn't said thank you.
EKAETTE:	Thank you, Mummy.
IDORENYIN:	What about Itoro?
CELIA:	She's sharing Ubong's. Where is Itoro?

EKAETTE: She's with Ubong. [*ENO jumps up and goes to the window.*]

ENO: I heard the gate. Daddy's home!

Both girls rush out of the room. IDORENYIN gets up, too. She looks questioningly at CELIA.

CELIA: I'll be down in a sec.

IDORENYIN leaves. CELIA closes the cases and leaves the room. She goes to UBONG'S room. It is empty, but the computer is on. Toy soldiers and other toys are scattered on the carpet. CELIA closes the door and continues downstairs. ANI is in the parlour. ENO and EKAETTE are seated on his lap. UBONG is seated on the chair next to them. ITORO is struggling with his briefcase.

ITORO: I'll put it in your room for you, Daddy.

CELIA: Isn't it a bit heavy for you, dear?

ITORO: No! I can carry it!

CELIA: OK. [*She goes over to ANI and kisses him.*] Welcome, darling. How was work?

ANI: Good.

CELIA: Your food is ready. Let me put it out. [*CELIA leaves.*]

EKAETTE: Daddy, can I take my phone to Abuja?

ENO: Daddy, Mummy said she can't take it!

EKAETTE: I won't lose it, Daddy, I promise!

ANI: You have to do what your mother says,
                    Ekaette. [*EKAETTE moans and hides her
                    face in his shoulder.*] How was school today,
                    Ubong?

UBONG: Fine, thank you.

ANI: Have you done your homework?

ENO: He doesn't have any. His school doesn't give
                    homework on Mondays and Thursdays.

ANI: Is that so?

UBONG: Yes, sir. [*ANI sighs. EKAETTE peeps out at
                    UBONG from ANI'S shoulder. UBONG
                    looks flustered.*] Yes, Daddy.

ANI: [*reaching over and patting him*] Don't worry.
                    With time you'll get used to it. What about
                    you two? I don't suppose you have any
                    homework.

EKAETTE *and* ENO: No!

ANI: [*smiling*] Pity.

EKAETTE: Pity? I like it!

ENO: Anyway, we're going to be in Abuja till
                    Friday. No homework this week!

*ITORO bounces back into the room. She pushes her way onto ANI'S
lap pushing ENO off in the process. ENO goes and sits in another chair.*

ITORO: I put it in your room for you, Daddy.

162

ANI: Thank you.

ENO: Itoro has homework.

ITORO: I finished it!

EKAETTE: [*looking at her in disbelief*] When did you do
                   it? [*CELIA comes in.*]

ITORO: In Ubong's room. Ubong helped me!
                   [*CELIA purses her lips.*]

CELIA: Darling, your food is ready.

ANI sets the two girls off his lap, gets up and leaves the room with CELIA.
The children run upstairs.

Fade.

Scene XXVI

It is night. The children are in their nightclothes in the upstairs parlour.
ANI and IDORENYIN are there, too.

ANI: Ubong, you choose tonight's film.
                             [*UBONG selects a DVD and holds it up.*] Go
                             ahead and put it on.

UBONG does so and all of them watch the film. Downstairs, CELIA
is in the kitchen with ATIM. ATIM finishes mixing the children's night
hot chocolate. She puts the mugs on a tray.

CELIA: Atim, did you lock the parlour windows?

ATIM: Yes, Ma.

CELIA: Are you sure? Two days ago when I checked,
                             they weren't properly locked. Go and check
                             again.

ATIM puts down the tray she had picked up and leaves the kitchen.
CELIA goes to the kitchen door and watches her disappear into the parlour.
She then quickly goes over to the tray, bringing out the plastic container
from the pocket of her bubu. *Taking a teaspoon from a drawer she carefully*
measures some of the powder out. As she is about to put it into the mug, she
hesitates. She returns some of the powder to the container, then puts what's
left on the spoon into the cup and stirs it in. She closes the container and
puts it back in her pocket. She goes to the sink and washes her hands and

the spoon, then dries the spoon and returns it to the drawer. She goes out of the kitchen just as ATIM is returning.

ATIM: They were locked, Ma.

CELIA: Good. You can never be too careful. [*She goes to the upstairs parlour and sits beside ANI.*] What film is this?

ENO: *The Lion King.*

EKAETTE: Ubong chose it.

CELIA: It's a good film. One of my favourites.

ANI smiles at her and reaches for her hand. CELIA smiles back. IDORENYIN sitting in another chair watches them, then turns back to the TV. ATIM comes in with the tray. The children take their mugs.

ENO: Ubong doesn't have a cup with his name.

ANI: We have to get him one.

They return to their positions sipping their drinks. CELIA glances at UBONG now and then. He makes short work of the drink and is draining his mug before the others finish. He goes and places it on the tray, then looks at CELIA.

UBONG: Thank you.

CELIA: You're welcome.

IDORENYIN: I keep saying it. Such lovely manners.

CELIA: This film is not going to end before 9 o'clock. You will have to stop it and finish up some other time. [*ENO looks up at the clock.*]

ENO: It's almost 9.

EKAETTE: Please let us finish it.

ANI: You don't want to be late for school tomorrow, do you? They'll just go to Abuja without you!

EKAETTE: Nooo! They will not leave without us! We're going to Aso Rock!

ITORO: Are you going to stand on a rock and greet the First Lady?

EKAETTE: How can we stand on a rock to greet the First Lady Itoro!

ENO: Aso Rock is the President's house. Isn't that so, Daddy?

ANI: Yes. Aso Rock is the name of the presidential dwelling. Although it is actually named after a real rock. Girls, your mother is right. You have to finish the film when you return.

ENO: That's OK. We've watched it before anyway.

CELIA picks up ITORO'S mug. It is still half full. She gives it to ITORO.

CELIA: Finish your chocolate, Itoro. [*ITORO drinks a little more, then gives the mug back to CELIA.*]

ITORO: I don't want any more.

CELIA: OK, everyone. Bedtime.

ANI: You can finish the film after school
                tomorrow, Ubong.

UBONG: Yes, Daddy.

*The children all leave the room after saying goodnight and kissing their
father and grandmother. CELIA leaves with them.*

IDORENYIN: I've discussed staying on longer with Celia.
                She said that it is fine.

ANI: I know. She told me.

IDORENYIN: Thank her again for me *o*. I think I'll turn in
                as well. Goodnight, my son.

ANI: Goodnight, Mama.

*IDORENYIN leaves. ANI switches the TV to CNN. In the bedroom
CELIA takes a brown and white handbag from among her other bags. She
puts some money in it, then looks around the room, goes to her closet and
stuffs the bag behind some shoes, leaving it barely visible. She goes back to
her dresser and sits writing out a list.*

Fade.

Scene XXVII

Morning. All the children are dressed and are having their breakfast. IDORENYIN and ANI are also at the table. CELIA is in the kitchen with ATIM.

CELIA: When you have finished with that, get me my brown and white handbag.

ATIM: Yes, Ma.

She leaves carrying a jug of water. Two lunchboxes are on the counter. CELIA opens one of them and takes out its bottle of Fanta. She opens it, then out of the pocket of her bubu brings out the hair gel container. She gets a spoon and quickly scoops up some of the powder. As she is about to put it into the drink, she hesitates. She withdraws the spoon, then takes it back to the drink where again she hesitates. Then shaking her head withdraws the spoon again and returns its contents to the little container. She quickly closes and returns the Fanta to the lunchbox. She opens a drawer and gets out a small black plastic bag. She ties the hair gel container tightly in the bag. She takes it to the big bin outside and throws it inside. Back in the kitchen she washes her hands and the spoon and joins the family at the dining table.

IDORENYIN: I've dished your food for you.

CELIA: Thank you, Mama. [*IDORENYIN gets up.*]

IDORENYIN: My knees are aching again. Let me go up and get my medicine.

CELIA: Atim can get it for you.

IDORENYIN: I'm not quite sure where I kept it last time.
                I have to go and look for it myself.

*IDORENYIN leaves the dining room just as ATIM enters with
CELIA'S handbag.*

CELIA: That took you a long time.

ATIM: Sorry, Ma, but it no dey with your other
                bags. I look, look before I find it inside
                closet with your shoes.

*CELIA takes the bag from her and brings out some money and gives it
to her.*

CELIA: That's for the things I want you to get from
                the market.

ATIM: Yes, Ma.

CELIA: Put Eno and Ekaette's travelling bags in
                the car.

*ATIM puts the money away in her pocket and goes and picks up the two
small suitcases from the corridor and takes them outside. IDORENYIN
returns. The girls have finished their food. UBONG still has food on his
plate.*

CELIA: Hurry up, Ubong. We have to start going.

UBONG: I've finished, Ma'am.

ANI: You've hardly eaten anything.

UBONG: I don't feel hungry.

IDORENYIN: Are you all right? You don't usually joke
                      with your food. [*UBONG twists and stretches
                      a little.*]

UBONG: I'm fine. I'm not hungry.

ANI: Are you sure you are OK? You look a little
                      dull.

UBONG: I'm fine, Daddy.

ANI: Well, if you're sure…

*IDORENYIN stares intently at UBONG and frowns. Everyone starts
leaving the dining room and heading outside. CELIA goes up to ANI.*

CELIA: I'll call his school later this morning to find
                      out how he is. If need be I can go for him
                      and take him to the hospital.

ANI: OK. Good. [*They go outside. He hugs ENO and
                      EKAETTE and kisses them on their foreheads.*]
                      Remember, both of you, to be on your best
                      behaviour. I want to hear good reports from
                      your teachers. Make us proud of you.

ENO *and* EKAETTE: Yes, Daddy. [*IDORENYIN hugs
                      them, too.*]

IDORENYIN: God grant you journey mercies. Go safely
                      and come back safely in Jesus' name.

ENO *and* EKAETTE: Amen.

They get into CELIA'S car. ITORO throws her arms around ANI'S legs.

ITORO: I'll be good, too, Daddy. [*ANI kisses her, too.*]

ANI: I know you will.

IDORENYIN: Come and give grandma a hug, too. [*ITORO goes and hugs her. Here. IDORENYIN gives ITORO some money.*] Don't cry about not going to Abuja.

ITORO: Thank you, Grandma.

ITORO joins her sisters in CELIA'S car. IDORENYIN goes over to UBONG and gives him some money, too.

UBONG: Thank you, Grandma.

ANI hugs and kisses UBONG, too, then UBONG enters the other car. He is alone with the driver. ATIM comes out with the lunchboxes.

ATIM: Itoro. Ubong. You forget your lunch.

CELIA: Ah, see me *sef.* I've forgotten all about that.

CELIA takes the boxes from ATIM and gives one to ITORO and one to UBONG.

ITORO: What of Eno and Ekaette?

ENO: We don't need lunchboxes today.

EKAETTE: We are going to have our lunch on the plane!

IDORENYIN goes up to CELIA.

171

IDORENYIN: Will you need the driver for anything this
                morning after he drops Ubong in school?

CELIA: If you want to go anywhere you are free to
                use him. I'll tell Atim to take a taxi from the
                market.

IDORENYIN: Thank you.

*CELIA enters her car. ITORO'S face is screwed up as though she is
going to cry.*

ITORO: I want to go on the plane Mummy.

CELIA: Don't worry. We will go, just us. And we
                won't take them. [*CELIA indicates ENO and
                EKAETTE with a nod.*] It will be just us.
                [*CELIA winks at ITORO.*] Right?

ITORO: [*smiling*] Yes. Yes. We won't take them. But
                we'll take Ubong.

CELIA: Yes. We'll take Ubong.

*ENO and EKAETTE giggle. ANI enters his own car, too. They drive
out one by one. IDORENYIN waves to each of them.*

Fade on the closing gates.

Scene XXVIII

SANDRA'S boutique. CELIA'S car is parked there, beside a spanking new salon car. CELIA is in SANDRA'S office with her.

CELIA: Sandra I have something to tell you, but before I do I have to beg your forgiveness.

SANDRA: [*smiling*] My forgiveness. I beg *jo*, be serious. If anybody should be begging for forgiveness it should be me, for taking you to that fake *babalawo* in the first place.

CELIA: That's just it. He isn't fake. I lied to you yesterday Sandra. When I went back to him and he explained about the protection, I did ask for my money. He didn't give it to me. Instead he offered me another option. The option of killing him.

SANDRA: So... what happened?

CELIA: I accepted that option.

SANDRA: You accepted to kill him.

CELIA: I'm not proud to say this, but yes I did.

SANDRA: [*looking shocked*] Cee! How can you even think of killing somebody?

CELIA:	I knew you would react like this which is why I lied to you. He charged 500,000 naira to give me a special powder that would do the job, but leave absolutely no trace. Not even with lab tests. When I complained about the 100,000 I had already given to him, he deducted it and said I should pay 400,000. Half now, and half afterwards. After I left you I got 200,000 from the ATM and went back to him. He gave me the powder. I am supposed to put one teaspoonful in Ubong's drink three times. After the second dose, he will be in hospital. After the third dose, nothing anyone does will save him.
SANDRA:	Celia, tell me you didn't do it.
CELIA:	I tried the first dose last night, but I couldn't bring myself to put an entire teaspoon. I put half. This morning I was about to put the second dose into his lunch drink when I stopped. I couldn't go through with it. I just couldn't.
SANDRA:	[*releasing a long breath*] Thank God for that!
CELIA:	What I was doing was punishing him for the sins of his parents. He had no say in whether or not he was brought into the world. He is an innocent child. As innocent as my own three. What's more, he himself is not even the type to offend anyone. And he likes Itoro so much. God forgive me for even thinking of such a terrible act.

SANDRA: Oh, Celia. I wish you had told me this yesterday. I would have talked some sense into you. What have you done with the powder?

CELIA: I tied it in a plastic bag and dumped it in the outside bin. Today is the day the waste people come to empty the bins, so it will be totally removed from my premises.

SANDRA: Good. But what are you going to do about the *babalawo*?

CELIA: I don't want his *wahalla o*! I will pay him his money complete. Then I don't want to ever see him again. In fact, if I can get the money, I'm willing to give it to him even right now, so I can just forget about it.

SANDRA: How much is left, 200,000?

CELIA: Yes. I've drained my account at the moment, but I'm expecting more money next week. That aside I just need to think up a story to tell Ani to get it from him.

SANDRA: Hmmm I think I can spare that amount. But, Cee, *na wa o*! What were you planning to say when he died? Surely you know all fingers of suspicion would point straight at you.

CELIA: I was planning to prostrate myself to Ani and declare my innocence. I know he would believe me. I didn't care about anyone else.

SANDRA: So how is Ubong now? After all, he took one
                   dose of the poison.

CELIA: Not a full dose. He seemed relatively OK this
                   morning though he couldn't eat much of his
                   breakfast. I'm planning to call the school in
                   about an hour to see how he's doing. If need
                   be, I'll take him to the hospital.

SANDRA: OK. [*She glances at her watch.*] Tell you what,
                   why don't we go to the bank now, so I can
                   get you the money. Then you can settle the
                   babalawo this morning and forget about him.

CELIA: Thank you, Sandra. And thank you for
                   forgiving me. [*They get up and SANDRA
                   brings out her keys.*]

SANDRA: You had me worried for a while back there.

CELIA: God forgive me. That's all I can say. Come
                   and show off your new car to me. [*SANDRA
                   laughs.*]

SANDRA: Yes *o*!

They leave the room.

Fade on the closed door.

176

Scene XXIX

ANI'S office. He is there working. The intercom rings. He puts it on speaker.

ANI: Funke.

FUNKE: Sir, your mother is here to see you.

ANI: OK. Let her come in. [*IDORENYIN enters and sits.*] What is it now, mother?

IDORENYIN: At first I didn't want to bother you with this, but the more I thought about it the more I realised that you need to know. A crafty tortoise can swallow the seed of knowledge but the fox will still get at it when he eats the tortoise.

ANI: Mama. I don't have time for adages. What is this about?

IDORENYIN: Celia is behaving like the crafty tortoise, hiding things from you. Are you aware that she's seeing a native doctor?

ANI: Celia does not patronise native doctors. She doesn't even believe in them.

IDORENYIN: But she went to one yesterday.

ANI: You must be mistaken, Mama. I repeat, Celia
                does not go to native doctors. Why even
                those eight years when we had no child, she
                did not go to them.

IDORENYIN: Is that what she tells you? Well, this time I
                saw her with my own eyes.

ANI: Mama, I thought you were staying to bring
                harmony, not discord into my home.

IDORENYIN: Why would I lie about this Aniekan? Eh?

ANI: I don't know, Mama. I don't know what
                you hope to gain. Celia is finally beginning
                to accept Ubong, and here you are trying to
                throw a spanner into the works.

IDORENYIN: The driver was there, too. He saw. Let me
                send for him so you can ask him yourself.

ANI: For you to see Celia at a native doctor's,
                you had to be there as well. What were you
                doing at a native doctor, Mama?

IDORENYIN: Me? Go to a native doctor? God forbid.
                Celia has been acting funny. The other day
                I saw her looking through the outside bin.
                When I asked her what she was looking for,
                she said her earring. But I saw her with a
                torn photograph that she had just taken out
                of the bin.

ANI: So? She decided not to throw away a picture.
                Why is that a big deal?

IDORENYIN:	It looked like a picture of Ubong. And the sound she made when she found it showed that that was what she was looking in the bin for. Not her earring. And I asked Atim if she had lost any earring and Atim said no.
ANI:	So maybe she simply didn't tell her.
IDORENYIN:	OK. Then why hide the fact that she was searching for Ubong's photograph in the bin?
ANI:	Who says she was hiding it? You've already made up your mind to be suspicious of everything she does.
IDORENYIN:	[*raising her hands in surrender*] All right. I can see there's no point in talking any more. Come and see for yourself.
ANI:	Come and see what?
IDORENYIN:	The driver is outside. He can take us to the place right now.
ANI:	I'm not going to any native doctor's place. Besides it won't prove anything.
IDORENYIN:	Why won't it prove anything? All you need to do is ask him…
ANI:	And I'm sure he will say what he's been told to say.
IDORENYIN:	Aniekan Umoh, are you suggesting that I, your mother, planned this? To what end?

ANI:	That I don't know. Right now, Mama, I need to get back to work. I have a client in the reception waiting to see me. [*ANI stands up*.]
IDORENYIN:	Ani…
ANI:	Mama, as far as I am concerned, this conversation is over. I need to get on with my work. [*IDORENYIN gets up*.]
IDORENYIN:	Just remember, my son, that all I want is what's best for you. [*IDORENYIN goes out. ANI resumes his seat.*]
ANI:	[*into the intercom*] Funke, send Mr Rogers in.
FUNKE:	Yes, sir.

Fade on ANI looking through some documents.

Scene XXX

The car park of a bank. CELIA and SANDRA come out of the bank and get into SANDRA'S car. SANDRA opens her handbag and gets out money which she hands over to CELIA.

CELIA: Thank you again. I should be able to pay you back next week latest.

SANDRA: So what are you going to do now?

CELIA: [*bringing out her phone*] Call the school. If he is all right, I'll go to the *babalawo*.

SANDRA starts driving while CELIA makes the call.

CELIA: Hello, madam, this is Celia Umoh. I'm calling about Ubong, I mean Ugochukwu Umoh... Yes, I want to find out how he is. He was not feeling so good this morning... Aah... I see... well, madam, what do you suggest?... OK... aah, can I call you back in a few minutes? Thank you. [*She ends the call.*] His class teacher says he complained this morning that he was feeling weak. She sent him to the sick bay to rest. She says she thinks he will be all right, but if I'm still worried I can come and get him.

SANDRA: I think you should go and get him and take him to a proper hospital. You don't know what was in that concoction. Don't take any chances.

CELIA: [*nodding*] I asked Baba what the powder was and he refused to tell me. [*She calls again.*] Hello, it's Celia Umoh again. I'm coming to get him… Yes. I want to take him to a doctor… I should be there in about half an hour… OK. Goodbye. [*She ends the call.*] Let me tell Ani. [*She makes another call. There is a long pause.*] Ani, I've called the school and spoken with Ubong's teacher. He had to be sent to the sick bay because he was feeling weak. I'm on my way to get him now. I'll take him to Mother of Our Saviour hospital. I'll call again after the doctor has seen him. [*She ends the call and turns to SANDRA.*] I got his voicemail.

SANDRA: I would have taken you to the school straight, but I have to get back to the boutique. The wife of the Commissioner for Education is coming. She always buys a lot and I like to be on hand personally for her.

CELIA: No problem. I'll go with my car.

SANDRA: Keep me posted.

CELIA: Definitely.

Fade.

Scene XXXI

The reception of a hospital. CELIA and UBONG are sitting, waiting. RECEPTIONIST comes up to them. She is holding a case file.

RECEPTIONIST: Please come with me.

CELIA and UBONG follow her to another room where NURSE 1 is waiting. RECEPTIONIST puts the case file on the table and leaves. NURSE 1 attends to UBONG, weighing him and taking his temperature. Then she leads them to the consulting room where they are met by DR IDIONG.

DR IDIONG: Hello, Ubong.

UBONG: Good morning, Doctor.

. DR IDIONG: Good morning, Mrs Umoh.

CELIA: Good morning, Dr Idiong.

DR IDIONG: How are your daughters?

CELIA: They are fine, thank you.

DR IDIONG: OK, Ubong, what is the problem?

UBONG: I was feeling very weak this morning.

DR IDIONG: Did you have breakfast?

UBONG: A little.

CELIA: He hardly ate any of it.

DR IDIONG: Have you had anything else to eat since
                then?

UBONG: The school nurse gave me a glucose drink.
                I feel better now.

DR IDIONG: Did you feel this way yesterday?

UBONG: No.

DR IDIONG: Have you ever had this kind of feeling
                before?

UBONG: No.

DR IDIONG: [*bringing out her stethoscope*] I want you to lie
                on that couch over there, and I'm just going
                to listen to your chest, OK? [*UBONG
                complies. DR IDIONG listens to his chest from
                the front and the back. Then she listens to his
                abdomen. She checks his eyes, mucous membranes
                and a few reflexes.*] OK, you can get up now.
                [*She helps him up and they return to their seats.*]
                I can't find anything wrong. The weakness
                is no doubt because you did not have much
                breakfast.

CELIA: He usually eats well. He had no appetite this
                morning.

DR IDIONG: How about now? What do you feel like
                eating?

UBONG:	I still have my lunch. I can eat that.
CELIA:	If you would rather have something else, just say. [*UBONG hesitates, looking at CELIA.*] You want something else don't you? What is it?
UBONG:	[*looking down, shyly*] Rice.
CELIA:	What type? White? Jollof? Fried? Coconut?
UBONG:	[*softly*] Any.
CELIA:	Doctor, I'd like you to keep him under observation for a while. And run tests on him.
DR IDIONG:	He doesn't really need to have any tests done at this point, except maybe blood glucose.
CELIA:	I still want some tests done on him.
DR IDIONG:	What tests do you want?
CELIA:	[*shrugging*] Blood tests. Comprehensive blood tests. I just want to make absolutely sure he is all right.
DR IDIONG:	OK. [*She brings out lab forms and begins filling them in.*] I'll have him admitted for observation then. Bloods will be taken once he's on the ward. As for the food [*she smiles at UBONG*] our restaurant is very good. I can vouch for their rice. It's excellent.

UBONG smiles back. DR IDIONG dials the intercom.

NURSE 1'S VOICE: Yes Doctor?

DR IDIONG: Please come.

NURSE 1 comes in and DR IDIONG hands over UBONG'S folder to her.

DR IDIONG: He is to be admitted for observation. And he has some blood tests.

NURSE 1 accepts the folder and smiles at UBONG and CELIA.

NURSE 1:   Please come with me.

CELIA: Thank you, Doctor.

UBONG: Thank you, Doctor.

DR IDIONG: You are both welcome. I will see you again later, Ubong.

They leave the consulting room with NURSE 1.

CELIA: Where's Matron?

NURSE 1:   She's out at the moment, but she will be back soon.

She leads them to the inpatient section of the hospital.

NURSE 1:   Please wait here. Someone will come to attend to you soon.

She shows them to the seats and leaves. CELIA brings out her phone. She makes a call.

CELIA: Ani, did you get the message I left on your voicemail?

ANI: I got it just now. I was about to call you. Have you taken him to the hospital?

CELIA: We are at the hospital right now. The doctor says he's fine, but I've asked for some tests to be done. I also want them to watch him for a few hours. When I pick Itoro from school, I'll bring him back home then.

ANI: OK. [*CASHIER approaches CELIA.*]

CELIA: I'll call you back, darling. My attention is needed now.

ANI: Let me talk to Ubong.

CELIA hands the phone over to UBONG and faces the young woman.

CASHIER: Good morning, madam. You need to pay a deposit for admission.

CELIA: How much?

CASHIER: 15,000 Madam. And 9,600 for the tests.

CELIA writes a cheque. Meanwhile, UBONG is talking to ANI.

UBONG: I feel fine now, Daddy. [*CELIA hands the cheque to CASHIER.*]

CASHIER: Thank you. I will bring you your receipt.

CASHIER exits. UBONG hands the phone back to CELIA. CELIA checks it then returns it to her bag.

CELIA: You don't mind staying in the hospital for a few hours, do you?

UBONG: No, Ma'am.

CELIA: Call me Aunty Celia.

UBONG: Aunty Celia.

NURSE 2 comes up to them and leads them to their room. It is a private room with a single bed. UBONG lies down. His schoolbag and lunchbox are kept on the nearby table. NURSE 2 puts on the TV and hands him the controls.

NURSE 2:   Someone from the lab will be in shortly to take some blood for the tests. [*She hands CELIA a booklet.*] This is our menu. He can choose anything he likes. I will be back to find out what he wants.

CELIA: He wants rice. [*NURSE 2 takes back the menu and turns a page.*]

NURSE 2:   These are our rice dishes. [*She shows it to him.*] Which one do you want? [*UBONG barely glances at it.*]

UBONG: Jollof rice.

NURSE 2:   With what? Fish, chicken or beef?

UBONG: Chicken.

NURSE 2:   Do you want salad, moi moi, or fried
                plantain?

CELIA: No salad for now. You can have moi moi or
                plantain.

UBONG: Plantain, please.

NURSE 2:   OK.

CELIA: How long will that take?

NURSE 2:   About thirty minutes.

*NURSE 2 leaves. There is a short knock and the door is opened.
CASHIER enters. She hands CELIA her receipt. As she leaves the
lab lady enters carrying blood collecting paraphernalia. CELIA stands
up. She brings a different phone out of her bag, and keeps it on the table
beside the bed.*

CELIA: This is Ekaette's phone. Call me if you feel
                uncomfortable or need anything before I
                return. Your father's number is in there,
                too, so you can call him if you wish. Do
                you know how to use the phone? [*UBONG
                picks up the phone and looks at it. He nods.*]
                Good. I will be off now.

UBONG: Goodbye, Aunty Celia.

CELIA: Enjoy your rest. See you later.

*CELIA exits. The lab lady is arranging her instruments. She then sits in
the seat CELIA vacated and takes UBONG'S arm and smiles at him.*

Fade.

Scene XXXII

The outside of ANI'S office. IDORENYIN is sitting in the car with the doors open. The driver ELIJAH is sitting on a seat under a nearby tree. ANI comes out and heads for his car. IDORENYIN gets out and goes to him. He stares at her surprised.

ANI: Mama. What are you doing sitting out in the car?

IDORENYIN: Waiting for you. I won't just sit back and watch you do things blindly. Whatever decision you make about your life is fine with me so long as I know you made it with full knowledge of all the facts. [*She grabs ANI'S arm.*] Ani, you will come with me to this place that I saw with my two eyes your wife go to. What you want to do after that is your business. [*IDORENYIN pulls ANI towards her car. He resists.*]

ANI: Mama, for God's sake stop this nonsense!

IDORENYIN: As your mother your welfare is my only interest. And if it's nonsense, what does it cost you to do it?

ANI: Mama, I'm about to go and inspect some properties…

IDORENYIN: [*almost shouting*] That can wait! The properties will still be there tomorrow or this evening. Ani, right now, you are coming with me.

ELIJAH has stood up and is hovering by the car. ANI allows IDORENYIN to lead him to the car. He enters the back.

IDORENYIN: Elijah, let's go back to that native doctor.

ELIJAH: Yes, Ma. [*He enters the car.*]

IDORENYIN: Oya, let's go.

They drive off.

Fade.

Scene XXXIII

The babalawo's *place. CELIA drives up and parks. She has her phone to her ear.*

CELIA:	Sandra? Hello… Yes, I'm at his place, but I've only just arrived. The traffic was terrible. Have you gone for Itoro yet?
SANDRA:	I'm at her school right now. I keep saying it, you pamper your mother-in-law too much. Agreeing to pick the girls so she can keep the driver all day. Why won't she want to stay in Lagos forever?
CELIA:	I'm just being cautious right now. When this Ubong issue settles, I'll take care of her. Please take Itoro to the hospital. Let her wait for me there with Ubong. They can keep each other company.
SANDRA:	Your feelings towards Ubong have really changed.
CELIA:	I have nothing against him anymore. In fact, every time I look at him I feel guilty. Let this all be over. I'll make it up to him… what did you say?
SANDRA:	I said what are you going to tell the *babalawo*?

CELIA:	[*glancing furtively at BABA'S hut*] Well, like I said, I just want this to all be over. I'll tell him everything is going according to plan. That I've given two doses and that Ubong is dying in the hospital as we speak. Then I'll give him the money and leave.
SANDRA:	What if he checks?
CELIA:	Why should he check? He won't suspect that I'm lying. And after this he'll never see me again.
SANDRA:	Good luck. See you when you return.
CELIA:	Thanks.

CELIA ends the call and alights from the car. She walks briskly to BABA'S hut, removes her shoes and enters. Shortly the other car drives slowly into the clearing. From inside the car ANI looks out at CELIA'S car.

IDORENYIN:	She's back again. Do you believe me now?
ANI:	There's probably a perfectly reasonable explanation for her being here.

ANI gets out. As he is about to slam the car door, IDORENYIN stops him, holds the door open and gets out through that same door. Once outside, she very quietly closes the door. In silence they walk to the hut. As they approach the door, they can hear voices inside.

CELIA'S VOICE:	I've come to give you the rest of the money, Baba.
BABA'S VOICE:	So soon? He can't be dead yet.

CELIA'S VOICE: Not yet. I've given him two doses and he is in hospital now. He is very sick. The poison is working very well, Baba. I'll give him the third dose this evening. He will be dead by tomorrow.

Shock shows on both IDORENYIN and ANI'S faces. IDORENYIN'S mouth is hanging open. Inside the hut, CELIA and BABA are seated as usual on the mat. CELIA hands over the money. BABA tosses it to one corner as usual.

BABA: Ugochukwu Umoh will be no more.

CELIA: Yes, Baba. He will no longer be a thorn in my flesh. My family will be as it was before he darkened my doorsteps. [*BABA looks puzzled.*]

BABA: Are you sure about this?

CELIA: [*frowning*] Of course I'm sure. That's why I'm bringing you the rest of the money.

BABA: He is very sick?

CELIA: That's what I said, Baba. Is something wrong? He's in the hospital. You can confirm that for yourself.

BABA: Oh, there is no need. Well done. [*CELIA stands up.*]

CELIA: Thank you again, Baba.

BABA: You are welcome.

As CELIA turns to leave, ANI and IDORENYIN enter. ANI looks furious. He launches himself at CELIA.

ANI: [*shouting*] Witch! Evil woman! I have been living with the devil!

ANI wraps his hands around CELIA'S throat. She grapples with him, trying to loosen his hold, choking. IDORENYIN joins and tries to loosen his hands. The babalawo, *after his initial shock, quietly disappears through another door at the end of the room. ANI is still shouting abuse at CELIA.*

IDORENYIN: Aniekan, leave her! I beg you! Don't soil your hands with her blood! She's not worth it!

Still ANI holds on, shouting insanely. CELIA'S knees start buckling. IDORENYIN runs outside.

IDORENYIN: Elijah! Elijah! Come quick!

ELIJAH runs into the hut with her. Together they manage to remove ANI'S hands from CELIA'S neck. By this time CELIA is lying on the floor.

IDORENYIN: Elijah, take him out of here!

ELIJAH tries to lead ANI outside. ANI shakes off his hands. He has stopped shouting, but is breathing heavily. IDORENYIN kneels beside CELIA. ANI abruptly turns and walks out of the hut. ELIJAH also kneels beside CELIA.

ELIJAH: Is she alive, Ma?

IDORENYIN: I'm not sure. I can't see her chest moving.

ANI'S VOICE: [*shouting from outside*] Driver! Driver!

ELIJAH leaves the hut. IDORENYIN grabs CELIA'S shoulders and shakes her. No response. IDORENYIN gets up and looks around, then quickly goes out through the same door BABA had gone through. IDORENYIN finds herself in a small backroom. There is a table, a chair and a thin mattress lying on the floor. Clothes, and a few utensils and books are scattered around. There are signs that someone did some hasty packing. The babalawo *is not there. IDORENYIN continues through another door at the other side of the room. This leads to a separate clearing. There are two drums of water. Fresh tyre tracks in the dirt indicate that a car has just recently left. IDORENYIN quickly scans the trees, then turns back inside. ELIJAH is kneeling beside CELIA again. IDORENYIN joins him. ELIJAH nods at IDORENYIN.*

ELIJAH: She's breathing.

IDORENYIN: Thank God. [*She shakes CELIA again.*] Celia! Celia! [*CELIA groans. IDORENYIN looks at ELIJAH.*] What did oga want?

ELIJAH: The car keys. He's gone.

IDORENYIN: Ah, how are we to get out of here?

ELIJAH: We can take madam's car.

IDORENYIN: Oh, yes. Where's her bag? [*They locate CELIA'S handbag and find the keys inside.*] Bring the car nearer.

ELIJAH goes out and drives CELIA'S car to the doorway. Together they help CELIA to her feet. She is moaning and rubbing her neck. They settle her in the back of the car then they enter and drive off. CELIA struggles to speak.

CELIA: Mama… Mama, please, it's… it's not like it seems. I didn't try… try to kill Ubong. I… swear I didn't.

She looks at IDORENYIN. IDORENYIN is silent, staring straight ahead. CELIA reaches for her hand. IDORENYIN pulls it away. CELIA starts crying, still rubbing her neck with her other hand.

CELIA: Mama… Mama… I have been… been a good daughter-in-law to you… you know I have, Mama… You have to help me beg Ani. Mama, please…

IDORENYIN: Beg Ani. Ha! Over my dead body. I will help him throw you out. I never wanted him to marry you in the first place. He spurned Justina, the girl I wanted him to marry, for you. You, who took eight years to have one child. Justina could have given him six children in that time. And to add insult to injury, you wanted my son to go to his grave without a son to carry on his name. Trying to kill an innocent child. You are reaping the rewards of your evil deeds. When I get to my son's house I will pack your things and dump them outside the gate. Rubbish with rubbish.

IDORENYIN hisses. CELIA withdraws the hand she had stretched towards her. She curls it in her lap and sits there sobbing and massaging her neck.

CELIA: I should have insisted on you going back to the village. Fool that I was, I was trying to be nice to you. I waited on you hand and foot, took you shopping repeatedly around

Lagos, went out of my way to prepare things I know you like to eat. [*She shakes her head.*] I should never have let you come in the first place. God! I even convinced Ani to give you the money when you said you wanted buy land and build another house in the village to be rented out. He thought that that might be too stressful for you. Till today we have not seen the land, not to talk of even one brick.

IDORENYIN: [*scornfully*] You, convincing Ani to give me the money? He would have given it to me regardless. He is my son. You don't know what it means to have a son because you have none. And what I did with the money is none of your business. It was my son's money. Hear me? [*She leans toward her and shouts it.*] My son's money! I thank God my son has a son, in spite of you. And he will have more once he marries again. This time I'll make sure he listens to me. And you better start praying Ubong survives. Because if he doesn't, nobody in this world will be able to keep Ani from dealing with you. Witch!

There is silence, broken only by CELIA'S sobs. Then her mobile phone rings. She answers it.

CELIA: [*hoarsely*] Hello? [*She clears her throat and tries again.*] Hello?

UBONG: [*sobbing*] Aunty Celia, Aunty Celia!

CELIA:	[*sitting up abruptly*] Ubong! Ubong! What is the matter? *IDORENYIN looks sharply at her.*
UBONG'S VOICE:	Aunty Celia!
CELIA:	Yes! Yes! It's me! What is the matter!
UBONG:	It's Itoro!
CELIA:	[*shouting*] What about Itoro?
UBONG:	I don't know. Aunty Sandra brought her. She was playing with me. Then she started crying that her tummy was hurting. I tried to fan her. She started vomiting. I called the nurse. She called other people and then took me to another room.
CELIA:	So where's Itoro now?
UBONG:	I think she's still in that room.
CELIA:	Is she all right now?
UBONG:	I don't know. They put me in another room.
CELIA:	Give the phone to a nurse. I want to speak to a nurse!
IDORENYIN:	[*to CELIA*] What is happening! What has happened to Itoro?
CELIA:	Nurse? This is Celia Umoh, Itoro's mother. What is the matter with my daughter?

NURSE 2'S VOICE: Mrs Umoh, you need to come to the hospital as soon as you can. The doctor will see you once you get here.

CELIA: Tell me now what the problem is!

NURSE 2:   I'm afraid I can't discuss anything over the phone, madam.

CELIA: Just tell me if my daughter is OK now.

NURSE 2:   Please get here as quickly as you can, madam. I am handing the phone back to your son now.

CELIA: No! Nurse! Nurse!

UBONG: She's gone Aunty Celia!

CELIA: OK, Ubong. [*She removes the phone from her ear.*] Elijah!

ELIJAH: Yes, madam?

CELIA: Step on it! Get me to Mother of Our Saviour Hospital immediately!

ELIJAH: Yes, madam. I will do my best. [*He speeds up.*]

IDORENYIN: Celia! What is the matter with Itoro? [*CELIA doesn't answer. She starts praying*].

CELIA: Our Father in Heaven. Hallowed be thy Name. Please, God, please. I confess my sins before you, Lord. Punish me if you will, Lord. I am but your humble servant.

But please, God, please, spare my innocent daughter. My sweet baby girl. Please, Father God...

CELIA continues sobbing. IDORENYIN brings out her own phone. ELIJAH overtakes rashly. There is screeching of brakes and sharp swerving as he narrowly avoids an oncoming car.

IDORENYIN: Elijah, take it easy! Do you want to kill us all!

CELIA: No! Don't slow down. I don't care if I die. Just get me to that hospital!

IDORENYIN: If you are dead, how will you get to the hospital? Unless it's to end up in their mortuary! Elijah. Drive fast, but for God's sake be careful!

ELIJAH: Yes, Ma. Sorry Ma.

CELIA continues sobbing and praying. IDORENYIN makes her call.

IDORENYIN: Ani? Have you heard anything from the hospital?

ANI'S VOICE: Yes. I called them. Ubong is fine.

IDORENYIN: What about Itoro?

ANI: What about her?

IDORENYIN: Ubong just called Celia. It seems something has happened to Itoro.

ANI: What! What has happened to her?

IDORENYIN:	I don't know. But it seems something has.
ANI:	Dear God. This is a nightmare. I'm almost at the hospital now. Still, I'll call them and try to find out what's going on. Talk to you later, Mama.
IDORENYIN:	I'm praying for you, Ani. You and all your children.
ANI:	Thank you, Mama. We need it.

IDORENYIN ends the call. She closes her eyes and starts praying softly. CELIA is still sobbing and praying.

Fade.

Scene XXXIV

The hospital. ANI drives in. He enters the reception. NURSE 1 is just passing. He accosts her.

ANI: Nurse, excuse me.

NURSE 1:   Yes sir?

ANI: I am Mr Umoh. My son, Ubong, is on admission here.

NURSE 1:   Yes, sir. Please follow me. [*NURSE 1 turns back. ANI follows.*]

ANI: Is my daughter Itoro here as well?

NURSE 1:   I will hand you over to Matron, sir.

ANI: [*getting angry*] Why can't you just answer me? A simple yes or no?

NURSE 1:   Please bear with me, sir. Matron will answer all your questions in a minute. [*NURSE 1 opens the door of a consulting room. DR IDIONG and MATRON are in there.*] Matron, this is…

MATRON: Mr Umoh.

MATRON jumps up and goes to ANI. NURSE 1 leaves. MATRON leads him to a chair. DR IDIONG also stands. She extends a hand to ANI who shakes it.

DR IDIONG: I'm Dr Idiong, sir.

ANI: Hello. [*ANI remains standing despite the chair MATRON offered him. He addresses them both.*] Is my daughter here?

MATRON: Yes, she is, but I'm afraid the news is not good.

DR IDIONG: I am very sorry to have to tell you, sir, that your daughter Itoro is dead.

ANI gasps. He abruptly sits in the chair.

ANI: [*shaking his head in disbelief*] That's impossible. Itoro was perfectly healthy this morning.

MATRON: She was with her brother who is on admission. It was he who raised the alarm.

DR IDIONG: When we got to the room she was gasping for breath. We did everything we could, but less than twenty minutes from the time we stepped into that room, she was gone.

MATRON: It was so sudden. I saw when she came. She was brought by a friend of your wife's who told us that she was to stay with Ubong and that your wife will pick them up in about an hour, an hour and a half. She asked us to arrange food for her. I was there in the room when she was choosing her meal.

She wanted the same thing her brother had, rice and chicken. She was completely okay. Thirty minutes later, we were just about to serve the food when we were called to the room, and she was gasping. I couldn't believe it!

ANI: [*still shaking his head in disbelief*] There's some mistake somewhere. It can't be my Itoro you're talking about. I want to see her. Take me to see her. [*DR IDIONG and MATRON lead him out of the consulting room.*] What about my son, Ubong?

DR IDIONG: Ubong is distraught about his sister, but other than that, he is medically fine.

They enter UBONG'S former room. Two schoolbags and lunchboxes are on the table. At one corner of the room is a drip stand with an IV infusion still hanging. On the bed is a small figure totally covered with a white bed sheet. MATRON folds down the sheet. ITORO is in her school uniform, her eyes closed, arms by her sides. ANI starts wailing and weeping.

ANI: Oh, my God! Oh, my God! No! No! No! [*He sits on the bed, picks ITORO up and cradles her in his arms.*] Why! Why! God, why!

ANI rocks ITORO back and forth as he continues weeping and lamenting. DR IDIONG and MATRON stay in the room with him. Then the door opens a little and NURSE 1 beckons to MATRON. MATRON goes out closing the door.

MATRON: What is it?

NURSE 1: Mrs Umoh and her mother-in-law are here Matron.

MATRON: Where are they?

NURSE 1:   At the reception.

MATRON: OK.

MATRON goes to the reception. CELIA immediately hurries towards her and IDORENYIN follows.

CELIA: Matron, Matron, please, where's my daughter?

MATRON: Celia, Mama. Come with me, please. [*They follow her.*]

CELIA: Matron, just tell me she's all right, please!

As they approach the room they can hear ANI still crying inside. CELIA and IDORENYIN look fearfully at MATRON.

MATRON: She's in there. [*She puts her arm around CELIA.*] Celia, I'm afraid she's, [*she takes a deep breath*] she's dead.

IDORENYIN lets out a long scream and collapses on the floor. CELIA stares at MATRON dumbly for a moment, then tears herself out of MATRON'S arms and bursts into the room. She rushes over to ANI and takes ITORO out of his arms. She shakes her.

CELIA: Itoro, wake up, Itoro! Baby, please! Open your eyes! [*She sits on the floor with ITORO and wails.*]

ANI: [*shouting*] Are you happy now? See the results of your deeds? Are you happy now?

MATRON helps IDORENYIN up. IDORENYIN staggers into the room. She sits with CELIA on the floor and she, too, tries shaking ITORO. The weeping and wailing crescendo. ANI leaves the room taking MATRON with him.

ANI: Show me Ubong's room.

Matron points to a room two doors down. ANI enters the room. UBONG is sitting on the bed looking miserable and scared. On seeing ANI he starts trembling.

UBONG: I'm sorry, sir.

UBONG starts crying. ANI sits on the bed with him and embraces him.

ANI: You have nothing to be sorry for, Ubong.

UBONG: I didn't know. I didn't know. I wouldn't have
                given it to her! I didn't know, sir!

ANI: I am your father, Ubong. Call me Daddy.

UBONG: Daddy. I'm sorry.

ANI: What wouldn't you have given her?

UBONG: My Fanta. After she drank it she started
                saying her tummy was hurting.

ANI pushes him away slightly so he can look into his face.

ANI: Your Fanta?

UBONG: My lunch Fanta. I didn't drink it at school.
                When Itoro came, she said she was thirsty

and I gave it to her. I'm sorry, Daddy! [*ANI looks thunderous.*]

ANI: It's OK, Ubong. You have done nothing wrong. Stay here. I will come and get you later. Have you eaten?

UBONG: [*nodding*] I ate before Itoro came.

ANI: All right. [*ANI hugs UBONG again and kisses him on the forehead.*] I will come back for you.

ANI goes back to the other room. MATRON and DR IDIONG are still in the room with CELIA and IDORENYIN. They have succeeded in getting them up off the floor and onto the bed. MATRON has her arm around CELIA and DR IDIONG around IDORENYIN. ANI bursts into the room. He wrenches ITORO from CELIA.

ANI: Do not put your filthy arms around this child. You killed her!

CELIA: Why would I want to kill my own child, Ani?

ANI hands ITORO to IDORENYIN. He grabs one of the lunchboxes and opens it. It contains only an empty Ribena bottle. He opens the second one. It contains uneaten sandwiches and an apple, but no drink bottle. ANI whirls round.

ANI: What happened to the bottle of Fanta that was in this lunchbox?

DR IDIONG: We ran some tests on it. When Ubong told us Itoro started complaining soon after drinking from it, even though she'd been vomiting, we took the precaution of washing out her stomach. Unfortunately that did not save her. We ran tests on the vomitus. By the time the results were out and we knew what we were dealing with, it was too late to administer any antidote. We then tested the Fanta bottle. [*IDORENYIN and CELIA stop crying. They both stare at the doctor.*] Both the vomitus and the Fanta showed high concentrations of arsenic. Arsenic is a deadly poison.

CELIA: That's impossible! That is absolutely impossible!

ANI: Why is it impossible? You wanted to kill Ubong. That is why you poisoned this Fanta. [*MATRON and DR IDIONG stare at each other open-mouthed.*] But your evil has come back to bite you. Ubong did not drink it. When the sister he loves was thirsty, he offered it to her. See what you have done to yourself? To this lovely little girl? You spawn of Satan! [*IDORENYIN starts moaning again.*]

IDORENYIN: [*shouting*] Oh, my God! Oh, my God! Oh! Oh! Itoro! My grandchild, my namesake. No! No! Itoroooooooooo! [*IDORENYIN continues weeping and lamenting.*]

CELIA: I swear to you, Ani; I swear on my life that I did not put anything in that drink!

ANI: Get out of my sight! [*He turns to MATRON and DR IDIONG.*] Get her out of my sight! Or I swear I will not be responsible for my actions!

MATRON quickly hustles CELIA out of the room. ANI also leaves the room. He goes outside, brings out his phone and makes a call.

GERRY: Hello Ani.

ANI: Gerry, my family is in crisis right now. I need a favour.

GERRY: Sure anything. What is the crisis?

ANI: My daughter Itoro is dead.

GERRY: You're joking!

ANI: I wish I was.

GERRY: What happened? Was she sick?

ANI: She wasn't. It's a long story. I'll tell you all of it later. Right now I need to make arrangements for the body. I'm in Mother of Our Saviour hospital. Ubong is here, too. Can you look after him for me this evening?

GERRY: Certainly. Shall I come and get him or do you want to bring him yourself?

ANI: Come and get him. I'll tell the hospital staff to expect you.

GERRY: Is there anything else you want me to do?

ANI: I'll let you know.

GERRY: How's Celia holding up?

ANI: That's part of the story. Talk to you later. Bye.

ANI ends the call and goes back into the hospital. He goes to ITORO'S room. IDORENYIN is still crying. No one else is in the room. He goes back out and speaks to a passing nurse.

ANI: Where can I find Matron or Dr Idiong?

NURSE 2:   Matron is in her office. Dr Idiong is in the consulting room.

ANI: Is she busy with a patient?

NURSE 2:   Let me check. [*She glances briefly into a consulting room.*] She's free. [*ANI enters the consulting room.*]

ANI: Doctor, I want to know the full details.

DR IDIONG: What I told you is basically it. It was so sudden. We had no chance to do much. Much of the bloods we took for tests ended up being tested posthumously.

ANI: Did you test the blood for the poison?

DR IDIONG: Once we found it in her stomach, we tested how much of it had gotten into her bloodstream. [*She opens a file and brings out a lab result form and shows him.*] She had a very high concentration in her blood, too. She was just five years old and weighed less than twenty kilograms. She didn't stand a chance.

ANI: What about Ubong? He's older and heavier. Could he have survived it?

DR IDIONG:	Not if he drank that same Fanta. The concentration was very, very high. [*ANI shakes his head.*]
ANI:	Where is the Fanta now?
DR IDIONG:	It's still in the lab. The bottle's almost empty though. Itoro drank most of it.
ANI:	Imagine what could have happened if he had shared that drink with his schoolmates.
DR IDIONG:	Thank God he didn't do that. Do you want to take the bottle?
ANI:	No. Please just keep it for now.
DR IDIONG:	All right [*She brings out another file and takes out two lab results.*] These are Ubong's test results. We took the liberty of testing him for arsenic, too, once we knew. [*She shows them to Ani.*] This one is his original blood tests. This second one is a urine test for arsenic. Urine is a better indicator of arsenic clearance rates. [*She points out an item.*] As you can see, he has it, too. But in his case the amount was very small. It is probably what made him unwell enough to reject his breakfast, but it was not enough to do him any real harm.
ANI:	What lasting effects can we expect from it?
DR IDIONG:	None. Arsenic in small doses has actually been used medically to treat certain

conditions. A single dose like this will leave no permanent effect.

ANI: Thank God for that. I will take both results.

DR IDIONG: [*giving him the papers*] I thought someone had accidentally put rat poison in the Fanta. But the concentration was so high I was puzzled. You are sure she deliberately tried to poison him?

ANI: Very sure. So you think it came from rat poison?

DR IDIONG: I'm not entirely sure it is in rat poison. I thought rat poisons today contained mainly anticoagulants to make the rats bleed to death. But maybe some brands still use arsenic, like the ones the street hawkers carry around. I just can't think of any other possibility.

ANI: Well, thank you for everything, Doctor. My friend Gerald Umana will be coming to pick Ubong. I would like you to admit my mother for the night. Give her a sedative if necessary. I doubt she'll get any sleep tonight otherwise.

DR IDIONG: I will do that.

ANI: I need to go now and make arrangements for Itoro. Can she stay where she is for now? DR IDIONG: She will be moved to another room at the back. But you need to have her taken away today.

ANI: I will. [*ANI and DR IDIONG both rise.*]

DR IDIONG: Please accept my sympathies, sir.

ANI: Thank you.

ANI leaves and goes to UBONG. UBONG is still sitting on the bed the way ANI had left him.

ANI: Don't you want to lie down for a while? [*UBONG shakes his head.*] OK. Do you remember Uncle Gerry?

UBONG: Yes, Daddy.

ANI: Uncle Gerry will be coming to take you to stay with him.

UBONG: [*looking down at his hands*] Yes, Daddy. [*He looks up.*] Don't you want me to stay with you anymore?

ANI: Of course I do. You will always stay with me Ubong. You are my son. Uncle Gerry is just keeping you for a few hours. You're coming home with me tonight.

UBONG: [*looking relieved*] OK. Can I stay with Aunty Celia instead?

ANI: Mmmm, it's better you stay with Uncle Gerry, OK?

UBONG: OK. [*He looks down at his hands again.*] Is Aunty Celia still angry with me?

ANI: She's not angry with you. I have to go now.
                Uncle Gerry will come for you. [*ANI hugs
                UBONG again and goes to the door.*]

UBONG: Daddy? [*ANI turns.*]

ANI: Yes?

UBONG: Will Itoro be OK? [*ANI releases a deep breath
                and thinks for a moment.*]

ANI: Itoro is OK now. She is with the angels.
                [*UBONG starts crying softly.*]

UBONG: Why can't she be here with us?

ANI: She just can't, but we have to believe she's
                at peace where she is. I will see you later.

ANI leaves the room.

Fade on UBONG still crying softly.

Scene XXXV

MATRON'S office. She and CELIA are inside. CELIA'S eyes are red and swollen. She is still crying. MATRON is leaning on the desk beside her. She is rubbing CELIA'S shoulders.

MATRON: Celia. It's enough. You will make yourself ill.

CELIA: What does it matter if I'm ill? What does it matter if I die even? Oh, maybe I should just die and be with my baby.

MATRON: What about Eno and Ekaette?

CELIA: Oh, poor girls! They don't even know what has happened yet.

MATRON: Do you want to call and tell them?

CELIA: [*shaking her head*] Let them enjoy their trip. They've been looking forward to it so much. Time enough for them to hear when they return.

MATRON: What do you want to do now? Are you going to return home?

CELIA: What home? Ani will not let me darken the doors of his house tonight.

MATRON: Where are you going to go and who is going to be with you? You should not be alone tonight.

CELIA: I'll call my friend Sandra.

CELIA brings out her phone, starts trying to dial, then drops the phone and bursts into fresh tears. MATRON picks up the phone.

MATRON: It's OK, Celia. [*She shows her the phone.*] Is this her number? [*CELIA nods. MATRON starts the call. Just then there is a loud knock at her door. She stops the call and opens the door.*] Who's banging on my door like… [*She stops when she finds herself facing two policemen.*]

POLICEMAN 1: Matron, sorry to disturb you. We are looking for Celia Umoh. [*CELIA comes to the door.*]

CELIA: I am Celia Umoh. Why are you looking for me? [*POLICEMAN 1 grabs her arm.*]

POLICEMAN 1: We have a warrant for your arrest.

MATRON: Arrest! [*The hospital employees gather nearby, watching.*] What charge? [*POLICEMAN 2 brings out the handcuffs.*]

POLICEMAN 1: [*twisting CELIA'S arms behind her back.*] For the murder of her daughter and the wilful attempted murder of her stepson.

They snap the handcuffs on, pinching her wrists. CELIA cries out in pain.

CELIA: It's hurting me! Take it off, it's hurting! I'll come with you without it!

MATRON: Can't you hear her? Take it off!

Both policemen ignore her. They half-drag CELIA out to their waiting police car. MATRON follows.

MATRON: What do you want me to do, Celia? Do you
                 have a lawyer I can call?

CELIA: Call Sandra!

MATRON: Which police station are you taking her to?

While POLICEMAN 1 answers MATRON, POLICEMAN 2 shoves CELIA, still complaining that her wrists are hurting, into the car.

POLICEMAN 2:   Be grateful you are still alive and can feel the
                 pain. Your daughter isn't so lucky!

POLICEMAN 1 and 2 get into the car with her and drive off. MATRON puts the phone to her ear and starts talking.

MATRON: Sandra?… This is the matron of Mother of
                 Our Saviour Hospital. I'm calling because…

Fade.

Scene XXXVI

The police station. SANDRA walks in and goes up to the desk.

SANDRA: Good evening, Officer.

POLICEMAN 3: Good evening, madam. What can I do for you?

SANDRA: I'm here to see Mrs Umoh.

POLICEMAN 3: [*pointing*] Go through that door. Turn left. You'll see some officers there. Ask one of them to direct you.

SANDRA follows his instructions and POLICEMAN 4 leads her to the cells. Through the bars CELIA can be seen sitting on a bunk bed with a threadbare mattress. There are four other inmates in the cell. SANDRA and the policeman walk up to the bars.

SANDRA: [*wrinkling her nose*] This place stinks!

POLICEMAN 4: Celia Umoh!

CELIA goes to the bars. The light from the corridor falls on her. Her face looks swollen. One eye is slightly closed from the swelling. Her neck, too, looks swollen. Both wrists are red and swollen. Her feet are bare.

SANDRA: Good heavens! What happened?

POLICEMAN 4:	You have ten minutes. [*He moves away*.]
SANDRA:	Who did this to you?
CELIA:	They say I resisted arrest and attacked the arresting officers. It's all lies. As they were taking me out of the car, I stumbled. They were dragging me so hard. I fell against one of them. They say I attempted to attack him, and he reacted instinctively. I was still handcuffed, mind you. The result is my bruised eye.
SANDRA:	What about your neck and wrists?
CELIA:	The handcuffs were really tight. I don't know if they used the smallest size or what. My neck was caused by Ani. He was so angry, he would have strangled me had it not been for Elijah.
SANDRA:	My God. And even your shoes. Why did they take your shoes?
CELIA:	They claimed it is a possible weapon, and they have to remove all harmful items from me. Have you brought a lawyer?
SANDRA:	I contacted one, but he said it's too late now to have a bail hearing. Until tomorrow.
CELIA:	I have to stay here till tomorrow?
SANDRA:	That's the same thing I asked him. He said the only way was to get to the chief of police to give the order to release you. I got Peter

to get in contact with him, but he refused to help. Peter thinks he has been told to make sure you stay in prison.

CELIA: Ani. He sold him the house he lives in two years ago. Gave him a really good deal on it. Since then they kept in touch. He no doubt went to him to have me arrested.

SANDRA: First thing tomorrow I'm going to organise bail. But I'm so sorry Celia, there's nothing I can do tonight. [*CELIA, leaning against the bars, just nods wearily.*] I got your handbag and phone from the hospital.

CELIA: Keep them. I'm not allowed to have anything in here.

SANDRA: But, Cee, what really happened? You told me you didn't put anything in the drink. You said you threw it away.

CELIA: Do you have a Bible in your bag?

SANDRA: Bible?

CELIA: Yes. Bible.

SANDRA: I have only this small New Testament.

SANDRA brings it out. CELIA takes it and places it carefully between her palms.

CELIA: I swear to you on this Bible that what I told you this morning is true. I did not put anything in Ubong's drink. I tied that hair gel container in a black plastic bag and threw it in the bin. [*She starts crying.*] I swear to you on my life, on the lives of my two remaining daughters. [*SANDRA covers CELIA'S hands with hers.*]

SANDRA: You don't have to swear like this, Cee. I believe you.

CELIA: Thank you. Thank God for you, Sandra.

POLICEMAN 4: Hey! Time up.

SANDRA: It's not even five minutes!

POLICEMAN 4: Time up. Are you going to leave willingly or do I have to get you forcibly removed?

SANDRA: *Na wa.* I'll leave. [*CELIA tries to hand her the Bible.*] No, keep it. It will bring you some comfort, especially the Psalms. And try to figure out what could have happened. What went wrong.

POLICEMAN 4: I will not ask you to leave again.

SANDRA: I said I'm leaving! I'll see you tomorrow, Celia. God be with you.

CELIA: Amen. Thank you again, Sandra. [*SANDRA leaves. CELIA goes back to the bed and gingerly sits. She opens the Bible and starts reading softly.*] The Lord is my shepherd, I shall not want…

SANDRA goes back to the reception of the station.

SANDRA: [*to POLICEMAN 3 at the desk*] Mrs Umoh
                   is in a terrible state. She needs medical
                   attention urgently.

POLICEMAN 3:   She's all right.

SANDRA: Have you seen her? She has been beaten...

POLICEMAN 3:   [*interrupting her*] Are you accusing us of
                   beating her, madam?

SANDRA: [*sarcastically*] Of course not. I wouldn't dare.
                   All I'm saying is she needs to be taken to a
                   hospital to see a doctor.

POLICEMAN 3:   If it's necessary the prison doctor will see
                   her tomorrow. She is not going anywhere
                   tonight. Good night to you, madam.

Without answering, SANDRA leaves.

Fade.

Scene XXXVII

The UMOHS' house. GERRY is in the upstairs parlour. The TV is on, but the volume is very low. ANI walks in and sits.

GERRY: That took a long time.

ANI: He didn't go to sleep immediately and I didn't want to leave him lying there awake and frightened.

GERRY: But he's asleep now. [*ANI nods, then he stretches wearily. GERRY picks up the glass on the side table and holds it up.*] I made this for you. You need a good drink. But you took so long to return, the ice is mostly melted. I'll go and refresh it.

ANI: No need. I'll take it like that. [*ANI accepts the glass from GERRY, and takes a long drink.*] You are right. I needed that. [*He lets out a breath.*] Thanks for staying tonight, Gerry.

GERRY: If you hadn't asked me, I would have offered to. You shouldn't be alone tonight, and even your mother is not around. How is she by the way?

ANI: Not good. When I went back with the undertakers, I checked on her. Her blood pressure's gone through the roof, with readings of 280/160. She's heavily sedated and on all sorts of antihypertensive medications.

GERRY: My goodness! 280/160! She could have a stroke!

ANI: I know. [*He sighs.*] That's all I need. To have to bury my daughter and my mother, at the same time.

GERRY: Pray against it, Ani. What about Celia? Is she still in jail?

ANI: Of course.

GERRY: Remember she is still the mother of your daughters. For their sake, temper punishment with mercy.

ANI: That is why I don't intend to pursue this any further. Tomorrow I'll call the police chief and withdraw all the charges against her. But let her suffer tonight. [*They are silent for a moment.*]

GERRY: I still can't believe Celia could actually try to kill a child. I've been looking at these lab results again. [*He indicates the lab results on a nearby table.*] Arsenic. Imagine. I thought I knew her. [*He shakes his head.*] It's incredible!

ANI: So imagine how I feel. I've been married all these years to a stranger. [*GERRY nods understandingly.*]

GERRY: How are Ekaette and Eno taking it?

ANI: I've spoken with them, but I haven't told
                them. It's not the kind of news to impart
                to children over the phone. I'll hold off the
                funeral until they return. Let them have the
                chance to say farewell to their sister. [*He
                stares unseeingly at the glass in his hand.*] To
                Itoro. My lovely little Itoro. Everywhere
                she went, people loved her. She was like
                a ray of sunshine. So lively. So generous
                of spirit. Look at how she took to Ubong.
                [*Tears start coursing down his cheeks.*] She had
                her whole life ahead of her. Every other
                week she changed her mind about what she
                wanted to be when she grew up. This week
                she decided she would be a pilot. [*He smiles
                sadly.*] So she could fly herself to Abuja any
                time she wanted.

GERRY: Ah, I see. [*ANI drains the glass.*]

ANI: I should go in and see what rest, if any, I
                can get.

GERRY: I think I'll turn in, too.

ANI: OK. Good night, Gerry.

GERRY: Goodnight, Ani.

Fade.

Scene XXXVIII

ANI'S room. CELIA'S clothes and other items are strewn on the floor and bed. Several drawers are open. ANI is sitting on the bed. CELIA'S bubu is on his lap. The bedroom door cautiously opens and GERRY looks in.

GERRY: I guessed you wouldn't be asleep. [*He comes into the room and his eyebrows go up at the state of it.*] What are you doing?

ANI: Trying to know the woman I called my wife. I've been hunting through her things looking for clues, anything that can tell me who she really is. And guess what I found? This. [*He holds up the little plastic 'Best Girl' container.*] It contains some white powder. I'm going to have it tested tomorrow. But I think I already know what the result will be.

GERRY takes it from him, opens it, looks in and closes it again. He scrutinises the container.

GERRY: Where did you find it?

ANI: In the pocket of this *bubu*.

GERRY: I don't know what to say. [*He shifts some things and places the container on a dresser top.*] You need to get some sleep, Ani. I brought this to help you. [*He shows ANI two white tablets.*]

These were prescribed for me. You know I sometimes have trouble sleeping. I just take two of these and I'm out like a light. And when I wake up in the morning, I feel well rested.

ANI: Thanks.

ANI gets some water from the room fridge and takes them. GERRY then helps him pack CELIA'S things to one side of the room. ANI starts yawning. He stretches out on the bed.

GERRY: See you in the morning.

He puts out the light and leaves.

Fade.

Scene IXL

It is morning. ANI, GERRY and UBONG are at the dining table. UBONG is in his school uniform. ATIM enters bearing a platter of eggs. ANI serves UBONG, then himself. GERRY serves himself. They start eating in a desultory manner. Only GERRY makes any inroads in his meal. ANI manages only a few bites. UBONG doesn't touch his food at all. ANI tries to encourage him.

ANI: Try a little of the food, Ubong. You need to keep your strength up. [*UBONG eats a little of the egg and drinks his tea.*] What's that tablet called, Gerry? I wouldn't have gotten any sleep without it. I'm thinking of getting my doctor to prescribe some for me.

GERRY: Rohypnol. It's the famous date-rape drug.

ANI: I can see why. It knocks you out.

There's knocking on the outside door. ATIM goes to answer it, then comes to ANI.

ATIM: Haruna say one woman name Ijeoma Nwankwo dey for gate.

ANI: Let her come in.

ATIM: Yes, sir.

She leaves and returns shortly with IJEOMA. ANI and GERRY get up to greet her. UBONG remains seated. IJEOMA rushes over to ANI and hugs him. She is crying.

IJEOMA: I heard about Itoro. I'm so sorry!

ANI: [*hugging her back*] Thank you.

IJEOMA: I couldn't believe it. I saw her just last week in your office. Such a lovely girl.

ANI: She certainly was. [*He disentangles himself from her.*] You remember my friend Gerry? [*IJEOMA looks up.*]

IJEOMA: Of course. Good morning, Gerry.

GERRY: Good morning, Ijeoma.

IJEOMA goes to UBONG and enfolds him in her arms.

IJEOMA: Are you all right?

UBONG: Yes.

ANI: Please join us for breakfast.

IJEOMA: [*wiping her eyes.*] Thank you, but I couldn't eat a thing. [*She pulls out the chair beside UBONG and sits.*]

ANI: At least have some tea. [*IJEOMA shakes her head.*]

IJEOMA: No, Ani. I can't handle anything right now.

ANI: We have to carry on. If we don't eat, we can't insist that Ubong eats. [*He looks at UBONG'S still full plate.*] His appetite is all but gone as it is.

IJEOMA: Try a little piece of bread, Ubong.

UBONG just remains looking down at his hands. He makes no move towards the bread.

IJEOMA: [*firmly*] Ubong, I said eat your bread. You need to have something in your stomach. [*UBONG reluctantly takes a bite. IJEOMA looks at ANI.*] How did it happen?

ANI: I'll tell you later. Where are you going from here?

IJEOMA: I'm taking the day off. I thought I'd spend it with Ubong.

UBONG: I'm going to school.

ANI: I wanted him to take today off, but he insisted he wanted to go.

GERRY: It's better that he goes. It'll take his mind off things.

ANI: How did you come?

IJEOMA: By taxi.

GERRY: I was going to take Ubong to school, but maybe you would prefer to go with him and the driver.

IJEOMA:	I can drive if you need the driver to do other things, and of course if there's a spare car.
ANI:	Yes, I do have a lot of things for him to do today. There's Celia's car. You could use that. I can get the driver to drop me off at the office first. My car is there.
GERRY:	There's no need for that. I can take you to the office.
ANI:	I want to stop off at the hospital and see Mama first.
GERRY:	No problem. I also want to see Mama.
IJEOMA:	Your mother is in hospital?
ANI:	Yes. This has all been a bit too much for her. [*He gets up.*] Come into the parlour, Ijeoma, let's talk. [*ANI and IJEOMA go to the parlour.*] I didn't want to discuss this in front of Ubong.
IJEOMA:	I understand. He's such a sensitive boy. This must be difficult for him. [*ANI nods.*]
ANI:	Very difficult. He loved Itoro.
IJEOMA:	I've heard some rumours – well, I call them rumours – that Celia had something to do with it. But that can't be possible.
ANI:	I have to be honest with you, Ijeoma, since it also involves Ubong. Itoro died of arsenic poisoning. It was in Ubong's lunch drink,

but as fate would have it, he did not drink it. [*IJEOMA gasps.*]

IJEOMA: Oh, God! How did it get there?

ANI: Celia put it.

IJEOMA: She wanted to poison Ubong?

ANI: Yes. I'm so sorry, Ijeoma. I had no idea she was capable of anything like this.

IJEOMA: [*shouting*] Heeey! Where is she now?

ANI: She spent the night in prison. She is probably still there.

IJEOMA: I don't want her anywhere near Ubong, Ani. You hear me? If she's coming back here, tell me, let me take my son away *o*!

ANI: She will never be allowed near him again. And she will never set foot in this house again.

IJEOMA: I will take him to school and go back for him. In fact, I'm going to take the week off. I'm going to stay with him *o*!

ANI: That's an excellent plan. I have a lot on my plate right now. And my mother's in hospital. I was thinking of asking Gerry to keep him after school. But you would obviously be better for him. I'll get the keys to Celia's car for you. The house keys are also on it. [*GERRY and UBONG enter the parlour.*]

GERRY: Ubong needs to start going.

ANI: Ubong, your mother will take you to school today, OK?

UBONG: Yes, Daddy.

ANI: Go to the car. I'll get the keys and meet you outside, Ijeoma.

GERRY, UBONG and IJEOMA go outside. ANI goes to the dining room.

ANI: Atim!

ATIM'S VOICE: Yes sir! [*She enters the dining room.*]

ANI: My wife is not to step into this house again, Atim. Do you understand me?

ATIM: Eno's mummy?

ANI: Yes. Eno's mummy. If I find that you have disobeyed me and let her in, I will send you back to the village. No matter what reason she gives, do not let her into this house. Do not take anything from this house to her or bring anything from her into this house. Is that clear?

ATIM: Yes, sir.

ANI:	If she calls on the phone, tell her you are not allowed to speak to her and hang up.
ATIM:	Yes, sir.
ANI:	Mama is in hospital. Pack some things to take to her. Beverages, fruit, bottled water. Take them to Gerry's car.
ATIM:	Yes, sir.

ANI goes upstairs. ATIM goes into the kitchen. Outside UBONG is sitting in front in CELIA'S car. IJEOMA and GERRY are standing beside GERRY'S car.

IJEOMA:	I can't believe people can be so wicked. And wickedness never pays. See what has happened now. She's reaping the fruits of her wickedness. Lord Jesus, thank you for protecting Ubong. You are all I have to look up to.
GERRY:	Well, I guess it just goes to show. No one ever truly knows the heart of another human being. Anyway, about your driving. I hope you are with your licence? The police and LASTMA have really been harassing motorists recently, even female drivers.
IJEOMA:	I should be with it. Let me check to be sure.

IJEOMA delves into her handbag and brings out the licence, looks at it, then hands it to GERRY. GERRY looks at it, too, and gives it back to her.

GERRY:	Good. [*ANI comes out.*]

ANI: Haruna! [*HARUNA comes to him.*] If
                        madam, my wife, comes here, do not open
                        the gate for her. I no want make she enter
                        this compound. You hear me so? No open
                        gate for her!

HARUNA: Yes, oga.

ANI: If I find out say you let her inside this
                        compound, I go sack you immediately.
                        Understand?

HARUNA: Yes, oga. Na because of the juju she do that
                        day, oga?

ANI: What juju?

HARUNA: Last week… Friday, no, Thursday. I see her
                        dey throw way something round the whole
                        house like this. [*He demonstrates.*] All the
                        time she dey talk something. I just know
                        sharp-sharp say *na* juju.

ANI: I see.

HARUNA: No worry, oga. She no go enter.

ANI: Good. [*He turns to IJEOMA.*] Here. [*He gives
                        her some money.*] I'm not sure how much
                        petrol is in that car. You may need to fill up.
                        [*He shows her the bunch of keys.*] These are the
                        house keys. This is the front door, this the
                        back. [*IJEOMA takes the keys.*]

IJEOMA: I'd like to visit your mother after dropping
                        Ubong in school, if that's all right.

236

ANI: I don't see why not. I'll let her know to
                    expect you.

IJEOMA gets into CELIA'S car. ANI leans in at the window.

ANI: Goodbye Ubong. Have a good day at school.

UBONG: Goodbye Daddy.

*IJEOMA drives off. ANI talks to ELIJAH while ATIM brings out a
covered basket which she puts in GERRY'S car. ANI then joins GERRY
in his car and GERRY drives off. ANI calls POLICE CHIEF.*

POLICE CHIEF: Mr Umoh.

ANI: Good morning, sir.

POLICE CHIEF: Good morning. Do you still want your wife
                    released today?

ANI: Yes. I can't pursue a case against her, because
                    of the effect it will have on my daughters.

POLICE CHIEF: That's true.

ANI: What about the native doctor who gave her
                    the poison? He is also culpable.

POLICE CHIEF: Definitely. He needs to realise he can't just
                    go around dispensing poison. I've sent my
                    officers to that place near Ijebu he's been
                    operating out of. That is obviously not his
                    true residence, but it may yield clues that
                    will lead us to him. I told them to go early,
                    and they are already there as we speak.

ANI:	Thank you, sir.
POLICE CHIEF:	Once again, accept my condolences.
ANI:	Thank you.

ANI ends the call.

Fade.

Scene XL

The babalawo's *hut. POLICEMEN 1 and 2 arrive in a police car. They look around the clearing then go to the hut. The door opens easily. They go in and look around. The mat is still on the floor. All other artefacts are still in the room. Jars, tins, bottles and plastic containers contain powdery substances, dried leaves and liquids. In one corner where BABA had thrown it, partially hidden under a stool, is the money. The policemen find it. They also look through the other room. Among the things there they find a 'Best Girl' hair gel container with some white powder in it. They also find the torn pieces of UBONG'S photograph. POLICEMAN 1 suddenly waves his colleague into silence.*

POLICEMAN 1:   Quiet! Quiet! I think I hear something. [*He goes to the outside door of the other room and listens.*] I hear a car. Someone is coming.

POLICEMAN 2:   If it's him, that makes our job easier. We can grab him as soon as he gets out of the car.

POLICEMAN 1:   Hide! If he is the one, I want to see what he does.

POLICEMAN 1 closes the door and peeps cautiously through the tiny window. A car drives into the second clearing. BABA gets out. BABA is dressed in ordinary trousers and shirt. His face and body are free of the usual paint. He looks quite young. He looks quickly around then walks briskly in through the back door. Pauses at the door and scans the room. He does not see POLICEMAN 1, who is hiding behind the table. He goes into the other room. POLICEMAN 2 is hiding behind the shrine.

BABA doesn't bother to scan this room but goes straight to the corner and searches under the stool. He straightens just as POLICEMAN 2 talks.

POLICEMAN 2:   Looking for this?

Startled, BABA jumps and whirls round. POLICEMAN 2 is holding up the money. BABA runs to the door and races into the other room and straight into the arms of POLICEMAN 1. He wrestles briefly but stops once POLICEMAN 2 grabs hold of him, too.

BABA: Please, officers, please. I haven't done anything.

POLICEMAN 1:   Then why did you run? Innocent men don't run.

BABA: Please you can just say you didn't see me. I'll make it worth your while.

POLICEMAN 1:   Shut up there! [*He handcuffs him, then leaves him for POLICEMAN 2.*] Take him to the car. I will bring these containers. The chief wants any substances found here to be tested.

POLICEMAN 2:   Yes, sir.

BABA: There's no poison in any of them *o*! I didn't give her any poison *o*!

POLICEMAN 2:   Eeeh? She just happened to get it somewhere else, *abi*? Come, let's go! You can explain that at the station.

POLICEMAN 2 leads BABA away.

Fade on POLICEMAN 1 packing the jars and tins into a carton they brought with them.

Scene XLI

*The hospital. GERRY and ANI approach the reception. ANI speaks to
RECEPTIONIST.*

ANI: Is Dr Idiong around?

RECEPTIONIST: She has not come yet, sir.

ANI: What about Matron?

RECEPTIONIST: She is around, sir.

ANI: Can you let her know I would like to see
                         her? I will be in Idorenyin Umoh's room.

RECEPTIONIST: Yes, sir.

*GERRY and ANI move on to IDORENYIN'S room. NURSE 3
is with her. IDORENYIN is lying on the bed. She is awake. They all
exchange greetings. NURSE 3 packs her trolley and leaves the room.
IDORENYIN sits up in bed. She looks frail and unwell. ANI hugs her.
GERRY keeps the basket on the table.*

ANI: How are you, Mama?

IDORENYIN: I don't know, my son. I woke up this morning
                         hoping it was all a bad dream. I asked the
                         nurse that came in and she confirmed that

the nightmare was real. Itoro. Itoro is really gone. Oh! Oh!

GERRY: Mama, you need to take it easy.

IDORENYIN: Easy! My granddaughter is dead!

ANI: Mama, you having a stroke will not bring her back to life. Gerry is right. You need to take it easy.

The door opens and MATRON comes in. Greetings are exchanged again.

MATRON: How are you feeling this morning, Mama? [*IDORENYIN leans back against the pillows and shakes her head.*]

MATRON: God is in control. Give it time.

ANI: I just want to see Matron for a minute, Mama. [*ANI and MATRON go out into the corridor.*] How is her blood pressure now?

MATRON: It went down in the night. At 4 a.m. the reading was 160/90 when she was sleeping. But it's on the rise again this morning. The reading that nurse has just taken is 180/100. [*ANI sighs.*] She's taking it really hard.

ANI: Please, you people must do your best. I don't want to bury her, too. Not now.

MATRON: We will do our best, and pray God will reward our efforts.

ANI brings out the small hair gel container from a plastic bag. He shows it to MATRON.

ANI: Matron, I want the powder in this container tested. I want to know what it is. [*He returns it to the bag and hands it to her.*] Be careful with it.

MATRON: I'll take it to the lab myself right now.

ANI: Thank you. [*ANI returns to the room.*]

IDORENYIN: Is there any problem?

ANI: I wanted her to test the contents of a plastic container I found among Celia's things.

IDORENYIN: Oh. Oh. How can anyone be so wicked? Gerry tells me you haven't told the girls. That's good. Let them hold on to their innocence a little longer. And I hear Ubong is taking it hard.

GERRY: He is, Mama. But I also said he's a child and therefore resilient. He'll bounce back.

ANI: I have to leave now, Mama. I'll come to see you again this afternoon.

IDORENYIN: I'd like to go home with you when you return. Or you can send the driver to pick me up if you can't make it.

ANI: Mama, let's just see how you are this afternoon before we make any decisions.

IDORENYIN: All right.

GERRY and ANI say their farewells and leave. IDORENYIN lies back on the bed.

Fade.

Scene XLII

The police station. SANDRA goes to the desk.

SANDRA: I'm here to arrange bail for Celia Umoh. My lawyer is on the way. [*POLICEMAN 5 looks bored. He doesn't look at, or answer her.*] Did you hear what I said?

POLICEMAN 5:   I heard.

SANDRA: So?

POLICEMAN 5:   So what? Did you ask me a question? [*He turns to a man who had just come in.*] Yes? What do you want?

SANDRA: You haven't finished attending to me!

POLICEMAN 5:   [*looking at her*] Madam, see those chairs over there? Sit there and wait for your lawyer. Yes, Mr man. What can I do for you?

SANDRA: [*raising her voice*] Excuse me! I want to see Mrs Umoh!

POLICEMAN 5:   Shouting at me is not going to help you. I've told you; go and sit over there.

SANDRA:	This is unbelievable! I'm going to take this up with…

SANDRA stops as CELIA emerges from another door escorted by a police officer.

SANDRA:	Celia!

POLICEMAN 5:	[*under his breath*] All these over-*sabi* women. Common good morning they can't even tell someone. [*To the man at the counter.*] Yes, Mr man, what is your problem?

SANDRA has gone over to CELIA.

CELIA:	They just came and told me this morning that I'm free to go.

SANDRA:	Just like that?

CELIA:	Just like that. I thought you had succeeded in arranging the bail.

SANDRA:	I haven't done anything. The lawyer is not even here yet. [*To the policeman who brought Celia out.*] Officer, what's going on?

POLICEMAN 4:	The charges against her have been dropped. Here are your possessions. [*He hands CELIA her shoes.*] You can go. [*POLICEMAN 4 goes back inside.*]

SANDRA:	I better call the lawyer and tell him not to bother coming. [*SANDRA makes the call while CELIA sits and puts on her shoes.*] Barrister… Ah, she's free *o*… They say the

charges have been dropped... I don't know.
I didn't ask... Yes... Thank you anyway. Bye.

SANDRA ends the call and scrutinises CELIA. She looks much the same as she looked the night before, but the swelling on her eye has reduced. However the area is dark. SANDRA touches it gently.

SANDRA: That must hurt.

CELIA: It does, but that's the least of my problems.
            I just want to get out of here.

They exit the station, get into SANDRA'S car and drive off.

SANDRA: I was thinking of taking you to my house,
            but is there anywhere else you would rather
            go? [*CELIA shakes her head, then winces and
            massages her neck.*]

CELIA: No. I'm pretty sure Ani would have left
            instructions that I should not be allowed
            into the house.

SANDRA: OK. Once you get to my place and get
            cleaned up as much as possible, and eat
            something, I'll take you to the hospital. You
            need to be checked over.

CELIA: I think I'm all right, but I do want to see
            Matron. I need to find out all the medical
            details about Itoro and Ubong.

SANDRA: Your mother-in-law is on admission there
            you know.

CELIA: [*sarcastically*] I wonder why. What could possibly be wrong with her?

SANDRA: I asked that but Regina didn't know.

CELIA: Regina told you? When?

SANDRA: Last night.

CELIA: How did she know?

SANDRA: You know Regina is busybody supreme. She minds everybody else's business. I think she was mostly calling on a fishing expedition. She wanted to pump me for information and tossed that morsel my way to try to loosen my tongue.

CELIA: What did you tell her?

SANDRA: Just that Itoro had passed on, but I didn't tell her how. Telling Regina anything is as good as putting it on CNN.

CELIA: Sandra, thank you very much for everything.

CELIA sniffles and starts crying softly. SANDRA reaches over and pats her knee.

SANDRA: I know it may not seem like it, but things will get better. Even between you and Ani. Have some faith.

They drive on not speaking, CELIA crying silently.

Fade.

Scene XLIII

IJEOMA drives to the hospital, parks and enters. She goes up to RECEPTIONIST.

IJEOMA: Good morning. I'm here to see Mrs Idorenyin Umoh.

RECEPTIONIST: Please have a seat. I'll get one of the nurses for you.

She leaves. IJEOMA doesn't sit. She stands idly looking around. RECEPTIONIST returns shortly with NURSE 3.

NURSE 3: Please follow me.

NURSE 3 leads IJEOMA to IDORENYIN'S room. IJEOMA enters.

IJEOMA: Good morning, Mama.

IDORENYIN: Ijeoma. How are you?

IJEOMA: I'm fine, Mama. I brought these few things for you. [*She shows IDORENYIN a bag of provisions.*]

IDORENYIN: Thank you. [*IJEOMA puts them away in the cupboard, then takes a seat.*]

IJEOMA: How are you feeling now?

IDORENYIN: I've been better. Still I don't want to stay in hospital any longer. When Ani comes this afternoon I'm going to insist he takes me home.

IJEOMA: Do you think that's wise? Maybe you should let the doctors decide…

IDORENYIN: No. I want to go home. [*IJEOMA sighs.*]

IJEOMA: It's such a terrible thing that has happened. [*IDORENYIN nods slowly.*]

IDORENYIN: Terrible. Absolutely terrible.

Fade.

Scene XLIV

SANDRA'S house. CELIA is in the parlour. She has cleaned up and is wearing a loose dress of SANDRA'S. The bruise on her face is still evident and there are plasters on her wrists. MAID enters and clears away the tray of food on the coffee table, exiting with it. SANDRA herself enters. She notices the still full plate of food being taken away.

SANDRA: You were still unable to eat much.

CELIA: I don't have the appetite.

SANDRA: Gerry called. He is on his way here and he wants to see you.

CELIA: Has Ani sent him to bring my things or what?

SANDRA: He didn't say anything like that. I think he wants to hear your version of events.

CELIA: I'll gladly tell him.

SANDRA: When he leaves we can then go to Mother of Our Saviour hospital. [*MAID re-enters.*]

MAID: Aunty, Maiguard say one Gerry dey find you.

SANDRA: Let him in. [*MAID exits.*] He must have been almost here when he called. [*MAID returns with GERRY. She shows him in and leaves.]* Gerry, welcome.

GERRY: Thank you, Sandra. Hello Celia. [*He studies her, noting her bruises.*]

CELIA: Hello, Gerry. [*They all sit.*]

SANDRA: What will you have? Tea? Coffee? Soft drink?

GERRY: No, nothing, Sandra. Thank you. Celia, what really happened?

CELIA: Gerry, I swear to you I did not poison that drink. I admit I got the poison from a native doctor and I admit that I put a little in Ubong's hot chocolate the night before. But...

GERRY: So you did try to poison him.

CELIA: I wish I could say I didn't, but yes, I did. I don't know what I was thinking, what devil entered me, but I came back to my senses, Gerry. In the morning, I threw the poison in the bin. I did not put any of it into his Fanta.

GERRY: You threw it into the bin?

CELIA: I tied it in a black plastic bag and threw it in the big outside bin, not even the kitchen bin. I didn't want it inside the house at all.

GERRY: Can you describe the container it was in?

CELIA: A small plastic container, with 'Best Girl hair gel' written on it, and a sketch of a woman's head.

GERRY: [*nodding thoughtfully*] Ani did a thorough search of your things last night, you know. He was, according to him, looking for clues to find out who you really are. He feels he no longer knows you.

CELIA: If I could turn back the clock and undo all this I would. Oh, God, how I would. I am telling you the complete truth, Gerry. I'm not holding anything back. I did poison the hot chocolate, God forgive me, but I did *not* poison that Fanta.

GERRY: So how did the poison get in it? I saw the test results. Ani showed me. That Fanta was loaded with arsenic. How come? [*CELIA throws up her hands helplessly.*]

CELIA: I don't know, Gerry. I swear to God I don't know.

GERRY: What about what happened at the native doctor's place? Ani says he heard you use your own mouth to tell the *babalawo* you had poisoned Ubong and he was almost dead.

CELIA: I was lying, Gerry! I decided I didn't want to have anything to do with the native doctor again! I thought it best to just tell him everything had gone according to plan, give him the balance of his money and leave! Oh,

God! Sandra, where's that Bible? I want to swear on it to Gerry!

SANDRA: Gerry, as for this, I can confirm that what she's saying is true. She and I had agreed that was the best way to handle the native doctor. Who knows what he could have done if he knew she had not gone through with the poisoning?

CELIA: And if I wasn't lying, how could I say that Ubong was dying? I took him to the hospital myself! I insisted that all those tests be done on him. Dr Idiong didn't think they were necessary! I knew all the time I was talking to Baba that Ubong was all right! I'm telling you the truth, Gerry. I swear to God!

GERRY: How did Itoro end up in Ubong's hospital room?

CELIA: I asked Sandra to help me pick her from school and take her to wait for me with him.

SANDRA: [nodding] Yes. [GERRY takes a deep breath.]

GERRY: I have to go.

SANDRA: When is the funeral?

GERRY: Saturday, because Eno and Ekaette are returning from Abuja on Friday.

CELIA: Gerry, please tell Ani what I've said. I didn't poison Itoro. [GERRY stands up.]

GERRY:	I will.
SANDRA:	How is Ubong?
GERRY:	Holding up. Ijeoma took him to school this morning.
CELIA:	Ijeoma took him to school?
GERRY:	She heard what happened and came this morning. She will take some time off work to stay with Ubong.
SANDRA:	You mean she's taking Ubong to stay with her?
GERRY:	No. She'll stay at the house with him. I have to leave now. I'll see you again soon, Celia.
CELIA:	Thank you for taking the trouble to come and hear me out.
GERRY:	You're welcome. [*GERRY exits.*]
CELIA:	Ijeoma is staying in my house. The next thing she'll want is to continue with Ani.
SANDRA:	Come. Let's go to the hospital now. Let them look you over and do a better dressing than these ones I did.
CELIA:	Ijeoma is after Ani. Eeeeh? Is that what all this is about? Is that why she killed my daughter? She must be the one who put that poison in the Fanta.

SANDRA: The Fanta was intended for her own son,
                 remember?

CELIA: That was just to make it look like I did it!

SANDRA: But when would she have put the poison?

CELIA: I don't know. But she found a way to! She
                 probably went to his school. Who knows?

SANDRA: And then told him not to drink it?

CELIA: Obviously! Not only that, she probably told
                 him to make sure all my girls drank it!

SANDRA: I don't know, Celia. I still don't see how she
                 could have done it. Anyway, let's go to the
                 hospital now.

SANDRA helps CELIA up and they leave.

Fade.

Scene XLV

ANI'S office. GERRY walks into the outer office. FUNKE is on the phone. She hangs up just as he walks in.

GERRY: Hello, Funke.

FUNKE: Hello, Mr Umana.

GERRY: How are you?

FUNKE: I'm fine. [*GERRY nods towards the inner office.*]

GERRY: How is he?

FUNKE: Not so good, I think.

GERRY: I don't think he should be working at a time like this.

FUNKE: I agree. I've called all his clients and rescheduled.

GERRY: So what's he doing in there?

FUNKE: He said he was reviewing some of our Lekki properties, but each time I go in there he seems to be just staring into space.

GERRY: Let me go and see him.

The inner office. ANI is sitting at his desk holding the ceramic dog. He remembers ITORO singing.

ITORO'S VOICE: 'How much is that doggie in the window?
                The one with the waggly tail…'

The phone rings. He puts down the dog and answers it. GERRY enters while he is still on the phone.

ANI: Hello… Good afternoon, Matron… Yes… I
                  see… Well, thank you very much, Matron.
                  Goodbye. [*ANI ends the call.*] Gerry, that
                  was the matron calling to let me know the
                  results of the tests they carried out on that
                  powder.

GERRY: What was it?

ANI: As I suspected. Arsenic.

GERRY: [*shaking his head*] My God.

ANI: No matter how many times I think about it,
                  it still seems unbelievable. [*He picks up the
                  ceramic dog again.*]

GERRY: I went to see Celia. She admits to putting
                  some of the powder in Ubong's hot
                  chocolate the night before, but categorically
                  denies poisoning the Fanta. She says she
                  came to her senses and threw the poison
                  away.

ANI: Ha! A likely story! But what else do you
                expect her to say?

GERRY: I know. But Ani if you think about it, this
                whole… [*he uses his hands to demonstrate
                while searching for the right word to use*] this
                whole drama, if you can call it that, doesn't
                make complete sense. It throws up more
                questions than it answers.

ANI: Questions like what?

GERRY: Let's say we accept that Celia poisoned
                Ubong's drink. Why did she take him to
                the hospital?

ANI: That's easy. To make it seem like she cares
                about him. That she tried to save him. So
                no one will suspect that she was responsible.
                And if you really think about it Gerry, she
                would have gotten away with it. The only
                reason the doctor suspected foul play
                with Itoro is because Ubong told them
                she complained shortly after drinking his
                Fanta. So they did blanket testing for every
                substance they could think of. When they
                found arsenic in Itoro's vomit, they tested
                the Fanta. Had Ubong drunk that Fanta in
                school, he would be dead before he could
                be taken to a proper hospital. And what with
                the confusion that would follow, the idea
                of testing him for poison would not even
                arise. And I, idiot that I was, would believe
                everything Celia told me. I would defend
                her to anyone who even suggested such a

thing. Hmm! She would get away with it cleanly.

GERRY: I stopped by the hospital on my way here and spoke with Dr Idiong. When Celia brought Ubong to see her, she says he was all right. All he needed was food. The blood tests that were carried out were done at Celia's insistence. Why would she do that? Why would she run the risk of them finding out he had arsenic in his blood?

ANI: They didn't test for arsenic with the original tests. It isn't something that is tested for as a routine. They only tested him for it after Itoro died.

GERRY: OK. But why did Celia allow Itoro anywhere near Ubong and the poisoned drink? She actually told Sandra to leave Itoro with Ubong after school.

ANI: Is that what she told you?

GERRY: Sandra corroborated it.

ANI: Sandra is her bosom friend. The two of them have been as thick as thieves since university! Of course she will lie for Celia!

GERRY: Even so, for whatever reason, the fact remains that Sandra picked Itoro from school. And she dropped her off in Ubong's hospital room. You'd think Celia would be more careful than that.

ANI: [*shrugging*] That was a mistake on her part. A very serious mistake. I see it as God's way of punishing her.

GERRY: I wish I could be as sure as you are about this. But I keep feeling like I'm overlooking something. Something that I ought to grasp, but haven't. And that this thing is the key to this whole mystery.

ANI: That's where your problem is. This is a very straightforward case and you are making a mystery out of it. Come down to earth, Sherlock Holmes. There is no mystery here.

GERRY: You know when Celia told me she had thrown away the container of poison, I immediately told her that you searched through her things last night.

ANI: Good. You caught her out in a lie. What did she say to that?

GERRY: Her response, or should I say, lack of response was puzzling. She said nothing about it. It was as if it didn't register with her that I was telling her you had found the poison.

ANI: [*bitterly*] Obviously she's very good at pretending. She's been pretending to me all these years. [*ANI'S phone rings again*] Hello? Good afternoon... Yes... I see... Certainly. I will come... Now?... I will be there. Thank you, sir. [*He hangs up.*] That was the police chief. His men caught the *babalawo*

261

this morning. They also tested several suspicious substances found in his hut. One of them was arsenic. He said he will tell me more when I come down to the station. The *babalawo* is about to be interrogated.

GERRY: I'd like to come with you.

ANI: Let's go.

ANI carefully returns the ceramic dog to its place on the table. He and GERRY leave the office together.

Fade.

Scene XLVI

Mother of Our Saviour Hospital. SANDRA drives in with CELIA. They alight and, as they walk towards the entrance, CELIA notices her car. She goes over to it, then back to SANDRA.

CELIA: Maybe the driver is here with Mama. If this can ever be resolved and my marriage stays intact, I will never allow her to come to stay again. Now I know her true feelings.

CELIA and SANDRA open the front door to enter and IJEOMA comes out. For a moment CELIA and IJEOMA look at each other. Then IJEOMA hisses and walks over to CELIA'S car, ostentatiously bringing out the keys and dangling them. CELIA gasps. She runs over to IJEOMA and launches herself at her.

CELIA: You planned this! You want to steal my husband and my home! [*IJEOMA fights back.*]

IJEOMA: Witch! You wanted to kill my son! God has punished you!

CELIA: You killed my daughter! I will scratch your eyes out today! I will kill you with my two hands! [*SANDRA tries to intercede and drag CELIA away.*]

SANDRA: Celia, leave her! God will judge her!

CELIA: I won't let you take my husband, too!

IJEOMA: I already have! What do you need a husband
                  for in prison?

*The guards at the gate rush over just as MATRON and NURSE 1 also
rush out. They succeed in separating the two women, but they are still
shouting abuses at each other. MATRON and SANDRA take CELIA
into the hospital. IJEOMA drives off.*

CELIA: She's driving my car! That murderess is
                  driving my car!

MATRON: [*to the hospital staff, who are gawking*] Don't
                  you people have work to do? [*They reluctantly
                  disperse.*]

SANDRA: Matron, please just take her to see the doctor.
                  She needs to be examined.

MATRON: [*to NURSE 1*] Get her case note and take it
                  to Dr Idiong. I'm taking her to the treatment
                  room.

NURSE 1:   Yes, Matron.

*MATRON and SANDRA support CELIA to the treatment room. They
help her onto the couch. CELIA goes from lamenting to praying.*

CELIA: Oh, God, help me. Show me the way. Show
                  me what to do now. Give me strength, Jesus.
                  Give me strength. [*DR IDIONG comes in.*]

DR IDIONG: Mrs Umoh.

CELIA: Doctor.

DR IDIONG: Can you stay still for a moment? I want to examine you.

CELIA: Doctor, Matron. I want to talk to both of you. I want you to tell me what happened to my little girl.

SANDRA: Celia, they can do that later. Right now let them examine you.

CELIA: I don't care what happens to me. I want to know about Itoro! That wicked devil poisoned my daughter!

DR IDIONG: I can't discuss anything until you've been treated, Mrs Umoh. So let's do just do this, then we can talk about Itoro.

CELIA: All right.

MATRON has organised instruments and dressing materials nearby. She and the doctor start removing the plasters from CELIA.

Fade.

Scene XLVII

The interrogation room of the police station. POLICE CHIEF and POLICEMAN 1 and 2 are there with the babalawo. *There are some papers in a file on the desk.*

POLICE CHIEF: You have given us your name as John Maduekwe and an Ikeja address. You are thirty- one years old. You read drama in University of Port Harcourt, and you are currently unemployed. Correct?

BABA: Yes, sir.

POLICE CHIEF: You say you are unemployed. But you have been working as a native doctor.

BABA: I was just trying to make *chop* money, sir.

POLICE CHIEF: By deceiving the public.

BABA: No, sir.

POLICE CHIEF: There are better ways of earning a living. And your method of being a native doctor is to dispense poison for your customers to use to kill people.

BABA: No, sir! I swear, sir, I have never given poison to anyone!

POLICE CHIEF:	Why are you bothering to tell such an obvious lie?
BABA:	It is not a lie, sir, I swear!
POLICE CHIEF:	Was Mrs Celia Umoh not a customer of yours?
BABA:	She was, but I never gave her any poison!
POLICEMAN 2:	Shut up! You're lying!
BABA:	No! I swear I'm not lying!
POLICE CHIEF:	Witnesses overheard a conversation you had with her. She informed you that the intended victim Ubong Umoh was dying from the poison you had given her to use on him.
BABA:	Sir. Sir, that woman has an agenda of her own. I don't know what she was talking about. There is no way that boy could end up in hospital from the powder I gave her. It was nothing more than vitamin C! I swear it is impossible for that boy to even end up in hospital!
POLICEMAN 1:	He did end up in hospital!
BABA:	Then she gave him something else. Something she did not get from me. I swear!
POLICE CHIEF:	You know we tested the powders and liquids we found in your hut.

BABA: Good. Then you know I'm telling the truth.
                 There is no poison there.

POLICE CHIEF: [*bringing out some papers from the file*] These are
                 the results of the tests. Thirteen items were
                 tested. Five were liquids; plain water, water
                 with menthol, cooking oil, engine oil and
                 soda water. Two were roughly ground dried
                 leaves. Six were powders. Five of the powders
                 were found with the other things in the
                 outer room. They were: brown face powder,
                 ground corn starch, fine sand, curry powder,
                 and talcum powder. The last powder, the one
                 found in the inner room, was arsenic.

BABA rises and POLICEMAN 2 drags him back to his seat roughly.

BABA: [*shouting*] No! No! That is impossible! Sir,
                 that is impossible!

POLICE CHIEF: [*pushing the papers towards him*] Here it is.
                 Look at it yourself! [*BABA stares at the paper
                 in disbelief.*]

BABA: No, no. This isn't true. This woman is setting
                 me up. I will not accept this. Sir, I am going
                 to tell you everything. Exactly as it happened.
                 I did not have poison in that house.

POLICE CHIEF: That is what you should have done from
                 the word go. Tell us everything instead of
                 wasting our time. Oya, start.

BABA: About a month ago…

Fade.

Scene XLVIII

POLICE CHIEF'S office. ANI and GERRY are waiting there.

GERRY:
The interrogation seems to be taking a long time.

ANI:
Maybe they are questioning him about his other customers. Celia can't be the only one. What is it? [*GERRY is frowning.*]

GERRY:
Remember what I said in the office? That I have this feeling that I'm missing something? Something I should be noticing. The feeling is still there, and I'm trying to think what it is. [*ANI glances at his watch.*]

ANI:
I have to meet with the pastor this evening. He wants to discuss the funeral arrangements. [*POLICE CHIEF enters.*]

POLICE CHIEF:
Sorry about that. Took longer than I expected. It has yielded some new developments. First of all you know I told you that one of the containers found in his house contained arsenic.

ANI:
Yes.

POLICE CHIEF: All the others contained harmless, even edible substances. The container with the arsenic was found in the second room. The man, his name by the way, is John Maduekwe, kept insisting that he did not give your wife the poison. That what he gave her was just vitamin C. He said he did not even have poison in the house. When confronted with the lab results, he opened up.

ANI: He admitted to giving her the poison?

POLICE CHIEF: No. This thing is more involved than that. According to Maduekwe, a woman approached him with a proposal. He is an actor who is jobless at the moment. This woman asked him to pose as a native doctor for a few weeks. She offered to pay him handsomely. She gave him an advance of 30,000 for himself and a further 200,000 to find a suitable place to rent for the charade. She was to pay him 10,000 for every week he carried on the role. He rented the house and decorated the outer room to fit the part. The inner room was where he kept a few items and spent time waiting for your wife. Whatever money he got out of your wife was his to keep. In addition, when everything had been successfully completed, he was to be given another 20,000 naira as bonus.

GERRY: What was the charade supposed to achieve?

POLICE CHIEF: He was told that Mrs Umoh would approach him looking for a way to handle the sudden emergence of an outside son into her family. He was to give her a powder to give to the boy that would produce whatever result it was that Mrs Umoh desired. The first time she came, he gave her plain water mixed with ashes and told her to sprinkle it around the house. She was to say whatever it was she wanted the water to do. She asked the water to make the boy mad apparently.

ANI: That must be what Haruna saw. This just gets worse and worse.

POLICE CHIEF: Needless to say, it did not work. His sponsor called and asked why he had not given the powder. He said he did not feel that Mrs Umoh at that stage would have been receptive to a powder that she actually had to give to the child. Moreover, she came with her friend, and the friend would definitely have been against it. But the sponsor grew angry and said he took an unnecessary risk. Because there was the possibility Mrs Umoh might not return. Your wife did return, but it was to demand that he refund her money. This time, she came alone. He then convinced her that the best solution to her problems was to kill the boy with poison. He would supply the poison. For this he charged her half a million naira in total. Your wife had already given him 100,000. He told her to balance 400,000, half then, and half afterwards. Then he took another risk. He did not give her the poison immediately. He wanted to have the money first. He felt that once she found out that the so-called poison was not working, she would not bring any more money. He wanted to get what he could before then. Mrs Umoh returned that same day with 200,000. He gave her a little plastic container with some whitish powder in it. He claims this container was given to him by the sponsor herself. And she told him it contained powdered vitamin C. He passed on the instructions that Mrs Umoh was to put one teaspoonful in the boy's drink on three occasions. After the third dose, the boy would die. Maduekwe says he was simply repeating verbatim what he had been told to say. He also told your wife that she would be safe because the poison was completely undetectable with lab tests. He claims he was shocked when Mrs Umoh returned the next day to tell him that the poison was working perfectly and that the boy was in hospital. He knows a child died from the poison, but he thinks it is Ugo who died. He doesn't know about Itoro.

ANI: Is he stupid? Someone gives you a suspicious powder to pass to someone else and you just accept it like that. I don't believe that. He knew he was giving Celia arsenic.

POLICE CHIEF: I would have agreed with you, but for one thing. The identity of the sponsor.

GERRY: Is it someone he did not know previously?

POLICE CHIEF: On the contrary. It is someone he has known for years. They attended the same university.

Which is why, according to him, he believed every word. [*He pauses and looks at ANI.*]

ANI: Who is it?

POLICE CHIEF: Ijeoma Nwankwo. Ugochukwu's mother. [*After a short moment of shocked silence ANI splutters into speech.*]

ANI: That is preposterous! Why would Ijeoma want to kill her own child?

GERRY: Does he have anything to support this story? [*POLICE CHIEF brings out a mobile phone.*]

POLICE CHIEF: He claims that this is Ijeoma's number. That they have been in constant touch with each other. There are two missed call from that number. Both were made at around 11 a.m. He was already in custody by then. [*He passes a piece of paper to ANI.*] Can you give me Ijeoma Nwankwo's number? [*ANI brings out his phone and writes a number on the paper.*]

GERRY: What was to be the whole purpose of the charade?

POLICE CHIEF: To discredit the present Mrs Umoh and get her out of the house, so Ijeoma could become the next Mrs Umoh. [*He compares the numbers and shakes his head.*] It's not the same number. That in itself doesn't entirely prove he's lying. Most people have more than one number these days. The next thing we want to do is bring Ijeoma in to answer some questions.

GERRY: Sir, to my mind he hasn't adequately explained everything. If his role in the plan was to pass on this powder to Celia, Mrs Umoh, he did that on Monday. Why did he still maintain the role? Why didn't he pack up shop, so to speak? He was still there yesterday when Celia returned to tell him the boy was dying.

POLICE CHIEF: He was to continue with the role until Ijeoma told him to stop. He was being paid ten thousand for every week it ran into and he has no job at the moment. So he did not mind continuing.

GERRY: All right. But yesterday he was told that Ubong was dying from the poison, a story he believed. Why did he not abandon the role then? I understand that he went back and was caught there this morning.

POLICE CHIEF: He did end the charade. He says he spoke with Ijeoma who assured him that Celia was lying. He returned to get the other 200,000 Celia had brought him. In the fracas that followed her visit, he forgot to take it.

GERRY: Does he have no other proof of Ijeoma's involvement other than this phone number?

POLICE CHIEF: No. He says Ijeoma never wrote him a cheque. It was cash throughout. She never went with him to rent the place. It's all in his

name. Or supposed name. He gave a fake
name and address.

ANI: What is the next step now, sir?

POLICE CHIEF: We will definitely keep him in prison while
we investigate further. But even if his story
turns out to be entirely true, he still has a lot
to answer for.

ANI: Ijeoma is supposed to be picking Ubong
up from school in another thirty minutes.
She will be bringing him to my house. That
would be a good time for you to get to her.

POLICE CHIEF: Yes. You go ahead. I have things to tidy up
here. When she is back in the house call me.
[ANI and GERRY rise and shake hands with
POLICE CHIEF.]

ANI: Thank you very much, sir.

POLICE CHIEF: I'm sure I don't need to tell you not to
breathe a word about any of this to anyone
at the moment.

ANI: We won't tell anyone.

POLICE CHIEF: Good. See you at your house.

They leave the office.

Fade.

Scene XLIX

The hospital. ANI and GERRY make their way to IDORENYIN'S room. They meet NURSE 3 in the corridor.

ANI: Hello, Nurse. How is my mother doing?

NURSE 3:   She is stable. But she is insisting she wants to go. She is even refusing to wear the hospital gown any more.

ANI: I see. [*ANI, GERRY and NURSE 3 continue down the corridor.*]

GERRY: Are you going to take her home?

ANI: If she refuses to stay, I have to.

GERRY: Who's going to look after her in the house?

ANI: She'll have to manage with Atim. At least she won't be alone.

ANI, GERRY and NURSE 3 arrive at IDORENYIN'S room, where NURSE 3 leaves them. IDORENYIN is as NURSE 3 said, dressed in her own clothes. ANI and GERRY greet her.

IDORENYIN: Ani, I've been waiting for you.

ANI: So I hear. How are you?

ANI takes her chart from the foot of the bed and looks through it. GERRY also looks at it over his shoulder.

IDORENYIN: My BP has come down.

ANI: I can see that. The last reading was 150/80.

GERRY: I see they did some blood tests on you, too.

IDORENYIN: Yes. And they said everything was all right. I feel better. I want to go home. I've hated hospitals ever since your father's illness and death.

ANI: All right, Mama. I'll take you home. Let me tell the nurse to get you discharged. [*ANI leaves the room.*]

IDORENYIN: Gerry, thank God you are here for him. How is he doing?

GERRY: Very well considering.

IDORENYIN: What about Celia? Has she come crawling back to beg him?

GERRY: Not that he has told me.

IDORENYIN: So she's not even sorry. What about the container Ani found in her *bubu*? Is the result of the test out?

GERRY: Yes. It contained arsenic.

IDORENYIN: I don't ever want to see her again for the rest of my life. [*ANI returns.*]

ANI: They are handling it. They anticipated it anyway, so it won't take long. Ijeoma came to see you.

IDORENYIN: Yes. She came twice.

ANI: Twice? Why?

IDORENYIN: I have my suspicions, but I don't want to say anything.

ANI: Ah, Mama, after a statement like that, you know you have to explain.

IDORENYIN: She's moving into the house to stay with Ubong, she's driving Celia's car, she's visiting me repeatedly. Do I need put two and two together for you, Ani? She brought me the things I've left behind in the cupboard. Let any of the staff who wants them have them.

GERRY: Mama, I take it you are not that keen on her filling Celia's shoes. Why not? After all, she is Ubong's mother. For him, it would be perfect. [*ANI stares at him.*]

IDORENYIN: At a time like this, that's what she's thinking of. At a time of tragedy like this.

ANI: Gerry. Are you saying you are in support of it?

GERRY: No, I'm not saying that. All I'm saying is that to someone looking at it objectively, it would seem perfect.

278

ANI: She and Celia got into a fight outside there in the parking lot.

GERRY: Are you serious?

ANI: Yes. She told me when I called her on the way over here, and Matron, too, just told me.

IDORENYIN: Nobody told me!

ANI: But they wouldn't, Mama.

IDORENYIN: Oh, what a disgrace. Two grown women. Where is Ijeoma now?

ANI: Picking Ubong up. We'll meet her at the house. [*MATRON and NURSE 3 enter.*]

MATRON: Here are your medications, Mama. [*She points out the tablets as she speaks.*] This one is to be taken daily, two tablets every morning with your breakfast. This white one is one tablet three times daily, and this last one is one at bedtime. It is to help you sleep. That's it. You are all set to go.

GERRY: What about the bill?

ANI: I've already settled that. [*MATRON checks to make sure nothing is forgotten.*]

MATRON: You are forgetting your provisions, Mama.

IDORENYIN: Deliberately. Matron, please give them to whoever wants them.

MATRON: All right, Mama.

MATRON and NURSE 3 walk with them as far as the entrance.
IDORENYIN, GERRY and ANI enter their car and drive off.

Fade.

Scene L

The UMOHS' house. IJEOMA, UBONG and ANI are at the dining table. IJEOMA is sitting in CELIA'S seat. She dishes for UBONG. ATIM comes in.

ATIM: Sir, Mama say she wan rest. She go eat later.

ANI: OK, Atim.

IJEOMA groans dramatically and touches a handkerchief to the light fingernail scratch on her face.

UBONG: Are you all right? [*IJEOMA smiles bravely at him.*]

IJEOMA: I will be. [*She looks at ANI.*] She just came at me like a bat out of hell. I wasn't expecting it at all. Shouting abuses. Oh, Ani, I can't even repeat some of the things she said.

ANI: You should have gone back and had the doctor or nurse look at your face.

IJEOMA: I just wanted to be out of there as fast as I could. I refused to fight her back. I just wanted to leave.

ANI: I apologise for her behaviour. And I insist on taking you to the hospital after the meal.

281

IJEOMA:	[*putting on another brave smile*] Thank you. But I don't want to make a fuss. I'll see how I feel. If it hurts too much, I'll go to the hospital.
ANI:	All right. Please excuse me a moment. I need to talk to Gerry.

ANI leaves the table. GERRY is outside on the veranda. He is on the phone. He ends the call just as ANI joins him.

ANI:	Won't you have something to eat?
GERRY:	Later. I'm not hungry right now. What time did the police chief say he's coming again?
ANI:	Any moment from now.
GERRY:	Is Ijeoma still at the table with Ubong?
ANI:	Yes. She doesn't suspect anything.
GERRY:	What about Mama?
ANI:	She's in her room resting. She says she will eat later.
GERRY:	You and I need to talk seriously. Let's take a walk outside. [*ANI and GERRY leave the veranda and walk slowly towards the gate. GERRY stops in the middle of the courtyard.*] You remember I kept saying something was niggling me and I couldn't quite put my finger on it?
ANI:	Yes. Have you figured it out now?

GERRY:	Yes, but it throws up even more questions. Before I go into that though, there's a different matter that has captured my attention. I need to know; did you speak with your mother today other than at the hospital this morning and just now when we went to get her?
ANI:	[*shaking his head*] Those are the only times I went to see her.
GERRY:	Did you speak with her on the phone?
ANI:	No. What's this about?
GERRY:	It's not a big thing, but when things don't seem to fit, I ask questions. While you were seeing to her discharge, she asked me if the result of the tests on that container you found in Celia's *bubu* were out.
ANI:	So?
GERRY:	She said the container you found in Celia's *bubu*. Who told her it was in Celia's *bubu*?
ANI:	Ah, ah, I must have. When I told her about it in the first place.
GERRY:	I was there when you told her, and I have an excellent recall for such details. You said, and I quote, 'the contents of a strange container I found among Celia's things.' Celia's things. That's what you said. You did not specify what things. So I ask again, how did she

know? Did you tell anyone other than me where you found that container?

ANI:	No.

GERRY:	Matron? When you gave it to her to test?

ANI:	No. I didn't discuss it with her at all. Just told her I wanted it tested.

GERRY:	So how did your mother know?

ANI:	[*shaking his head*] What the hell are you suggesting Gerry?

GERRY:	I'm not suggesting anything! I don't know what to suggest! All I'm saying is I don't like questions that have no answers.

ANI:	I'm sure there's a simple explanation. I'll just ask her. You can't for one moment believe she put it there.

GERRY:	[*shrugging*] I don't know what to believe any more. There are so many other things that don't fit. Like Celia's lack of reaction when I told her you searched her things. She maintains that she threw the plastic container away. It was as though she did not expect you to find it among her things. A scenario that would make sense only if someone else put it there.

ANI:	What are you trying to do? Clear Celia at my mother's expense? Gerry! Be careful!

GERRY: Ani, pipe down. Look. This is me. Gerry.
                The same Gerry who has been your friend
                since secondary school. The same Gerry
                who spent a school holiday with you and
                enjoyed your mother's generous hospitality!
                Why would I now want to run her down?
                Why? Go ahead and ask her how she knew.
                I'll be even happier than you if she can give
                a plausible explanation! [*ANI briefly covers his
                face with his hands.*]

ANI: I will ask her in your presence. There is
                a perfectly reasonable explanation. You'll
                see. [*He takes a shuddering breath.*] Probably
                Ijeoma told her.

GERRY: And how did Ijeoma know?

ANI: I don't know. But she's mixed up in this
                somehow.

*POLICE CHIEF and POLICEMAN 1 arrive in the police car.
HARUNA opens the gates for them. ANI welcomes them and all four
men go into the house.*

Fade.

Scene LI

ANI goes into the dining room. UBONG and IJEOMA are still there.

ANI: Atim!

ATIM'S VOICE: Sir!

ATIM comes into the dining room. ANI goes over to UBONG and speaks softly to him.

ANI: Ubong, I want you to finish your meal upstairs, OK? Your mother and I need to see some people.

UBONG: Yes, Daddy.

ANI: Atim, take his food to the upstairs parlour, and stay there with him.

ATIM: Yes, sir.

ATIM brings out a tray and packs UBONG'S food on it. She and UBONG leave the room.

IJEOMA: Somebody came. I heard the car. Who is it?

ANI: It's the police. They want to talk to us. They are interviewing everyone and you are Ubong's mother.

IJEOMA: Of course.

IJEOMA follows him to the parlour where the two policemen and GERRY are waiting.

ANI: These are the officers who wish to speak with you, Ijeoma. Gentlemen, this is Ijeoma Nwankwo.

IJEOMA: Officers, I'm willing to do anything I can to help.

POLICE CHIEF: That will be much appreciated. I'll go straight to the point Miss Nwankwo. We have in custody the native doctor Mrs Umoh was seeing. [*IJEOMA looks startled.*] He is the man who supposedly supplied her with the poison. He, on the other hand, is pointing the finger at you.

IJEOMA: At me!

POLICE CHIEF: He claims you hired him to carry out an elaborate charade on Mrs Umoh.

IJEOMA: He is lying!

POLICE CHIEF: He says you paid him 30,000 naira and gave him a further 200,000 to rent and decorate the building appropriately.

IJEOMA: All lies! I don't even know him!

POLICE CHIEF: His name is John Maduekwe. He claims he knew you from university.

IJEOMA: The name means nothing to me. Officer, lots of people knew me in university!

POLICE CHIEF: He also claims you gave him the poison that he passed on to Mrs Umoh. That it was all your doing.

IJEOMA: It's not true, Officer! None of it is true! [*She looks beseechingly at ANI.*] Ani, please tell them none of it is true! Why would I give someone poison to use on my own son?

POLICE CHIEF: OK. We would like you to come down to the station with us. Maybe when you actually see him it might jog your memory and help you tell us why he has singled you out for such allegations.

POLICE CHIEF looks at the POLICEMAN 1 and nods. POLICEMAN 1 starts fiddling with the phone he had in his hand.

IJEOMA: [*looking frightened*] Come down to the station!

POLICE CHIEF: It's the normal procedure where such serious allegations are involved. You need to come and give us an official statement. [*IJEOMA turns beseechingly to ANI again.*]

IJEOMA: Ani... [*The phone in IJEOMA'S handbag starts ringing. Everyone turns and looks at the bag.*]

POLICE CHIEF: [*shouting, as IJEOMA reaches for it*] Stop! Don't touch that bag! Officer, bring that bag here!

POLICEMAN 1 dives towards IJEOMA and grabs the bag. The phone stops ringing. He hands the bag to POLICE CHIEF. As POLICE CHIEF looks through the bag, realisation dawns on IJEOMA. She looks even more frightened. POLICE CHIEF brings out two phones.

POLICE CHIEF: [*to POLICEMAN 1*] Make that call again. [*One of the phones starts ringing again.*] That's OK. [*POLICEMAN 1 ends the call.*] Ijeoma, you say you do not know this man, yet his number is in your phone under the name John M. He had two missed calls from your phone this morning. According to the call logs on both phones, you have been in touch with him frequently. In fact, yesterday you spoke with him several times, one of the calls lasting twelve minutes. [*He looks up at her.*] What did you discuss for twelve whole minutes with a man you say you don't know?

IJEOMA: I... I... [*IJEOMA lapses into silence.*]

POLICE CHIEF: Yes? You what? [*IJEOMA stays silent looking down at her hands.*] Well, if you have nothing to tell us, then we have to accept that everything he says is true. That means that you gave him the poison he handed over to Mrs Umoh. The poison that ultimately resulted in a child's death. We have to charge you with murder.

IJEOMA: [*immediately shaking both her head and her hands*] No! No! I did not give him any poison! He's lying about that! What I gave him was vitamin C powder only! I don't know anything about the poison! [*She stops.*]

289

POLICE CHIEF: Go on.

IJEOMA: I didn't mean for anyone to die. I swear to God, I didn't give him any poison! He was to give it to Celia to give to Ugo. Why would I want to poison my own son?

POLICE CHIEF: Do you admit to giving him 200,000 naira to rent a house and pretend to be a native doctor?

IJEOMA: Yes. But not the poison. I didn't give him the poison.

POLICE CHIEF: And what was the aim of the charade? [*IJEOMA doesn't answer.*] To get Celia out of the house so you could become Mrs Umoh? [*IJEOMA still doesn't answer.*] Answer me!

IJEOMA: Yes. [*She looks at ANI.*] I'm sorry. I didn't mean for anyone to die. I don't know where he got the poison.

ANI: So when you found out my daughter had died, why didn't you tell all this? To help us get to the source of the poison?

IJEOMA kneels in front of him. When she puts her hands on his feet, he pushes them off and gets up.

IJEOMA: Ani, please… [*POLICEMAN 1 grabs her and pulls her to her feet.*]

POLICEMAN 1:   Come! You are coming to the station with us!

They take her out to the police car. She is still begging. Begging ANI, begging POLICEMAN 1, begging GERRY.

POLICE CHIEF: [*to ANI and GERRY*] I need to contact Celia Umoh again. She needs to be re-interviewed in light of these new developments. Where can I find her?

ANI: She is staying with her friend Sandra Edo.

POLICE CHIEF: Is that Peter Edo's wife?

ANI: Yes.

POLICE CHIEF: He called me yesterday, perhaps at his wife's bidding. Tried to persuade me to release Celia. OK. I'll contact you with any new developments.

ANI: Thank you again, sir.

They shake hands then the policemen drive off with IJEOMA. IDORENYIN watches them leave from an upstairs window. ANI and GERRY enter the house. IDORENYIN closes the curtains.

Fade.

Scene LII

ANI and GERRY enter the parlour.

ANI: Let's go and see Mama. I want to put to rest
            the question of how she knew.

GERRY: Don't you think you should let her rest a bit
            first? Remember she only just came back
            from the hospital.

ANI: She has been resting since then. She should
            be OK to answer a single question. Gerry, I
            want to finish with all these issues entirely
            by the time Eno and Ekaette return. Then I
            will bury my daughter and focus on carrying
            on with my remaining three children.

GERRY: OK. But I think you should go alone. It will
            seem too much like an inquisition if we go
            together.

*ANI goes up to IDORENYIN'S room, knocks and enters.
IDORENYIN is sitting at the dresser looking through some papers. She
puts them away as he enters.*

IDORENYIN: I was just about to come and see you. I saw
            the police car and them taking Ijeoma away.
            What happened?

ANI:	Ijeoma is behind it all. She hired a man to pretend to be the native doctor Celia went to see. [*IDORENYIN shakes her head.*]
IDORENYIN:	Now I've heard everything. Imagine. And what was the purpose?
ANI:	What you said in the hospital. She wanted to be my wife.
IDORENYIN:	How did the police find out she was involved?
ANI:	They have the native doctor in custody. He told them.
IDORENYIN:	I pray to God that everyone involved in Itoro's death will get their just reward. People think they can just do anything, but there is a God. And He's watching.
ANI:	Amen to that. Mama, Gerry told you the container I had tested this morning contained arsenic.
IDORENYIN:	Yes. He did. Celia, too, will get her just reward.
ANI:	How did you know I found it in her *bubu*?
IDORENYIN:	You told me.
ANI:	I didn't actually mention that I found it in her *bubu*.
IDORENYIN:	Yes, you did. Ani, how else would I know?

ANI: I don't recall…

IDORENYIN: I do. You said you found it in her *bubu*. Like
                         I said, there is no other way I could have
                         known. [*She frowns.*] What is this about?

ANI: You are right. I must have said so. Are you
                         ready to eat something now?

IDORENYIN: I don't have any appetite, but I will try. Ani,
                         why are you asking me about this?

ANI: It's nothing, Mama. I simply didn't
                         remember I'd told you. But I remember
                         now. Shall I have Atim bring something up
                         for you or do you want to come down?

IDORENYIN: Send her to me let me find out what there
                         is, first.

ANI: [*standing up*] I'll do that.

IDORENYIN: Are you sure everything is all right? I mean
                         about the *bubu* issue.

ANI: Yes. Everything is all right. I'll see you later.

*ANI leaves. IDORENYIN stares at the door for a while then brings out
the papers she had just put away. She sits there staring at them.*

Fade.

Scene LIII

GERRY is on the veranda again. He makes a call.

CELIA:	Hello, Gerry.
GERRY:	Hello, Celia. Can you tell me how you knew about the native doctor?
CELIA:	Sandra heard about him from a friend. He was supposed to be very good.
GERRY:	Has Sandra herself used him before?
CELIA:	No.
GERRY:	Do you know the friend who recommended him?
CELIA:	Regina Olusola.
GERRY:	Thomas Olusola's wife?
CELIA:	Yes.
GERRY:	Is Sandra there?
CELIA:	Yes. Shall I hand her the phone?
GERRY:	Yes. [*Shortly SANDRA comes on the line.*]

SANDRA:	Hello, Gerry.
GERRY:	Hi, Sandra. Celia says Regina Olusola told you about the native doctor.
SANDRA:	Yes. She was so effusive about him. He'd apparently worked wonders for her. I should have remembered Regina tends to exaggerate if she thinks it improves the story.
GERRY:	Did she mention the problem he helped her with?
SANDRA:	The US authorities. She said he gave her a charm which worked wonders.
GERRY:	And when did he do this?
SANDRA:	About five months ago.
GERRY:	[*thoughtfully*] Five months. When did Regina tell you about it?
SANDRA:	Not long. Two weeks ago I think.
GERRY:	What led to her telling you this?
SANDRA:	Eeem, I can't exactly remember. She came to the boutique and bought some things. Then we got talking. I don't think it was anything specific.
GERRY:	Had you yourself been there prior to taking Celia there?

SANDRA:	No, but Regina gave me very thorough directions. We found the place easily.
GERRY:	How long have you known Regina?
SANDRA:	About two years, when she and her husband moved to Lagos. We move more or less in the same social circle. Celia has known her longer. Her husband, Thomas, and Ani attended the same secondary school. But you know that. You attended the same school, too.
GERRY:	Yes. We meet every year at our Old Boys' Association meetings. They were in Abuja before moving here. Let me speak to Celia again. [*CELIA comes back on the line*]
CELIA:	Gerry.
GERRY:	Is there anything else you can tell me?
CELIA:	About Regina?
GERRY:	About anything or anyone that might shed some more light.
CELIA:	I can't think of anything else Gerry.
GERRY:	I hear Ani's mother brought you back from the *babalawo's* place after Ani overheard your conversation. What did you talk about on the way back?
CELIA:	That was when I found out just how much my mother-in-law hates me. She still has her

heart set on a village girl for Ani. Or maybe she is endorsing Ijeoma now. After all, Ijeoma has done what I couldn't. Produced a son. Is she still there in the house?

GERRY: Mama?

CELIA: Ijeoma.

GERRY: Not at the moment.

CELIA: Gerry, I swear to you that I did not poison that Fanta. I am telling the truth, Gerry.

GERRY: I know you are, Celia.

CELIA: Thank you for believing me.

GERRY: I'll talk to you again. Bye.

CELIA: Goodbye. [*GERRY ends the call as ANI comes out to the veranda.*]

ANI: Are you talking to yourself?

GERRY: I was just on the phone.

ANI flops down into a chair. He looks tired and rubs his eyes.

ANI: I spoke with Mama, then checked on Ubong.

GERRY: What did Mama say?

ANI: That I told her.

GERRY:	You told her.
ANI:	Yes. And that's what must have happened. There's no other explanation. None that makes a jot of sense. So let's just leave it at that.
GERRY:	OK. Fine. However, there is one more thing we need to discuss.
ANI:	What?
GERRY:	Before the police came I told you I had finally figured out what was bothering me. Today at the hospital when I saw your mother's blood results, it fell into place.
ANI:	So what was it?
GERRY:	You are blood group A, like your mother, like me. I found that out three years ago when you roped me into participating with you in that blood drive your church organised to help the local hospitals. This morning I saw Ijeoma's driver's licence. It says she is group O.
ANI:	So?
GERRY:	I saw Ubong's test results. He is group B. I called a doctor friend of mine and he explained the ABO blood grouping system to me in great detail. I won't bother you with all the jargon, but the long and short of it is that a group O person and a group A

person cannot produce a group B child. Ani, Ubong is not your son.

ANI: What? What? Are you sure about this?

GERRY: I'm sure about your blood group and I'm sure about Ubong's blood group. So if Ijeoma's licence is correct, Ubong's father is someone who is either group B or AB.

ANI: I don't believe this. Gerry, are you sure? Are you sure you're sure?

GERRY: This is the age of DNA testing, Ani. It's easy enough to confirm.

ANI: Oh, God.

ANI gets up abruptly and storms into the house, grabs his car keys. GERRY follows him.

GERRY: Where are you going?

ANI: To the police station. I want to confront that bitch. [*GERRY grabs the keys from him.*]

GERRY: Take it easy, Ani. Let me do the driving.

ANI: All right. But step on it!

GERRY: I will.

ANI and GERRY get into the car. IDORENYIN is again watching through the window as they drive off.

Fade.

SCENE LIV

The police station. IJEOMA is in the interrogation room. POLICE CHIEF is with her. IJEOMA has a document in front of her that she is reading. She looks up.

POLICE CHIEF: Do you have anything to add to that?

IJEOMA: No, sir. He hands her a pen.

POLICE CHIEF: Sign it.

IJEOMA signs. POLICE CHIEF puts the statement away. POLICEMAN 2 enters the room with JOHN MADUEKWE. On seeing IJEOMA he starts shouting.

JOHN MADUEKWE: Ijeoma! You gave me poison and said it was vitamin C!

IJEOMA: I did not give you any poison! You connived with Celia to kill my son! You wicked man!

JOHN MADUEKWE: Who is the wicked one? You wanted your own son killed! And you want me to take the blame for it! I won't! I swear before God and man that I handed over the container exactly as you gave me!

POLICE CHIEF: If it was to be a harmless substance you were to give to Celia, why couldn't you provide it yourself? Why wait to collect it from Ijeoma?

JOHN MADUEKWE: Ijeoma said she wanted Celia to give him something beneficial while thinking all the time that she was harming him. She said that would give her something else to laugh at Celia about.

POLICE CHIEF: It's easy enough to get vitamin C. Why didn't you get it yourself? Why wait for Ijeoma to supply it?

JOHN MADUEKWE: She told me she already had vitamin C powder in her house, so there was no need for me to go looking for it again.

POLICE CHIEF: Ijeoma is this true?

IJEOMA: Yes. All of that is true. And I gave him the vitamin C powder, Officer. I didn't give him any poison!

POLICE CHIEF: Maduekwe, how do you explain the arsenic that was found in the second room?

IJEOMA: Ha! He even had more of it!

JOHN MADUEKWE: You put it there! Officer, she put it there to incriminate me! I did not have any poison in that house! I don't know what you hope to gain by telling all these lies, Ijeoma. All I know is the truth will come out!

IJEOMA: The only time I went to that house was when you took me there immediately after renting it. I never went there again. I didn't want to risk running into anyone. I never went back there again!

POLICE CHIEF: Not even to check if he was setting up the place adequately?

IJEOMA: He studied drama in university. So I left it to him. He showed me pictures of it when he was done.

POLICEMAN 1 comes into the room. He has a short whispered conversation with POLICE CHIEF then sits.

POLICE CHIEF: Ijeoma, you told us you bought the vitamin C powder from Rightway Pharmacy. My officer is just back from there. They say they don't sell vitamin C powder. That they never have. My officer also asked around at other chemists. The answer was the same. None of them stock vitamin C powder.

JOHN MADUEKWE: Oh, ho!

IJEOMA: Oh, I'm sorry, Officer. I bought the tablets and crushed them.

POLICE CHIEF: You seem to think I'm a fool. At no time during your interview did you mention crushing tablets. You consistently talked about vitamin C powder. Even to the extent of telling us you bought the powder from Rightway. You don't seem to appreciate that a child is dead! Dead because of this powder you are lying about! I am asking for the last

	time. Where did you get that powder? The truth this time!
IJEOMA:	Someone gave it to me.
POLICE CHIEF:	Why did you say you bought it from a pharmacy?
IJEOMA:	I didn't realise vitamin C powder is not readily available in pharmacies. I thought a big pharmacy like Rightway would surely have it.
POLICEMAN 1:	They have vitamin C tablets, effervescent tablets, syrups and injections. They don't have powder.
POLICE CHIEF:	Who gave it to you? [*IJEOMA hesitates*.] You are trying to think of another lie! No one gave it to you. You got the poison yourself!
IJEOMA:	No, sir! Someone did give it to me!
POLICE CHIEF:	Who!
IJEOMA:	Regina Olusola. She told me it was vitamin C powder.
POLICE CHIEF:	Why did she give it to you?
IJEOMA:	I mentioned it to her and she said she had vitamin C powder in the house.
POLICE CHIEF:	Who is Regina Olusola?

IJEOMA: Thomas Olusola's wife. They own Olusola Transport.

POLICE CHIEF: What is your relationship to her?

IJEOMA: She was my mother's sister.

POLICE CHIEF: Was?

IJEOMA: My mother is late. She died when I was five. Since then Aunt Regina has been looking out for me.

POLICE CHIEF: Was she then aware of this plan to get someone to pretend to be a native doctor?

IJEOMA: Yes. She gave me the money to finance it.

POLICE CHIEF: [*to POLICEMAN 2*] Take him back to the cell.

JOHN MADUEKWE: Officer, you see I am innocent of that poison! You see, sir!

POLICEMAN 2: Come on, let's go! [*He takes him out of the room.*]

POLICE CHIEF: [*to POLICEMAN 1*] I want Regina Olusola brought in for questioning.

POLICEMAN 1: Yes, sir. [*He leaves the room.*]

POLICE CHIEF: I am running out of patience with you Ijeoma. You have been lying to us and withholding information from the beginning. This time

	I want the truth, the whole truth with nothing left out. Is that clear?
IJEOMA:	Yes, sir.
POLICE CHIEF:	Start from the beginning. Who came up with the idea?
IJEOMA:	Aunt Regina. Things have not been going well for me. The business I tried to do did not work out. She thought the best thing was for me to get married…

Fade.

Scene LV

The reception of the police station. ANI storms in with GERRY behind him. He goes up to POLICEMAN 3 at the desk.

ANI: Good evening, Officer.

POLICEMAN 3:   Good evening, sir.

ANI: I'm here to see Ijeoma Nwankwo.

POLICEMAN 3:   Chief is busy with her right now.

ANI: Please can you tell him that I am here, and I have information that may be pertinent to the interrogation he's conducting right now? My name is Aniekan Umoh.

POLICEMAN 3:   Please wait here.

POLICEMAN 3 leaves the room. GERRY sits, but ANI paces up and down.

ANI: What's taking so long?

GERRY: He's only been gone five minutes.

ANI: It doesn't take five minutes to deliver that message. [*POLICEMAN 3 returns.*]

POLICEMAN 3:   He says I should take you to his office to wait
                 for him.

ANI: Did you say I have information pertinent to
                 the investigation?

POLICEMAN 3:   Yes. And he said I should take you to his
                 office. Follow me.

ANI is about to say something again, GERRY stops him.

GERRY: Let's just do as he says. We can't expect him
                 to just break off an interrogation. Come.

*GERRY takes ANI'S arm. They follow POLICEMAN 3 out of the
room. Shortly afterwards CELIA and SANDRA enter the reception.
They sit and wait. POLICEMAN 3 returns.*

POLICEMAN 3:   Yes, madam. [*CELIA goes up to the desk.*]

CELIA: I am Celia Umoh. I was told to come to the
                 station.

POLICEMAN 3:   By whom?

CELIA: The police chief. He called me and said he
                 wanted to see me at the station.

POLICEMAN 3:   Have a seat. Chief is busy at the moment. I
                 will let him know you are around. [*CELIA
                 returns to the seat.*]

CELIA: I dread this place.

SANDRA: I'm surprised you agreed to come back here.

308

CELIA: It's because the police chief called himself.
              And he said new information has come to
              light that favours me.

SANDRA: Let's hope they have found out who did it.

Fade.

Scene LVI

The OLUSOLAS' residence. POLICEMAN 1 and POLICEMAN 2 drive up to the gate. MAIGUARD looks at them through a slot in the side gate.

POLICEMAN 1:   Open this gate!

MAIGUARD: Officer, please, make I go tell oga first. I no fit open the gate like that. I beg.

POLICEMAN 1:   Oya, go and tell him we wish to see his wife.

MAIGUARD: Yes, Officer.

MAIGUARD disappears inside. Shortly he returns with THOMAS.

THOMAS: Officers. What seems to be the problem?

POLICEMAN 1:   Good evening, sir. We would like to have a word with your wife.

THOMAS: What about?

POLICEMAN 1:   We are not at liberty to discuss that with you, sir.

THOMAS: This is my wife we are talking about, and you're telling me you are not at liberty to discuss. OK. Then you are not at liberty to see her. [*He turns to go back inside.*]

POLICEMAN 1: Sir! Sir! [*THOMAS waits.*] We are investigating a serious incident, and your wife's name has come up. We wish her to come to the station and give us a statement.

THOMAS: What is the incident?

POLICEMAN 1: I cannot tell you that, sir. But it is in her best interests to come with us and tell us how her name came to be mixed up in this.

THOMAS: Why does it have to be at the station? If it is a statement you want, it can be done here. She doesn't have to come there.

POLICEMAN 1: It is normal procedure for statements to be taken at the station, sir.

THOMAS: Indeed. And since when do you stick rigidly to procedure? I don't know what incident you are talking about, but my wife is not going anywhere with you. If it is a statement you want, you can either take it here, or not at all. Excuse me officers. I have to get back to my meal. Tell my maiguard to inform me of your decision.

THOMAS goes back in. POLICEMAN 1 makes a call.

POLICE CHIEF: Yes?

POLICEMAN 1: Mr Olusola is refusing to let his wife come down to the station, sir. He says we should either take her statement here, or not at all.

POLICE CHIEF: What arrogance! Don't take any statement. They want to do this the hard way. Let us oblige them. Go back and arrest her as an accessory to the murder of Itoro Umoh. Cuff her and bring her in. If her husband tries to stop you, cuff and bring him in, too, for obstruction.

POLICEMAN 1: Yes, sir.

POLICEMAN 1 ends the call. He discusses briefly with POLICEMAN 2 in low tones then goes to MAIGUARD.

POLICEMAN 1: Tell your oga we will take the statement here.

MAIGUARD: Yes, Officer. [*He goes inside then returns shortly.*] Oga say make you enter. [*He begins to open the big gate.*]

POLICEMAN 1: Leave the gate. We are not driving in.

They enter through the small gate and go up to the front door. Before they can ring the bell it is opened by SERVANT.

SERVANT: Madam dey parlour. Come.

SERVANT leads them to the parlour. REGINA is sitting in one of the chairs. THOMAS is beside her. REGINA stands up.

REGINA: Officers. I don't know what this is all about.

POLICEMAN 2 goes up to her, grabs her hands and pulls them behind her back.

POLICEMAN 2:   Regina Olusola, you are under arrest for
                 conspiracy in the murder of Itoro Umoh!
                 [*THOMAS jumps up from his seat.*]

THOMAS: What! [*POLICEMAN 2 snaps the cuffs on.
                 REGINA screams.*] You said you were coming
                 to take a statement! This is preposterous!

*With one policeman on either side, REGINA is led out of the house.
REGINA'S two boys come to the doorway and start crying and shouting
when they see their mother in cuffs.*

THOMAS: [*to the boys*] Go back inside! [*He turns to
                 MAIGUARD*]. Lock the gate! Lock the gate!

POLICEMAN 1:   If you lock this gate, I will call for back-up
                 and we will arrest everybody in this
                 compound! [*MAIGUARD hesitates.*]

THOMAS: Let them go! [*MAIGUARD opens the gate.*] I
                 will get to the bottom of this! You can't just
                 treat innocent citizens this way! Where is
                 the proof of these allegations? Where is the
                 arrest warrant? [*Neither policeman answers.
                 They put REGINA into the car.*] I'm following
                 right behind, Regina! Don't worry! [*The
                 police car drives off.*]

THOMAS: [*to MAIGUARD*] Open the gates!

*He runs back in and drives out. He takes off after the police car with tyres
screeching.*

Fade.

313

Scene LVII

The police chief walks into his office. ANI jumps up.

ANI: Sir.

POLICE CHIEF: Sit down. Sit down. Sorry to keep you waiting but I had to finish that interview. That woman tells a different story every time. It's incredible. You said you had some information.

ANI: I have just found out that I may not be the father of her son after all.

POLICE CHIEF: How did you find this out?

GERRY: Through his blood group.

POLICE CHIEF: I didn't know you could tell paternity through blood group.

GERRY: Not in most cases, but this time it is obvious.

POLICE CHIEF: So this is yet another lie she has told.

GERRY: What is her story this time?

POLICE CHIEF: She said it was just vitamin C powder in the container she handed over to Maduekwe.

She claimed to have bought it in Rightway pharmacy. When we confronted her with the fact that Rightway does not sell vitamin C powder, she changed her story. She now says she was given the powder as it was in the container by her co-conspirator, her aunt, who even told her to tell Maduekwe how Celia should use it.

ANI: Who is this aunt?

GERRY: Let me guess. Regina Olusola.

POLICE CHIEF: Yes. How did you know?

ANI: Wait a minute. Are we talking about the Regina who is married to Thomas Olusola?

POLICE CHIEF: The very same one. How did you know, Gerry?

GERRY: Sandra recommended the native doctor to Celia. But Sandra herself was told about him by Regina.

POLICE CHIEF: Aha. That is one of the things I wanted to ask Celia about.

GERRY: What's more, Regina claimed to have used the services of this native doctor five months ago. We know he is a fake *babalawo*, and five months ago he was not even a *babalawo*. Regina was lying. Why? There could only be one reason.

POLICE CHIEF: To get Celia to go to him. But why not tell it to Celia directly? What if Sandra had failed to pass on the information?

GERRY: Maybe they had a back-up plan. Personally, I think Regina did not want to be seen as being directly involved.

ANI: But once the police started investigating, it would have come out, as it has. She couldn't escape being mentioned.

GERRY: I don't think it was supposed to come out. If Maduekwe had not been greedy, he would not have returned to the hut for the money. Had he not returned, he would not have been caught by the police. Ijeoma would not be brought in, and it is she who mentioned Regina. I don't think Maduekwe knew about Regina. He dealt with Ijeoma only.

POLICE CHIEF: I disagree. The moment that boy died, as was obviously the plan, the investigation would be so intense, we would find Maduekwe. It might take us a while, but we would find him. And all would then come out, just as it has.

ANI: I don't understand why they wanted to poison Ubong. He's their flesh and blood.

POLICE CHIEF: According to the story Ijeoma is now telling, they didn't intend to poison anyone. She says the powder was supposed to be vitamin C. That an anonymous source was to inform you that Celia was trying to harm Ubong using native medicine. And a native medicine charm was to be placed in his school bag for you to find.

ANI: That sounds pretty weak. There are any number of reasons why I might not buy that story or send Celia packing.

POLICE CHIEF: That was to be the start. Sowing seeds of suspicion in your mind.

ANI: All that effort and money just to make me suspicious?

POLICE CHIEF: Suspicion doesn't make for a harmonious marriage. It was the first step to getting Celia out.

ANI: So who ultimately provided the poison? Regina?

POLICE CHIEF: So it seems at this point, though Ijeoma is still insisting it came from Maduekwe.

GERRY: I have my doubts about that. This thing is too involved. Maduekwe has nothing to gain by poisoning Ubong.

POLICE CHIEF: That's just it. No one involved has anything to gain by poisoning Ubong. No one except Celia.

ANI: But Celia had to get the poison from one of them.

POLICE CHIEF: Regina is being brought in for questioning. She should be here anytime now. I'll have someone take you to Ijeoma while I see to Mrs Olusola. [*He leaves the room.*]

ANI: There's always the possibility Celia got the poison herself somewhere else, when she suspected the one the *babalawo* gave her wasn't working. As the chief has pointed out, she is the only one with something to gain from actually poisoning Ubong.

GERRY: Time works against that theory. She collected the stuff from Maduekwe Monday afternoon. Tuesday morning, Ubong's Fanta was poisoned. That leaves no time for Celia to even conclude that the original powder would not work, much less start looking for another source.

POLICEMAN 5 comes and leads them to the cells and leaves them. IJEOMA comes to the bars.

GERRY: What a smell.

IJEOMA: [*crying*] Ani. Thank you for coming, Ani. Ani, please forgive me. I only wanted to be your wife. I love you. I did not give Celia the poison. I swear to you. Forgive me please, for the sake of our son.

ANI: Which son?

IJEOMA: Ubong. Our son, Ubong.

ANI: Ubong is your son. I accept that. But he is
            not mine.

IJEOMA: Why are you saying this, Ani? Are you
            making a joke?

ANI: Do I look like I'm laughing? You thought I
            would never find out!

IJEOMA: Who is telling you these lies? Ubong is
            yours! There was nobody but you in my
            life when he was conceived. Oh, Ani, you
            can say anything to me, but not that! Gerry,
            please tell him!

GERRY: What exactly am I to tell him, Ijeoma?

IJEOMA: That Ubong is his! He even looks like him!

GERRY: That's just a coincidence, because he is not
            his. His blood group proves that.

IJEOMA opens and closes her mouth. No sound comes out.

ANI: Lost for words? Can't think of any more
            lies? I'm going to have DNA tests done.
            [*IJEOMA remains silent.*] You were calling
            Celia names. You are worse than she is. And
            for your information, I would never in a
            million years have married you! [*IJEOMA
            starts crying again.*]

IJEOMA: Ani. Ani. All this must be a mistake
            somehow. Ubong is yours.

ANI: [*to GERRY*] Let's go!

ANI and GERRY leave. As soon as they move out of sight, IJEOMA'S crying abruptly ceases. She looks contemplative.

Fade.

Scene LVIII

The front room of the station. CELIA and SANDRA are still sitting there. The POLICE CHIEF comes in. CELIA and SANDRA get up.

POLICE CHIEF: Mrs Umoh.

CELIA: Sir. You said you had new information that might benefit me.

POLICE CHIEF: Yes. Let us… [*He stops as REGINA is brought in.*]

SANDRA: Regina?

POLICE CHIEF: Mrs Umoh, I'm afraid I have to ask you to wait a little longer.

CELIA: All right. [*SANDRA goes up to REGINA.*]

SANDRA: Regina, what's happening?

REGINA: Sandra. Celia. I don't know what is happening. They just came to the house and brought me here.

SANDRA: In handcuffs?

POLICE CHIEF: Bring her through to the interrogation room.

REGINA, POLICEMAN 1 and 2 and POLICE CHIEF disappear inside. THOMAS rushes in shortly. He stops short at the sight of CELIA.

CELIA: Thomas!

THOMAS: What happened to you?

SANDRA: She was 'resisting arrest' [*She makes air quotes with her fingers.*]

THOMAS: What? [*He goes to POLICEMAN 3 at the desk.*] Where is my wife? She was brought in just now!

POLICEMAN 3:   Have a seat, sir. She is being interrogated.

THOMAS: [*pointing to CELIA*] If you can do that to a woman who has just lost her child, I don't want you interrogating my wife! I demand to see her right now!

POLICEMAN 3:   Have a seat, sir! I will let the interrogating officers know you are here. [*He makes a call on the intercom.*]

SANDRA: But why have they brought Regina in? They must have said why when they took her.

THOMAS: They said it's something to do with your daughter's death, Celia. But they must be mistaken. Regina couldn't possibly have anything to do with that.

CELIA and SANDRA look at each other. ANI and GERRY enter the reception from inside.

| THOMAS: | Ani. Gerry. What's going on here? |
| CELIA: | Hello, Ani. |

ANI looks her over, noting the bruises. He doesn't reply her greeting.

ANI:	Thomas. Why are you here?
THOMAS:	Regina's being questioned.
ANI:	I see.
THOMAS:	Ani, I'm so sorry to hear about your daughter, but what does that have to do with my wife?
ANI:	Maybe she will tell us that.
THOMAS:	The police said your daughter was murdered.
ANI:	Yes. She was poisoned.
THOMAS:	That's terrible! Who would do a thing like that?
ANI:	That's what the police are trying to find out.

Fade.

Scene LIX

The interrogation room. REGINA, POLICE CHIEF and POLICEMAN 1 and 2 are in the room. The intercom rings.

POLICE CHIEF: Yes?… No. Let him wait. [*He turns back to REGINA. The handcuffs have been removed.*] Yes, Mrs Olusola. You say that while you admit that Ijeoma Nwankwo is your niece, you deny everything else that she said.

REGINA: I don't know what Ijeoma is playing at. Why she is saying I am involved in all this. I am not. Officer the only thing I know is that two months ago Ijeoma told me she wanted to try setting up another business. The first one she tried was a failure. This time she said she wanted to open a beauty salon. I gave her 400,000 naira to help her.

POLICE CHIEF: You knew nothing about her plan to hire John Maduekwe to pretend to be a native doctor?

REGINA: Nothing whatsoever! I am shocked to hear it!

POLICE CHIEF: What about her statement that she got the container of poison from you?

REGINA:	That is a complete lie, officers!
POLICE CHIEF:	But what can she hope to gain by lying against you? You, her aunt, who has been helping her?
REGINA:	I wish I knew, Officer.
POLICE CHIEF:	Did you know she has a son?
REGINA:	Yes.
POLICE CHIEF:	Do you know who his father is?
REGINA:	She never directly said who his father is, but there was a boy she was hoping to marry at the time. I assumed he was the father. I hear though that he was denying it on the grounds that Ijeoma was sleeping around. But now she is saying the child's father is Aniekan Umoh. I don't know how true that is.
POLICE CHIEF:	What's the name of this person she wanted to marry?
REGINA:	Chijioke... Chijioke... something. Something Eze I think.
POLICE CHIEF:	Where is this Chijioke Eze?
REGINA:	I hear he got married. I don't know where he is now.

POLICE CHIEF: Well, that is it then, Mrs Olusola. You are free to go. Please accept my apologies for the rough handling you have suffered.

REGINA: [*Looking relieved*] Apology accepted. [*She rises.*]

POLICE CHIEF: That is gracious of you. [*POLICEMAN 2 escorts REGINA towards the door.*] Oh, by the way, madam. Can you tell me how you were able to describe in detail the directions to the native doctor to Sandra Edo?

REGINA: I described it to Sandra?

POLICE CHIEF: In great detail. Following your directions, she found John Maduekwe.

REGINA: There must be some mistake. I don't remember describing anything to her.

POLICE CHIEF: You also told her that you yourself had used the services of Maduekwe five months ago to help you with a problem you had at the US consulate.

REGINA: Nothing like that happened. Yes I had some dealings with the US officials, but why would I see a native doctor about it? I don't believe in native doctors, Officer.

POLICE CHIEF: So Mrs Edo is lying?

REGINA: She is mistaken, Officer.

POLICE CHIEF: Very well. Goodbye, Mrs Olusola.

REGINA leaves the room. POLICEMAN 1 is holding the intercom phone.

POLICEMAN 1:   Ijeoma is asking for you. She says there are things she didn't tell you and she wants to make a complete confession.

POLICE CHIEF: Does she? I wonder why. Bring her in here.

POLICEMAN 1:   Yes, sir. [*He turns to go, then turns back.*] Sir, do you believe Mrs Olusola is innocent?

POLICE CHIEF: Of course not. She is lying through her teeth. Unfortunately, I have nothing to hold her on at the moment. Let her go. Something will turn up, and when it does, I personally will go back for her.

POLICEMAN 1 gives a small smile as though relishing the thought then leaves the room. POLICEMAN 2 comes back in.

POLICEMAN 2:   Sir, Mr Olusola is demanding to see you.

POLICE CHIEF: What for? He has got his wife back.

POLICEMAN 2:   He says he wants an explanation for the way his wife was handled and brought here.

POLICE CHIEF: I don't have time for him. Tell him I'm busy. Any complaints he has he should put into writing and it will be processed through the official channels.

POLICEMAN 2:   Yes, sir.

He leaves. IJEOMA is brought in by POLICEMAN 1.

POLICE CHIEF: Yes Miss Nwankwo? What have you to tell me?

IJEOMA: [*tearfully*] Sir, if I have not been totally honest with you it's because I'm afraid.

POLICE CHIEF: Afraid of what?

IJEOMA: What will happen to me. I did not provide that poison, but I'm afraid you will not believe me.

POLICE CHIEF: If you were honest from the beginning, you would be more believable. What is it you want to tell me now?

IJEOMA: When I told you an anonymous source was going to tell Ani about the juju, that wasn't true. The source was not to be anonymous.

POLICE CHIEF: Who was the source?

Fade.

Scene LX

The station front room. ANI, GERRY, CELIA and SANDRA are still there. THOMAS is arguing with POLICEMAN 2.

THOMAS: If he wants it in writing, I shall give it to him in writing! I will follow this matter up to the end. You cannot treat innocent citizens like this!

POLICEMAN 2 doesn't answer. THOMAS takes REGINA'S hand. They say goodbyes to the others and leave. ANI goes up to POLICEMAN 2.

ANI: Is the police chief free now?

POLICEMAN 2: No. He's still busy. Shall I tell him you want to see him when he's free?

ANI: Yes.

POLICEMAN 2 nods and goes back inside. ANI starts pacing. CELIA goes up to him.

CELIA: Ani, please, I'm begging you. I swear I did not try to poison Ubong.

ANI: And you did not also try to make him mad.

CELIA: I did, but even then I knew deep inside
                   that it was all rubbish. I am so sorry for
                   everything I did. But please believe me, on
                   Tuesday morning I threw that poison away.
                   I did not want to hurt him anymore. I took
                   him to hospital to be treated. To make him
                   completely well.

ANI: So how come I found the poison in the
                   pocket of the *bubu* you wore that morning?
                   [*CELIA frowns.*]

CELIA: That's not possible. I threw it away, Ani.
                   I threw it away in the big bin outside the
                   kitchen!

ANI: Get away from me, Celia. I'm not interested
                   in hearing your lies or your excuses.

POLICEMAN 2 comes out again. He indicates ANI and GERRY.

POLICEMAN 2:   Sirs, the police chief will see you now.
                   [*SANDRA stands up.*]

SANDRA: What about us? We've been waiting here for
                   ages!

POLICEMAN 2:   Please. Have patience a little longer.

*POLICEMAN 2 leaves with GERRY and ANI. SANDRA and
CELIA sit again and continue to wait.*

Fade.

Scene LXI

The interrogation room. IJEOMA is still there with POLICE CHIEF and POLICEMAN 1. POLICEMAN 2 enters with GERRY and ANI. They sit.

POLICE CHIEF: There's a new twist to the tale. Ijeoma tells us there is yet another conspirator. I wanted you to hear it from Ijeoma herself. [*GERRY brings out his phone and fiddles with it.*]

ANI: [*to IJEOMA*] And you couldn't tell us this before? Who is it?

GERRY gives his phone to POLICE CHIEF, who looks at it then at GERRY in surprise.

IJEOMA: [*with relish*] Your mother.

ANI: Be careful what you say about my mother, you witch!

POLICE CHIEF: Ani, let's step outside a minute.

ANI: I want her to stop using that lying mouth of hers to say nonsense about my mother!

POLICE CHIEF: You can tell her that when we return. She's not going anywhere. She will still be here. I want a word with you and Gerry outside.

The three of them leave the room. [*They go into the corridor.*]

POLICE CHIEF: Ani, you are shocked that Ijeoma is mentioning your mother, but your friend here isn't. He wrote her name on his phone and showed me just as Ijeoma was telling you. Gerry, it seems you are one step ahead of us all the way. Please explain.

ANI: Is it because of that *bubu* thing?

GERRY: It's more than that. Too many things did not make sense.

POLICE CHIEF: What *bubu* thing?

ANI: I found the container of arsenic in Celia's *bubu* last night.

POLICE CHIEF: Why didn't you tell me this?

ANI: I was so sure Celia had poisoned that drink that I looked on it merely as confirmation. I didn't see that it could make any difference to the investigation.

POLICE CHIEF: How does your mother come in?

GERRY: When Ani took the powder to the hospital to be tested this morning, I was in the room when he told Mama about it. He told her he had found it among Celia's things. But when we returned to take her home this afternoon, Mama asked me about the result

332

of the test on the container Ani found in Celia's *bubu*.

POLICE CHIEF: I see. How did she know it was in the *bubu*?

GERRY: Exactly. Ani didn't talk to her again before we returned.

POLICE CHIEF: Did you try asking her for an explanation?

ANI: I did. She insisted I had said I found it in Celia's *bubu*. I didn't want to believe unimaginable things about my own mother. I convinced myself that I must have said so. Gerry obviously still did not believe it.

GERRY: You know what I was like in school Ani. My memory of it was word-perfect. I did not *think* you said 'Celia's things'. I *knew*. Therefore I knew immediately Mama was hiding something.

POLICE CHIEF: I see. You said there were other issues.

GERRY: Yes. Celia keeps insisting she did not poison Ubong's drink. And that she threw the poison away. She could be lying of course. But if she did poison that drink, then Itoro's death makes no sense. I said this before, Ani, that she would move heaven and earth to make sure her own daughter could not come in contact with Ubong and that Fanta. She knew how close they had become. But instead we have her telling Sandra to drop Itoro with Ubong after school. Not only that, she drives away from the hospital leaving Ubong's lunchbox in the room with him. A lunchbox containing a lunch he had not eaten and a drink he had not drunk. If she knew that drink was poisoned, it would be the easiest thing in the world for her to take the box with her, knowing that Itoro would soon be in that room with him. [*POLICE CHIEF nods slowly. GERRY continues.*] To my mind though, the most damning thing against your mother Ani, is the fact that she was the one who took you to the *babalawo's* place. If you think about it Ani, why did she do that? You were reluctant to go. You told me she waited hours for you in the car park. Why such perseverance? To simply show you a *babalawo's* hut? And the case against Celia started from there. Had you not made that trip, you probably would disregard anything anyone said against her.

POLICE CHIEF: But how did Mama know Celia was going to be there at that particular point in time?

GERRY: I don't think she knew. I think the plan was to get Ani face to face with Maduekwe who would then incriminate Celia. Meeting Celia there was a bonus. It made things easier.

ANI: I can hardly take this in. All this would mean my mother is endorsing Ijeoma to take over from Celia. But that isn't the case. You heard yourself in the hospital. She doesn't want Ijeoma to be my wife.

GERRY: I wondered about that. It did not seem to fit. At first I thought it might all be an act and she would later turn around and support her. But there is one scenario where it fits.

ANI: Which is? [*GERRY takes a deep breath.*]

GERRY: I'm reluctant to even say it. Ani, look, this is pure conjecture, OK? I don't have a shred of proof.

ANI: All right. What is the scenario? [*GERRY takes another breath.*]

GERRY: If we are to believe Celia did not poison Ubong's Fanta, then the next step is to also believe that she did throw the poison into the bin. I mean, why lie about one and not the other? That raises two obvious questions; who actually poisoned the Fanta and how the container ended up in her *bubu*. I'm sure I'm not alone in thinking that both questions should have the same answer. If we say that answer is Ijeoma, where did Ijeoma see Ubong to poison his drink? She did not go to his school that day. She did not go to the hospital. And why would she want to kill her own son? The son that she saw as her passport to you and a better life? She also did not come to the house yesterday, so she couldn't put anything in Celia's *bubu*. Rule out Ijeoma. Regina and Maduekwe are even more unlikely. And the same argument applies to them. They had no access to Ubong or the *bubu* that day. It's also hard to come up with a motive for

335

either of them. And that leaves only Mama. The likeliest scenario is for the poison to be added in the house before Ubong left for school. Of the people in the house that morning, rule out yourself, rule out the children, rule out Atim. We agree to rule out Celia. Again that leaves only Mama. But I didn't want to believe it. What grandmother would deliberately kill her own grandchild?

POLICE CHIEF: Except that he is not truly her grandchild.

ANI: But Mama did not know that. She accepted Ubong as her own flesh and blood.

GERRY: And that had me stumped for a while. But that still left unanswered the question: who put the poison in the Fanta? And the other question: how did Mama know about Celia's *bubu*? Put the two questions together and there can only be one answer that fits them both. Mama. A famous detective once said: if you rule out the impossible then what's left, however improbable, must be the answer. So I focused on finding out why she would attempt to poison her grandson. Her son's only son. It couldn't be only to discredit Celia. When I found out Ubong is not your son, I started wondering if Mama knew.

POLICE CHIEF: So? Does she know?

GERRY: I think she does. But I cannot prove it. I said before, that this scenario is pure conjecture.

336

ANI:	A conjecture that leaves Celia innocent.
GERRY:	Not entirely. She admits to putting the powder in his hot chocolate the night before.
POLICE CHIEF:	So how did he survive the night?
GERRY:	She said she put very little. She was told to put one teaspoon, but she put half. [*ANI shakes his head.*]
ANI:	I had that powder tested. Even half a teaspoon would have seriously harmed him. She's lying. Your problem, Gerry, is that you believe everything Celia says.
POLICE CHIEF:	Let's hear from Ijeoma. [*They re-enter the interrogation room.*] So Ijeoma, at what point did Ani's mother enter the plan?
IJEOMA:	From the beginning. A month ago when I learnt that she was in Lagos visiting, I arranged to see her. I took pictures of Ugo and showed her. She cried when she learnt that she had a grandson. I met her a few times after that and discussed the chances of me becoming Ani's wife. She was very receptive to the idea, and asked me how I planned to get rid of Celia. I told her I would come up with a plan. When Aunt Regina and I came up with the native doctor idea, Mama said she liked it. She knew Celia used native doctors in the past when she was trying to have a child. Once Celia took the bait and brought the powder to

the house, Mama was to take Ani to the native doctor. He would confess everything to Ani. As proof, there was the photograph of Ubong Celia had torn up there in the hut. There was also another 'Best Girl' hair gel container, exactly like the one John gave Celia that he was to show Ani. When Ani returned to the house, he would find exactly that same type of container with Celia. That would clinch it.

POLICE CHIEF: And these empty hair gel plastics were to contain vitamin C?

IJEOMA: Yes. They were to contain vitamin C. Nobody was supposed to die. So there would be no need to test the powders. We would let Ani assume they were harmful. Once Celia was sent packing, Mama was to help convince Ani that marrying me would be best for Ubong.

GERRY: What if Celia did not go to Maduekwe? Sandra may have failed to tell her. Or simply forgotten. Or Celia may not want to go. What then?

IJEOMA: Aunt Regina would then tell Celia herself about John, and try to persuade her. If Celia still did not go, we would still continue as if she had. Mama would plant the hair gel container among her things and go ahead and take Ani to John. John would tell Ani that Celia had visited him and show him the other hair gel container just as planned.

GERRY: Celia obviously, would deny it all. What if despite everything, Ani believed her?

IJEOMA: I'd move on to plan B. Ubong would still be in the house and Ani wouldn't know that I had anything to do with the native doctor issue. I'd take fertility pills and use Ubong to see Ani often and try to get him to sleep with me again, hoping for another pregnancy.

POLICE CHIEF: Why didn't you just go with plan B from the beginning? That was simpler, less risky, less expensive, too.

IJEOMA: It wasn't guaranteed to get Celia out of the house. And that's what I really wanted. And there was always the possibility that Ani might refuse to sleep with me again with Celia still in the picture.

ANI: Everything I've just heard is your word only. If my mother denies it all, what proof do you have?

IJEOMA: She took you to the *babalawo's* place.

ANI: That doesn't prove she was part of any plan. She saw Celia go there.

POLICE CHIEF: You still haven't told us why arsenic was substituted for vitamin C.

IJEOMA: I don't know why John did that!

POLICE CHIEF: You still maintain that it was Maduekwe's doing?

IJEOMA:	Yes! Aunt Regina would never give him arsenic to give to Ubong. Why would she?
GERRY:	Why are you telling us this now?
IJEOMA:	I want to come clean about my part in this. I will admit to everything I did. But I did not poison Itoro. I did not supply any poison. Poison was not part of the plan. I am telling you the truth. I am telling you the whole truth.
ANI:	Not quite the whole truth. You have not admitted that Ubong is not my son. Remember I can prove it with DNA.
IJEOMA:	You have to believe me, Ani, I thought he was yours. The timing and everything fit. I swear you were the only one in my life at the time. It was just one night when I got drunk at a party that it must have happened. I'm telling you the truth, Ani. [*ANI looks at her scornfully.*]
ANI:	Truth? You don't know the meaning of the word.
IJEOMA:	I am telling you the truth now, I swear! I wouldn't push someone's child on you! I believed he was yours!
ANI:	I've heard enough. I need to go. I have to meet my pastor. [*He gets up.*] Chief, thank you very much. [*POLICE CHIEF also rises.*]

340

POLICE CHIEF: I will conclude the interview and then see your wife. [*POLICE CHIEF, GERRY and ANI go out into the corridor again.*] You go ahead with the funeral arrangements.

ANI: Will you be interviewing my mother?

POLICE CHIEF: Tomorrow. Let me know what time would be convenient for me to come and see her.

ANI nods dully. He and GERRY go through to the reception. CELIA and SANDRA are no longer there.

GERRY: [*to POLICEMAN 3 at the desk*] Have Mrs Umoh and her friend gone?

POLICEMAN 3:   The chief said to let them wait for him in his office.

GERRY: Ah. I see.

GERRY and ANI leave the station.

Fade.

Scene LXII

It is night. The UMOHS' house. GERRY drives in with ANI. ATIM opens the front door. He and ANI enter.

ATIM: Welcome, sir.

ANI: How is Ubong? ATIM: He dey sleep.

ANI: What of Mama?

ATIM: She dey her room.

ANI: Did she eat anything?

ATIM: She eat smaaaall, like this. [*She demonstrates using two fingers to indicate a small gap.*]

ANI: Gerry, do you want anything?

GERRY: No. I'm fine.

ANI: All right, Atim. You can go to bed.

ATIM: Goodnight, sir.

ANI: Goodnight. [*They lock up and go upstairs.*]

GERRY: Shall I bring some more sleeping tablets for you?

ANI: If you can spare some more. I forgot to get
                     some from the hospital.

GERRY: I'll bring you some.

*GERRY goes into his room. ANI checks on UBONG. He is fast asleep.
ANI adjusts the sheet over him and watches him a while. Then he goes to
IDORENYIN'S room. IDORENYIN is lying on the bed, eyes closed.
As ANI turns to go out, she calls to him.*

IDORENYIN: Ani. [*ANI turns back.*]

ANI: I thought you were asleep.

IDORENYIN: I've been drifting in and out. How did it go
                     at the station?

ANI: [*after a moment's silence*] Not good, Mama.
                     Ijeoma is saying you were part of a plot to
                     get Celia out of my house.

IDORENYIN: Heeey! She is lying *o*! I don't know anything
                     about any plot!

ANI: She says you were in it from the beginning.
                     That your role was to take me to the native
                     doctor, which you did.

IDORENYIN: My son, she is lying! She knows I took
                     you to the native doctor. I told her in the
                     hospital. She is now twisting it to seem like
                     a plan. The only reason I took you there was
                     because I saw Celia go there!

ANI: Celia claims she did not put poison in
                     Ubong's Fanta on Tuesday.

343

IDORENYIN: Why are you telling me this? Of course Celia
              will lie about it!

ANI: Even so, there are things that don't fit,
              Mama. I am going to ask you outright. The
              suggestion has been made that you poisoned
              that drink. Mama, did you? [*IDORENYIN
              starts sobbing.*]

IDORENYIN: I can't believe you, Ani, can ask me that.
              You believe that I can poison your son, my
              grandson! Oh! How have I come to such a
              terrible pass in life that my own son can ask
              this of me! [*ANI starts getting angry.*]

ANI: Mama, my daughter is dead! She is
              dead because someone put poison into
              Ubong's drink! Up till now, despite all the
              confessions I'm hearing left and right, no
              one is admitting poisoning that drink! I
              want to know who did it! [*IDORENYIN
              cries harder.*]

IDORENYIN: Oh, they have poisoned your mind against
              me! That you can ask me this!

ANI: So you are saying you had no hand in Itoro's
              death? [*IDORENYIN raises both arms to the
              ceiling.*]

IDORENYIN: As God is my witness, I had no hand in
              Itoro's death. If I am lying may God strike
              me down!

*IDORENYIN collapses on the bed, still sobbing. ANI rests his face in
his hands and talks to himself.*

ANI: God, what do I do now?

IDORENYIN'S crying abruptly stops. ANI turns to her. She is lying on the bed. Her eyes are rolled back in their sockets. A fixed grimace is on her face. She is jerking.

ANI: Mama! [*He grabs her and raises her.*] Mama! Her breathing is laboured and audible. Saliva trickles out of one corner of her mouth.

ANI: [*shouting*] Gerry! Gerry! Gerry! [*GERRY comes rushing in.*]

GERRY: My God! What happened?

ANI: We have to take her to the hospital quick!

Together ANI and GERRY carry IDORENYIN out of the room. ATIM and UBONG have woken up and are standing in the upstairs corridor watching. UBONG starts crying.

GERRY: Atim, run downstairs and open the doors for us. Tell Haruna to open the gate! [*ATIM disappears downstairs.*]

UBONG: What's wrong with Grandma!

ANI: Grandma will be fine. We just need to take her to the hospital. Go and wait in your room. Atim will come and stay with you.

UBONG goes into his room. ANI and GERRY carry IDORENYIN out to the car. They lay her on the back seat.

ANI: Atim, lock up, then go and stay with Ubong until I return.

345

ATIM: Yes, sir.

ANI sits in the back with IDORENYIN'S head on his lap. He wipes her mouth. GERRY drives through the gates.

Fade on HARUNA closing the gate.

Scene LXIII

Morning. GERRY drives into the UMOHS' compound. He and ANI slowly get out of the car. They stretch tiredly. ATIM and UBONG come to the front door. UBONG is in his school uniform. ANI holds out a hand to him and he rushes into his arms. They enter the house together.

ATIM: Good morning, sir.

ANI: Good morning, Atim. How was the night?

ATIM: No problem, sir.

ANI: Did you get any sleep?

UBONG: She slept in my room.

ANI: That's good isn't it? You were not alone.

ATIM: How is Mama?

UBONG: When is she coming home?

ANI: Not for a while, Ubong. She needs to stay with the doctors for now.

UBONG: [*fearfully*] She's not going to the angels, too, is she?

ANI:	Let's pray she doesn't. Now, are you ready for school?
UBONG:	Am I going to school today? I wore my uniform, but I don't know.
ANI:	Yes, you are. You don't want all your classmates to learn things and leave you out, do you?
UBONG:	No. Who will take me to school?
ANI:	Elijah. Have you had breakfast? [*UBONG nods.*] Good. Get your schoolbag and your lunchbox.

UBONG goes and gets the items. ATIM brings out a tray with tea and coffee things.

GERRY:	Atim, you are a treasure.

ANI sees UBONG off to the car then returns to the parlour. He and GERRY make themselves coffee. GERRY flops into an armchair.

GERRY:	It never rains but it pours.
ANI:	A massive stroke. It's not entirely surprising. Her blood pressure was out of control.
GERRY:	But did she have a high blood pressure problem before all this?
ANI:	No, not at all. This all started with Itoro's death. Now not only is Itoro dead, I don't know if my mother will live or die.

GERRY: And the doctor's prognosis is that we just
            have to watch and see if she will survive it.

ANI: Even if she does, she will be an invalid for
            the rest of her life.

GERRY: At one stage I wasn't sure she would even
            make it through the night.

ANI: Yes, it seemed to be touch and go there for
            a while.

GERRY: Ani, did anything happen last night in the
            room to make her blood pressure shoot up
            like that?

ANI: I was questioning her about Ijeoma's
            assertions. She denied them all. Said Ijeoma
            was lying. I asked her if she poisoned
            Ubong's Fanta. She said no. [*He sips his
            coffee. GERRY gives a shrug of acceptance.*]

GERRY: OK.

ANI: You know the funny thing is, I asked her to
            tell me if she had no hand in Itoro's death.
            She swore to God that she had nothing to
            do with it. Said God should strike her down,
            or something like that, if she was lying. That
            was the last thing she said. Then she had the
            stroke. [*They are both silent.*]

GERRY: So what are you thinking? That God did
            strike her down?

ANI:	I'm confused, Gerry. Somehow I still don't want to believe it. Now I'll never know. Even if she recovers, it's doubtful she'll ever talk again. [*They are silent again then ANI drains his cup.*] I need to go and sort through her things. I have to take some of them to the hospital. She's going to be there a while.
GERRY:	Shall I come and help you?
ANI:	No need. I just want to throw a few things together.
GERRY:	What about the rest of her things?
ANI:	They can wait. She's not going anywhere for a while.

ANI leaves and goes upstairs. GERRY makes himself another cup of coffee, stretches himself out on the settee and sighs. As he sips his coffee he hears ANI calling him from upstairs.

ANI'S VOICE:	Gerry! Gerry, come here!
GERRY:	I'm coming!

GERRY runs up the stairs. ANI is in IDORENYIN'S room. He is seated at her desk, the drawer of which is open. He has some papers in his hands.

GERRY:	Ani, what is it?
ANI:	Take a look at these.

ANI gives him the papers. GERRY sits on the bed and looks through them.

GERRY: Oh, my God!

ANI: You were right all along. She knew Ubong
            wasn't mine.

GERRY: But where did she get these? A copy of his
            original birth certificate, showing Chijioke
            Otobueze as father. [*He turns to the other
            document.*] A copy of a school report from
            his original school. 'Third term class one
            report for Ugochukwu Otobueze.'

ANI: One thing Ijeoma did not lie about was his
            brilliance. He came first in that report.

GERRY: Ani, oh my God, Ani, did you notice the
            dates? [*ANI leans over to look again.*]

ANI: What dates?

GERRY: The date of this school report. He was in
            class one just last year! He should have been
            in class two last year! And look at the year on
            his birth certificate. Ani, Ubong isn't eight
            years old. He's seven!

ANI: No wonder he's so small. Ijeoma!

GERRY: When she decided to pass him off as yours,
            she had to rectify the dates.

ANI: The affair was over and she had left my
            employ long before she became pregnant.
            No doubt she came up with this scheme
            because of Ubong's superficial resemblance
            to me.

GERRY:	How long has Mama had these?
ANI:	I think the answer to that is in this letter. ANI hands him some further papers. [*GERRY reads through and shakes his head in wonder.*]
GERRY:	'Peace Of Mind' Consultancy? What are they?
ANI:	A sort of detective agency apparently. That's a detective report.
GERRY:	Your mother hired a detective? How did she know how to go about getting one?
ANI:	Don't ask me.
GERRY:	Your mother is full of surprises!
ANI:	And check out the date of that report.
GERRY:	Over a month ago!
ANI:	Long before I even knew of Ubong's existence.
GERRY:	Wait a minute. That can't be right? Ijeoma said she told Mama about Ubong a month ago. But we are looking at a report written before that about Ubong!
ANI:	Surprise, surprise. Ijeoma is lying – again. Mama knew about Ubong more than a month ago. She knew about him before she came here from the village.

GERRY:	This gets more and more bizarre.
ANI:	Well, Gerry. You're the one who's been figuring it all out. I have a headache. I'm depending on you to make sense of this!
GERRY:	Right. Where do I start?
ANI:	What I don't still get is why Mama wanted to kill Ubong. Even if he's not mine, why kill him? And, Gerry, you need to see the way she behaved with him. You would swear she loved him. She was so partial to him, she was even sometimes unfair to the girls!
GERRY:	Maybe that was part of the whole plan. No doubt that would upset Celia even more.
ANI:	Of course, yes. It did.
GERRY:	Giving Celia even more incentive to get rid of Ubong, while at the same time removing any trace of suspicion from Mama herself.
ANI:	But why actually try to kill him, Gerry? Why not be satisfied with putting suspicion on Celia without killing him? [*GERRY puts down the papers and stares off into space thinking.*]
GERRY:	Good question. I don't know. Maybe to get at Ijeoma.
ANI:	It's got to be more than that. Does this prove that Mama is the one who poisoned the Fanta?

GERRY: By itself, no. However, there is something
                   I wanted to discuss with you. At the police
                   station you said Celia was lying when she
                   says she put only half a teaspoon of the
                   powder into Ubong's night chocolate.

ANI: I didn't show you that test result, but even
                   half a teaspoon of that poison would make
                   him seriously ill.

GERRY: [*nodding*] So does that mean Celia is saying
                   she poisoned his night chocolate when in
                   fact she didn't? Why lie against herself?

ANI: So…

GERRY: So she has to be telling the truth. She did
                   put half a teaspoon of that powder into
                   Ubong's hot chocolate. But as we can see, it
                   had almost no effect on him. Why? Neither
                   Regina, Ijeoma nor John Maduekwe accept
                   responsibility for supplying Celia with
                   arsenic. They maintain that they gave her
                   harmless vitamin C. Of course, with the
                   death of a child hanging over their heads,
                   none of them will eagerly admit to supplying
                   the poison. But the fact remains that Celia
                   used the powder she was given, and nothing
                   happened. Therefore the powder Celia got
                   from Maduekwe is not the same powder
                   that was used in Ubong's Fanta, nor was it
                   the same powder that was later tested at the
                   hospital. At some point between her putting
                   the half teaspoon in the night, and Ubong
                   leaving the house the next morning with his
                   lunchbox, the powder was substituted.

ANI: And only one person could have done that
                substitution. My mother.

GERRY: As I said before, it makes no sense for Regina,
                Ijeoma or Maduekwe to truly target Ubong.
                Seemingly only Celia would have a motive
                for that. Celia, or, as we now know, Mama.

ANI: And it seems Celia has been telling the truth
                all along. GERRY: So far, everything she
                said stands up under scrutiny.

ANI: And she is telling the truth, too, when she
                says she was lying to Maduekwe?

GERRY: That, too, stands up under scrutiny. She
                left Ubong in perfectly good health in
                the hospital. An hour later she is telling
                Maduekwe he is dying. She was definitely
                lying. In a way, Celia is lucky Ubong did not
                touch his lunch, because if Ubong had died,
                nobody would believe Celia didn't poison
                that drink herself.

ANI: So can you piece together this whole sorry
                story from the beginning?

GERRY: I can try. But before I do I want us to do a
                thorough search of this room.

ANI: Do you have anything particular in mind
                you expect to find?

GERRY: Yes. Where did you find these papers?

ANI: In this top drawer.

GERRY: Almost in plain sight.

ANI: She knows I'd never riffle through her things like that.

GERRY: You might not. But what about Celia? Or even Atim? House helps have been known to pry into things that are none of their business.

ANI: Probably she brought them out of hiding only after she came back from hospital.

GERRY: OK. But even then, if she was bold enough to leave them just lying there, maybe she brought out other things as well.

GERRY and ANI start looking through the drawers. Nothing special is revealed. They check the wardrobe.

ANI: What is it that you expect to find? [*He brings down IDORENYIN'S suitcase.*]

GERRY: The rest of the poison. [*ANI stops what he was doing and stares at him.*]

ANI: Are you serious?

GERRY: Where do you think ordinary individuals can lay their hands on arsenic?

ANI: Dr Idiong suggested rat poison. But she wasn't sure.

GERRY: I am. I checked it up. I found two brands of rat poison with arsenic as their main ingredient, available in some of the larger supermarkets.

ANI: This suitcase is locked. I'm going to break it. Atim!

ATIM: Sir! [*She comes to the door.*]

ANI: Bring me the hammer from downstairs. [*ATIM exits.*]

GERRY: Well, that's it. We've looked everywhere else.

ATIM returns with the hammer. ANI breaks the lock and hands back the hammer to her. She leaves with it. They open the suitcase. There are clothes in it. They sift through the clothes. There are some letters at the bottom of the suitcase, lying on a tied yellow-and-black striped plastic bag. They bring out the letters and the bag. They open the bag and find two small packets of rat poison in it. One packet is empty. The other half empty.

ANI: You are right again. Here it is. She used up an entire packet. [*He reads aloud.*] 'Contains arsenic trioxide 52%. Warning. This product is poisonous. Use strictly according to instructions for the elimination of rodents. Keep out of reach of children, pets and domestic animals. Keep away from food and water. Always wash hands thoroughly after coming in contact with product. Should accidental ingestion occur, seek immediate medical attention.' [*He drops the packet.*] There it is, boldly written that it's meant for rats, but my mother, my own mother, deliberately gives it to an innocent child. [*GERRY has been scanning through the letters.*]

GERRY: These letters are all from someone called
            Etima. Who is Etima? [*ANI takes the letters
            and looks through them.*]

ANI: Etima. She's the girl Mama has been hinting
            I should take as a second wife. She's the
            daughter of her friend in the village. She has
            certainly been keeping in touch with her.
            These are a lot of letters.

GERRY: It appears that since you refused to take the
            hints, Mama decided to do something about
            it. Here in one letter Etima says she hopes
            she won't end up waiting in vain for you like
            Justina. Justina? That name sounds vaguely
            familiar.

ANI: She was the first village girl my mother
            chose for me. She really tried to push her
            on me during those years Celia and I had
            no children.

GERRY: What became of Justina?

ANI: I think she eventually got married.

GERRY: Ani look at this. Look at this letter. [*GERRY
            passes a letter over to ANI. ANI reads it.*] It
            mentions that Etima's brother works for
            'Peace Of Mind' consultancy. Apparently
            they're not actually a detective agency,
            merely a group of people willing to do just
            about anything a client wants them to.

ANI: How in the world do they come up with a
            name like 'Peace Of Mind'? What a travesty.

GERRY: It seems Etima's brother himself did the research on Ubong for Mama. And, procured the rat poison as well. See this paragraph? [*GERRY shows it to ANI.*]

ANI: And all this was... [*he looks at the date*] six weeks ago.

GERRY: Ijeoma did not come to see Mama when she came here. She went to her in the village. I wonder why she lied about that.

ANI: Maybe she wanted it to seem unplanned. Or maybe lying˙ is just second nature to her. Why though did Mama have Ubong checked out?

GERRY: Something must have made her suspicious of Ijeoma's story.

ANI: Or it could simply be Etima and family not wanting this new complication. So they decided to check it out, and gave Mama their findings. [*GERRY nods.*]

GERRY: Very likely. They devised a plan to use this new competition to permanently get rid of Celia. Mama played along. It seems she never really liked Celia. Everything is falling into place. I think I can piece it together now. [*ANI sits back in the chair.*]

ANI: So tell me.

GERRY: About six weeks ago, Ijeoma goes to your village and tells your mother Ubong is your son. Etima and brother soon discover this is not so. They plan with Mama to use this to their advantage. You have proved stubborn in the past when it comes to marrying the girl she chose. She makes plans to come to Lagos for a long visit. Ijeoma tells her about the fake *babalawo* plan. She agrees to go along with it. But she knows the powder supplied will not be poisonous. She, or more likely Etima and her brother, decide that actually killing Ubong removes not only Celia but Ijeoma and Ubong himself as well. Celia is to get the blame for everything. On Monday, Mama is told that Celia has collected the powder. Tuesday morning, she finds an opportunity to put the real poison into Ubong's Fanta. When everybody leaves, she searches for the hair gel container Celia got from Maduekwe. She finds it in the bin where Celia threw it. Brings it out, puts the poison in, and leaves it in Celia's *bubu* for you to find. If you didn't find it on your own, she would find a way to lead you to it. She comes to your office and drags you down to the *babalawo's* place. She gets some incredible luck. You run into Celia apparently admitting to the crime. You drive off leaving them there. I think that is when Mama left some arsenic in the other room for the police to find. That would explain the source of the arsenic and leave Ijeoma, Regina, and Maduekwe blaming one another. Everything is going perfectly, then it all starts falling apart. Itoro, not Ubong, dies. The shock of that sends Mama's blood pressure soaring. She tries to rally the next day, but Ijeoma goes to visit her twice. Ijeoma who is no doubt expecting her support. Not only that, with Celia sent out of the house, Ubong becomes untouchable. She dares not try anything against him for now. All she can do is wait for things to die down. Then maybe she can find a way to let you know Ubong is not yours. Meanwhile she lets you know she doesn't want Ijeoma for a daughter-in-law. Then she makes the *bubu* mistake. When you ask her, she tries to brazen it out, insisting you told her. She knows when Ijeoma is taken away by the police. She waits. Then you come back and question her again about her involvement. She launches into what was probably a well-rehearsed denial. Her plan was to admit nothing. Unfortunately, she got too worked up. Her BP shot up, and she had a stroke. [*After GERRY stops speaking, ANI is silent for a moment.*]

ANI: That about covers it.

GERRY: Yes. But one thing bothers me though. Ubong had a tiny amount of arsenic in his system, as shown by the test. That means the powder Celia was given could not have been just vitamin C. There was some arsenic in it. A minute quantity. Not enough to kill him. My question is: who put it, and why.

ANI: I can't answer that. My headache is intensifying. I'll sort the things to take to the hospital later.

GERRY: Do you have any pain pills?

ANI: I have paracetamol. That should do. [*He stands.*]

GERRY: I'll bring the sleeping tablets, too. You need a good sleep. [*ANI and GERRY leave the room together.*]

ANI: You, too.

ANI closes the door.

Fade.

Scene LXIV

The police station. SANDRA and IYABO walk into the reception.

SANDRA: [*to POLICEMAN 3*] Sandra Edo. The police chief is expecting me.

POLICEMAN 3:   Follow me.

POLICEMAN 3 leads SANDRA and IYABO to POLICE CHIEF'S office and leaves them there.

POLICE CHIEF: Mrs Edo, welcome. Have a seat. You said on the phone that you had some information for me. [*SANDRA and IYABO sit.*]

SANDRA: Yes. You mentioned yesterday that it is my word against Regina's when I said she told me about the *babalawo*.

POLICE CHIEF: Yes.

SANDRA: Well, it's not. This is my shop assistant, Iyabo. She says she heard Regina that day she was telling me.

POLICE CHIEF: [*to IYABO*] Is that so?

IYABO: Yes, sir. I was attending to a customer in the changing room. They were standing in the aisle beside the changing room. I heard them.

POLICE CHIEF: So what exactly did you hear?

IYABO: I didn't know what they were talking about at first. I heard Mrs Olusola giving my madam the directions to a place near Ijebu. I only realised it was to a native doctor when madam asked her if the charm he gave her really worked. And Mrs Olusola said yes. That it was almost like a miracle.

SANDRA: Let Regina try denying that!

POLICE CHIEF: All she has to say is that you coached her. After all, she is your employee.

SANDRA: I didn't coach her!

POLICE CHIEF: That won't stop her from saying you did. I will still ask her about it, but it won't carry much weight.

IYABO: It's not only me who heard.

SANDRA: Who else heard?

IYABO: Aunty, the customer. She was right there beside me. When Mrs Olusola mentioned the US embassy, she parted the curtains a little and peeped out at the two of you.

SANDRA: Who was the customer?

IYABO: The wife of the Commissioner for Education.

SANDRA: Of course! I remember she had just left with her purchases. I didn't know she had returned. You told me later.

POLICE CHIEF: And she heard?

IYABO: She heard everything. She looked at me and like, rolled her eyes. Then we concentrated on the clothes.

POLICE CHIEF: [*passing a paper to SANDRA*] Give me her contact details. [*SANDRA writes on the paper using information from her phone.*] I will follow it up.

SANDRA: It galls me to hear Regina is calling me a liar.

POLICE CHIEF: Let's see what she has to say about this. Thank you for coming. [*He escorts them out.*] Where is Celia?

SANDRA: She went to church. She's having a special prayer session with the pastor. After that she's going to the mortuary. She says she wants to spend the rest of the day with Itoro and say her personal goodbyes to her.

POLICE CHIEF: I see. Well, goodbye. I will let you know if this yields any results.

SANDRA: I hope it does. Goodbye.

SANDRA and IYABO leave.

Fade.

Scene LXV

The OLUSOLAS' house. POLICE CHIEF and POLICEMAN 1 and 2 arrive at the gate.

POLICEMAN 1:   [*to MAIGUARD*] Tell Mrs Olusola the chief of police wishes to see her.

MAIGUARD goes inside and returns with REGINA.

REGINA: Yes, Officers?

POLICE CHIEF: New information has come to light that necessitates your coming to the station again, madam.

REGINA: I've told you everything I know. I have nothing new to add. Ijeoma is telling you lies.

POLICE CHIEF: The new information is not from Ijeoma Nwankwo.

REGINA: Who is it from?

POLICE CHIEF: I cannot discuss that here. You need to come down to the station.

REGINA: My husband is not in at the moment. I cannot leave my children unattended.

POLICE CHIEF: There are servants in the house and a guard at the gate. Are you telling me you take your children with you whenever you go anywhere?

REGINA: I don't feel comfortable leaving them unattended. Or coming to the station without my husband.

POLICE CHIEF nods to POLICEMAN 1, who promptly goes behind REGINA and grabs her arm. REGINA tries to dodge.

POLICE CHIEF: I thought you were going to cooperate.

REGINA: You can't do this again! My husband said you had no right last time. You had no warrant!

POLICE CHIEF: [*to POLICEMAN 2*] Officer, bring the warrant. [*POLICEMAN 2 hands him the warrant as POLICEMAN 1 cuffs REGINA.*] Here is a duly signed warrant for your arrest. It is all above board and legal.

REGINA: What am I being charged with?

POLICE CHIEF: Same thing as before. Accessory to the murder of Itoro Umoh.

REGINA: I want to call my husband!

POLICE CHIEF: You can do that from the station. Put her in the car, let's go.

They enter the car and drive off.

Fade.

Scene LXVI

The UMOHS' residence. GERRY, ANI and UBONG are at the table.

ANI: How was school, Ubong?

UBONG: I didn't get all my maths right. I got five out
                of ten.

ANI: Don't worry. With practice you will get it
                right next time.

UBONG: Teacher said if we are good, and pray for
                good things, God will answer our prayers.

ANI: That's true.

UBONG: I am going to be very good. And I'm going to
                pray for Itoro and Aunty Celia, and Ekaette
                and Eno and Grandma to come back.
                [*GERRY and ANI exchange glances.*]

ANI: OK. Eno and Ekaette will be back tomorrow.

UBONG: What about Itoro and Aunty Celia and
                Grandma?

ANI: Itoro can't come back. Grandma and Aunty
                Celia may not be able to come back just
                now. Grandma is very sick. You can pray

for her to get better. That will be a great help. [*UBONG'S face crumples and he starts sniffing.*]

UBONG: Please, I want Itoro to come back. [*ANI holds out his hand to him.*]

ANI: Come here. [*UBONG goes and sits on his lap.*] Sometimes it's just not possible for us to get exactly what we want. We have to learn to be happy with what we have. I will be here. Eno and Ekaette will be here. [*ATIM brings in a dish.*] Atim, too, will be here.

ATIM: Sir?

GERRY: It's OK, Atim. He's not calling you. [*ATIM leaves.*]

ANI: Ubong, you know you are safe with me here. I will never let anything bad happen to you. [*UBONG nods.*] I'm going to ask you some questions, and I don't want you to be afraid to tell me anything. OK? [*UBONG nods again, but he looks apprehensive.*] How old are you?

UBONG: [*hesitantly*] I am... eight years old.

ANI: Is that your true age, Ubong? Or is that what you were told to say? [*UBONG is silent. He hides his face in his hands. ANI gently removes his hands and tips his face up again.*] You don't need to be afraid, Ubong. Nothing is going to happen to you. Are you really eight years old? [*UBONG starts crying.*]

UBONG:	She will beat me.
ANI:	Who will beat you?
UBONG:	Aunt Ijeoma. [*He gasps and immediately covers his mouth.*] Mummy, I mean Mummy.
GERRY:	You are used to calling her Aunt Ijeoma, aren't you? Not Mummy. [*UBONG sobs harder.*]
UBONG:	She didn't like me calling her Mummy. She said it made her old.
ANI:	When did she tell you to start calling her Mummy?
UBONG:	Not long before she brought me here. She came to the house and said from now on I should call her Mummy. Each time I forgot, she beat the back of my hands with a stick. [*He rubs his hands together, remembering.*] It's painful. Please don't tell her I didn't call her Mummy. [*ANI and GERRY exchange glances again.*]
ANI:	[*soothingly*] Don't worry. She will never know. [*He dries UBONG'S tears with his handkerchief.*]
GERRY:	And she also told you to say you are eight years old when you are really seven, right? [*UBONG nods.*]

UBONG: She changed my school. And put me in
                class three. She said she will beat me if I tell
                anyone I am not eight years old.

GERRY: How are you coping in class 3?

UBONG: OK. But I will not be first this term. There
                are many things I don't know. Like today's
                maths. By next term, I will know. Are you
                going to tell my Mummy?

ANI: No. What's more, your mother will never
                beat you again. That's a promise.

UBONG: Thank you, Daddy.

ANI: Do you want to try a little more of your
                food now?

UBONG: OK. [*UBONG nods and returns to his seat to
                resume his meal.*] I'm glad you're my daddy.

ANI smiles.

Fade.

Scene LXVII

The police station. POLICE CHIEF goes into the interrogation room. REGINA and POLICEMAN 1 and 2 are waiting.

POLICE CHIEF: So have you spoken with your husband?

REGINA: Yes. He is on his way here. He says I should say nothing to you until he arrives.

POLICE CHIEF: You are within your rights to say nothing. However, if you do not explain away the allegations against you, we will have no option but to put you in the cell while we commence full proceedings against you.

REGINA: What are these allegations?

POLICE CHIEF: Sandra Edo maintains her story that you told her about the native doctor that she in turn told Celia about.

REGINA: I have already told you that is not true.

POLICE CHIEF: Yes, so you said. However you forget that this conversation took place in Sandra's boutique. You were overheard by another customer. She saw you, and she heard what you said. And she has given us a statement to that effect. He pushes the statement towards her. [*REGINA reads it. Her face crumples.*]

REGINA: Oh, my God.

POLICE CHIEF: Are you still insisting that all three of them are lying?

REGINA: Thomas will kill me!

POLICE CHIEF: Why? Is he not involved as well?

REGINA: No! He knows nothing about it! In fact, yesterday I swore to him that it was all a mix up. That it had nothing to do with me! He will kill me *o*!

POLICE CHIEF: Did you plan with Ijeoma Nwankwo to poison her son, Ubong, through Celia Umoh?

REGINA: Nooo! Nobody was to actually be poisoned!

POLICE CHIEF: What was to happen?

REGINA: Her husband, Ani, was to catch her apparently trying to poison Ugo and send her packing, but no actual poison was to be involved. It was all just an attempt to get Celia out and Ijeoma in.

POLICE CHIEF: Who came up with this plan?

REGINA: Ijeoma. She came to me crying because the boy she set her cap on married someone else. In three months she will be thirty. She was desperate to do something about it.

POLICE CHIEF: So whose idea was it to pass her son off as Ani's?

REGINA: Ijeoma's of course. How was I to know that she had been sleeping with Ani when she was working for him?

POLICE CHIEF: How did she get the job with him in the first place?

REGINA: I heard from Thomas that Ani was looking for a secretary. Ijeoma had just finished secretarial school. I told her to apply. I was going to ask Thomas to put in a word on her behalf, but Ani employed her straight off.

POLICE CHIEF: So he never knew you were related to her?

REGINA: No. It just never came up. Besides, Thomas and I were living in Abuja at the time.

POLICE CHIEF: Ijeoma says this whole native doctor scam was your idea.

REGINA: That's not true.

POLICE CHIEF: Did you finance it?

REGINA: Yes. I gave her 400,000.

POLICE CHIEF: And you provided the so-called vitamin C?

REGINA: Officer, I did not provide the poison that killed that child. Wherever Celia got that from, it wasn't from me.

POLICE CHIEF: So you maintain that it was vitamin C powder?

REGINA: Yes. I brought it from India several years ago and forgot about it for a long time. When I found it again in the back of the cupboard and saw it had not expired, I decided to use it.

POLICE CHIEF: So it was only vitamin C that you gave Ijeoma? [*REGINA hesitates.*]

REGINA: Officer, the truth is, there was some arsenic in the vitamin C, but a very tiny amount. We read that arsenic can actually be beneficial to humans in small amounts. And we felt it would carry more weight if Ubong actually tested positive for a poison. Then nobody could doubt that Celia wanted him dead. But I assure you, Officer, that we were very careful. The amount we put was so small, even if Celia gave him the entire powder, it could not kill him.

POLICE CHIEF: When you say we, are you saying Ijeoma was aware of this?

REGINA: Yes!

POLICE CHIEF: Did John Maduekwe ever know of your involvement?

REGINA: No. I was the silent partner.

POLICE CHIEF: Was anyone else involved in this plan?

REGINA: Ani's mother. She was the one to make Ani aware of Celia's activities.

POLICE CHIEF: Did she know of your involvement?

REGINA: No.

POLICE CHIEF: How did you get her to agree to this?

REGINA: Ijeoma went to see her in the village…

POLICE CHIEF: When?

REGINA: About… six weeks ago I think. It was common knowledge how desperate she was for Ani to have a son. Ijeoma presented her with a ready- made son. She fell for it.

POLICE CHIEF: Ijeoma told us about your involvement, but was reluctant to mention hers. Why do you think that was?

REGINA: [*shrugging*] Knowing Ijeoma, I'm sure she thought she had something to gain. Maybe she thought that for Ubong's sake Ani's mother would see to it that she was released or something. Officer, what's going to happen to me now?

POLICE CHIEF: Thanks to all this, a child is dead. You will not be charged with the murder but other charges will be brought against all those involved, including you. [*The intercom rings. POLICE CHIEF answers it.*] Yes? We are bringing her out. [*He hangs up.*] Your husband is here. [*To the policemen.*] Take her to the visiting room. Let him see her there. [*REGINA moans as they lead her out.*]

REGINA: Thomas will kill me…

Fade.

Scene LXVIII

The UMOHS' house. GERRY knocks and enters ANI'S room. ANI is stretched out on the bed.

ANI: Gerry. You still have more of those tablets? Or have I finished them all?

GERRY: I still have some. I'll get it for you.

ANI: The police chief thinks Ijeoma decided to confess about Mama's involvement only when she realised we knew about Ubong. Up until then she was hoping we would let her go free for his sake.

GERRY: What are the charges being brought against her? [*ANI shakes his head.*]

ANI: Fraud charges only. Against the three of them. No point bringing murder into it. They did not actually kill Itoro. And I don't want to press any charges against Celia. After the funeral though I'm going to press charges against Etima and her brother. They provided the rat poison. They are not going to go scot-free.

GERRY: True. How's Ubong?

ANI: He's sleeping now. But he's still tearful. Tonight again, he prayed for everyone, especially Itoro to come back home.

GERRY: He really loved her. It's hard for an eight, no, seven-year-old to accept the finality of death.

ANI: You know, I wonder what kind of mother Ijeoma was to him. She had very little to do with him. She kept him with relations. When each one got tired, she shifted him to another one. From the little he says about it, I gather they mostly treated him like the house help.

GERRY: What are you going to do about him now?

ANI: I'm keeping him. I brought him into this house and I told him to call me Daddy. I'm not going back on that. He has no father that can be identified, and I can get the courts to declare Ijeoma an unfit mother if she tries to make a fuss.

GERRY: Why should she? She's used to other people keeping him.

ANI: I will officially adopt him. [*GERRY nods.*]

GERRY: That's an excellent idea. Ani, what about Celia? [*ANI looks at him.*]

ANI: You obviously have something in mind. Say it.

GERRY: I know what she tried to do originally was terrible. But she did not follow through with it. She came to her senses. In the end, she was incapable of actually killing someone.

ANI: You know, if the powder Maduekwe gave her was the real thing, she could have killed Ubong before she came to her senses, as you put it.

GERRY: No. From my calculations Mama had to have put about a tablespoonful of the poison in that 250ml Fanta bottle to achieve that concentration. That mug holds about the same quantity. The half teaspoonful Celia put it could not possibly kill him. It would make him sick, yes. But in the absence of further poisoning, he would recover.

ANI: [*shrugging*] All right.

GERRY: You know it's ironic the way things work out. Had Celia not poisoned Ubong's night chocolate, Ubong would have died the next day. Think about it. The little arsenic that was in his system put him off food the next day. Without that, he would have eaten a hearty breakfast. In school, he wouldn't be in the sick bay drinking glucose. He would eat his lunch and drink his Fanta.

ANI: I never looked at it like that.

GERRY: Celia is sorry, Ani. And she has to live with the knowledge that she, in some way, contributed to her own daughter's death.

That's a heavy enough yoke for any woman to bear.

ANI: I had already decided to forgive her. For Eno and Ekaette's sake. Ubong is finding it so hard to deal with Itoro's death. Imagine what it is going to be like for those two. Plus, their grandmother is critically ill in hospital. They don't need to lose their mother as well.

GERRY: No, they don't. I think that's a wise decision. I'll go get you the tablets. [*He pauses at the door and looks back at ANI.*] You know Ani, you are not altogether blameless.

ANI: What do you mean?

GERRY: If you hadn't slept with Ijeoma all those years ago…

GERRY leaves the sentence hanging, goes out and closes the door. ANI closes his eyes.

Fade.

Scene LXIX

The Umoh's compound. It is the day of the funeral. Mournful music plays throughout. No actual words are audible from the crowd of people gathered there although their lips can be seen moving. The mournful music covers all speech. A small coffin is lowered into a freshly dug grave. The pastor says the final rites over it and like everything else, his actual words are not heard. ENO, EKAETTE and UBONG are clinging to CELIA. ATIM is standing beside them. All of them are crying. ANI throws a shovel of dirt on the coffin. He is crying, too. The pastor finishes the final rites, and the grave diggers take up shovels and start returning the soil into the open grave. The choir sings. The men make short work of filling up the grave. They pat down the soil, making it level and neat. The marble headstone is uncovered. The mourners place heaps of flowers and other offerings on the grave. CELIA places ITORO'S Barbie doll on the grave. She sobs bitterly. Next to it, ENO places a little teddy bear in a transparent plastic covering, EKAETTE a small doll's house. UBONG places some toy soldiers among the flowers. ANI adds the little ceramic dog. People start dispersing. Some offer their condolences to the family before leaving. Close friends and family accompany them into the house. The marble headstone bears the drawing of a cherub holding a dove in cupped hands. Below it the inscription:

OUR LITTLE ANGEL HAS JOINED GOD'S ANGELS
REST IN PEACE
MISS ITOROABASI IDORENYIN UMOH
11 FEBRUARY 2004–6 MAY 2009.

The mournful music finally dies away.

Fade.

Scene LXX

It is night. The UMOHS' bedroom. CELIA and ANI are in bed, but neither of them is sleeping.

CELIA:　　　　　What are your plans for Ubong?

ANI:　　　　　Next week I'm starting full adoption procedures. He will be my son.

CELIA:　　　　　No. He will be our son. He is not Itoro, and he can never take the place of Itoro. No one can. But he can have his own place, and he will help ease the pain of her loss. He is such a lovely boy. I can't say often enough how sorry I am for what I tried to do to him. Pastor has given me fasting and prayer for three days.

ANI grunts an acknowledgement. They are silent for a while.

CELIA:　　　　　Ani, I want to thank you again for your generosity towards me. Not many people would forgive in this situation. Much less trust me enough to allow me to continue caring for Ubong. When Eno was born, I declared before everyone that I would be a perfect mother to her. I now realise how arrogant that sounds. We are all human. None of us is perfect. How could I then presume to become a perfect mother? The best I can hope for is that God will grant me the grace to be a good mother to Eno, Ekaette and Ubong. If I can achieve that, I will be content. [*ANI grunts again.*] I am looking on today as the start of a new chapter in our lives. Henceforth, I intend to keep no secrets from you again. Therefore, I have a confession to make. [*ANI turns to look at her.*] You remember when I had that miscarriage two years ago? I had to have an operation. You were told I had an ectopic pregnancy. That wasn't true. I had a hysterectomy. My womb was removed. I begged the doctor not to tell you. [*She takes a deep breath.*] I can never have another child, Ani.

CELIA and ANI stare at each other. ANI does not look surprised.

ANI: I know that, Celia. I've known that for two years.

CELIA: What! How did you know?

ANI: Three days after the operation, I went to the consulting room to discuss your progress with the doctor. The room was empty. I was about to leave when I saw your case note on his desk. I read through it.

CELIA: You've known all this time!

ANI: Yes.

CELIA: Why didn't you say something?

ANI:	What should I have said? You were so upset about it that you were prepared to hide it from me.
CELIA:	I'm sorry, Ani.
ANI:	It would have served no purpose to bring it up with you afterwards.
CELIA:	You don't mind not having any more children?
ANI:	Itoro's birth was very difficult for you. I told you afterwards we should not have any more.
CELIA:	I thought you were just saying that because that was what the doctor recommended.
ANI:	Is that why you decided on your own to try again? The result was the miscarriage, and the operation. You could have died in the process.
CELIA:	I thought I'd try just that last time to see if I could have a boy.
ANI:	When I saw in your case note that your uterus had been removed, I was actually relieved. [*They are silent again for a while.*]
CELIA:	It just goes to show. All this time I thought I was deceiving you. I was deceiving myself. No more. No more secrets.
ANI:	Put off the light, let's try and get some sleep.

CELIA switches off the light. Darkness descends on the room.

CELIA'S VOICE: I love you, Ani.

ANI'S VOICE: I love you, Celia.

Fade.

THE END

More from Uduak E Akpabio

Little Devils

Life is comfortable but a little dull for nine-year-old twins Ekom and Chike, who live with their widowed mother, Ima, and teenage aunt, Mfon, in Lagos, Nigeria. What the twins want more than anything is for their mother to spend time with them, but Ima, unaware that she is neglecting their emotional welfare, is more concerned with running her late husband's successful import/export business, Across Borders. While Ima is away, it falls to beautiful, but naive Mfon, to take care of the twins.

When Mfon becomes distracted by the attentions of an unscrupulous man, the twins, with no mother figure offering guidance, are led astray by Chike's unprincipled friend, Michael, who happily encourages them into deeper and deeper trouble.

Ima, away overseas on business, has no clue that her family back home is teetering on the brink of disaster. When matters come to a head, will she be able to re-establish respect and authority with her children and sister before it is too late? Little Devils is a play that explores the importance of communication and trust within the family, showing that money does not necessarily lead to happiness.